BEING
FISHKILL

BEING
FISHKILL

RUTH LEHRER

CANDLEWICK PRESS

Copyright © 2017 by Ruth Lehrer

First edition 2017

Library of Congress Catalog Card Number pending
ISBN 978-0-7636-8442-6

17 18 19 20 21 22 BVG 10 9 8 7 6 5 4 3 2 1

Printed in Berryville, VA, U.S.A.

This book was typeset in Bembo.

Candlewick Press
99 Dover Street
Somerville, Massachusetts 02144

visit us at www.candlewick.com

For Amy, who understood
why we had to sample Yodels

1

My mother named me after a New York highway sign, passing through, passing by, not even stopping to squeeze out my blue body. Going north on the Taconic Parkway, she lay on the back seat and pushed. As I gushed onto gray vinyl, she caught a glimpse of the Carmel/Fishkill exit sign and decided it was not just a highway sign but a cosmic sign, and I was Carmel Fishkill. She even did away with my inherited surname, her name, Jamison, and let me battle my way through six grades of school under the sign of Fishkill.

Overconfident boys used to call me Caramel, like the candy. "Stick-in-your-teeth-Caramel can't afford a dentist," they would taunt, tossing chewed gum at me in the cafeteria. When I was Carmel, school lunch was the low point of every day. I had no quarters for lunch on a tray. If I brought lunch, which was rare, my paper bags always contained a bizarre combination of whole cans of sardines and bags of Cheez Doodles.

I decided that in seventh grade, at the new school, in the new school year, I would own that hard-sounding last name. Fish—cold and scaly. Kill—dangerous, you-don't-want-to-fuck-with-me dangerous. I would be Fishkill Carmel.

So when school started in September, my life as Fishkill also began. The very first day, I decided I deserved lunches like those belonging to the girls with pretty lunch bags and cartons of chocolate milk. I strolled down the cafeteria aisles and surveyed tables. If I saw something that struck my fancy—a chocolate cookie, a hot-dog roll, a Yodel—I took it and gave the kid a look that just dared him to scream. I decided to be fair and only take one item from a tray. I never took from kids with free-lunch passes, only the ones who bought pizza and cookies, which meant their parents gave them money, so they could buy another pizza or cookie. I could tell the free-lunch kids by their sneakers: ragged toe holes, the same as me. After a few weeks on my new Fishkill diet of thievery, my nails grew longer and my hair lost its thin, wispy fingers. Grown-ups didn't call me *boy* so often.

As Fishkill Carmel, I instantly developed a left jab and a right hook that rivaled those of TV mobsters, and there were no more caramel-candy jokes. The first week of seventh grade, I punched a boy so hard, he hit the concrete with a crack that turned his face turquoise. It was much better to be Fishkill Carmel.

The last week of September, I met Duck-Duck. It was lunchtime, and she had a peanut-butter-and-jelly sandwich cut corner to corner in two neat triangles. Triangle sandwiches always taste better than rectangle sandwiches. I could see it was chunky peanut butter, and the grape jelly oozed out the sides just enough that the bread was only the slightest bit sticky and her pink napkin was still clean. I wondered if she always got pink napkins or if she'd had a birthday party and it was left over. My hand darted out. Quick like a fish, Duck-Duck's hand came down on mine.

"What's the secret password, creep?" she said, squeezing my fingers, not hard like a fist but just gentle enough so the jelly wouldn't go all over.

I could have socked her with my other hand, but her shiny little earrings—bubbles of starry blue water—distracted me. And she smelled like a vanilla wafer with hot cocoa on the side. I couldn't think of a smart password.

"Gimme," I said, and immediately felt stupid. Fishkill wasn't ever supposed to feel stupid.

"Not a chance," said Duck-Duck. "What's your name?"

Here was an opportunity to use my practiced hard stare.

"Fishkill Carmel," I snarled. But it was hard to swagger with one hand on peanut butter and jelly and the scent of vanilla wafer in my nose.

"Cool," she said. "I'm Duck-Duck."

Duck-Duck? I wanted to say, but I was sensitive to bad names, strange names, mismatched names. I'd never seen this girl before. She must have just moved to town. Maybe from another country or even another planet.

"It's my gang name," she said, and flicked her blond hair with a small hand.

I didn't even think to doubt her then. Fishkill didn't care about other people, but if the gang was big, maybe I ought to be a little careful.

After Grandpa died and Social Services descended on us, I watched a cop show in the Department office while my mother made excuses and tried to fill out paperwork. The cops attempted to outwit gang members who drove convertibles, wore dark glasses, smoked cigarettes, and spit in the gutter. I liked the spitting. I'd never seen anything like that in the little town of Salt Run, New York, though.

"What gang?" I said.

"The G.R.s."

"G.R.s?"

"The Gumbo Rumbles, featuring Duck-Duck Farina. If you're in the know, you just call us the Grrs. Take your hand off my sandwich." She squeezed my fingers again, her soft hand over my hard one. I could feel the white bread bubble under my knuckles.

She had blond eyelashes too, and no one I knew had such blue eyes. My grandfather had had mean black ones, but he'd been dead for two years, and I was glad. My mother claimed her eyes were hazel, but they were really just the color of light mud, the same as mine. Though without a mirror at home, it was hard to remember my own exactly, since I was inside them.

"Off!" commanded Duck-Duck.

I released my grip, even though I was truly hungry and lunch period was almost over.

Duck-Duck pulled out another small pink napkin, peeled

a soggy peanut-butter-and-jelly triangle off the wax paper, and took a bite.

"Here," she said, and she handed me the other half. "Grrs like a little good publicity every once in a while."

The bell rang, and she ran off with her lunch box and her pink napkins and her blue eyes, my fingers still sticky with jelly.

When Grandpa was still alive and living at Birge Hill with me and my mother, he called me Carmela and hit me with the hitting stick. It was a thick wooden walking stick he kept at the front door just for hitting, just because he could. When Grandpa was still alive, we ate sardines and canned tomato soup every day for a year. When he died of a heart attack so sudden it was like hitting the Delete key, the food got a little better, but not much.

The Social Service ladies came around for a whole six months after he died, wanting to know what was in the refrigerator and if I got to school on time. They lectured us about the importance of good communication and paying bills, and they noticed if the kitchen floor was dirty. They complained about how far we lived from town. They wanted me to cut my scraggly brown hair and wash my hands more often.

"You look like a boy," they said. "Don't you want to be pretty?"

For those six months, we kept the floor clean, I went to school, Keely kept an honest job, and finally the Department of Social Services said we could be a closed case and they wouldn't come around anymore. I've always thought my mother and I were just that, a closed case—nothing ever changed. Not now, not never. I didn't have her last name, so when I grew up, no one would know we were ever a case at all.

The second time I tried to steal Duck-Duck's lunch, she had a cold waffle with jam. It struck me as an odd meal, but the crisp, browned edges spoke of a real waffle iron, and the toasted top was covered with real jam made from whole cherries. This time, I didn't try to snatch it—I sat down across from her and stared at the waffle.

"Did you know gang graffiti is one of the hardest codes to crack in the world? Cops spend days deciphering just one word," said Duck-Duck. She licked up a wet cherry and eyed my hands.

"Why is it so hard?" I asked, still looking at the waffle.

"For one thing, we spell our names and certain words differently," she said. "Cops don't have much imagination, so it's hard for them to find us in the phone book." She took another bite. "Like, how do you think I spell my name?"

"Like the bird," I said. "But twice."

"Nope. I spell it *D-U-K-D-U-K*. It's more exotic, and the cops will never find me." Duck-Duck took a sip of milk. A carton of milk cost sixty cents. "Want some waffle?"

I had already imagined those wild ducks in flight, so I couldn't picture her without the *c*'s: *Duck-Duck*. I nodded and held out my hand, and she tore her waffle along one of the dotted waffle lines. She evened out the cherries too, so that there were two whole cherries on my half. She slid it onto my palm, and, just for a second, her warm fingers touched mine. It felt like the cherry tree itself giving me lunch.

The third time I tried to steal Duck-Duck's lunch, she asked me to write my name in blood. In case she ever needed my signature, she said.

"Blood?" I said. "It has to be blood? Why?"

"Blood," she said firmly. "Anything else lacks commitment. But ketchup will work in a pinch."

"I'm not in your gang," I said. I wasn't sure if I wanted to be or not, even if it was a real gang. Fishkill Carmel was tough all on her own. On the other hand, it was the first time Duck-Duck had wanted something from me, and I was quickly learning that it was hard to say no to her.

"But you want to audition to be in it, right?"

"Audition?" I said, stalling.

"You have to sign your name in blood before I can tell you our secret signs and passwords."

Duck-Duck opened her lunch box and surveyed its bounty. Her blond hair hung down like a shining curtain, shielding the contents from my view. She handed me a fistful of grapes and continued.

"We only accept the best, most nasty. You strike me as having great potential," she said, and dug out the most beautiful lemon cupcake I had ever seen.

No one had ever told me I had great potential before. My schoolwork was average, my athletic skills unremarkable. The only gift I found I had was the ability to knock a boy to the dirt in the time it took a teacher to look away. Personally, I was very proud of this new skill, but no one, kid or grown-up, gave me credit for the achievement.

She looked up from cupcake heaven. "What do you say?"

I had no idea how to respond. I ate a grape.

"Blood oathing is only the first of several trials," she said. "You need to pass all of the trials in order to become a full-fledged Grr member. You have to prove you're worthy." She licked her little finger, which had grazed the lemon icing.

"Did your mother make the cupcake?" I asked; for some reason my heart was pounding. I saw what looked like candied lemon peel on top of the frosting.

"No, she bought it," said Duck-Duck, and she plunged her pink fingers into the little cake, separating it into two pieces with gooey mathematical precision.

When my mother picked up dessert, unusual in our life of church-pantry food, she put it away in the metal bread box, giving me a slice the thickness of a postcard every day until it was gone. It always seemed to disappear much faster than it should, even though she swore she had only been eating slivers too.

"Okay," I said, and accepted the golden cake. Lemon cream trickled from the middle. It tasted like the iced-sugar lemonade I once stole from the August county fair.

"Meet me after school at the famous people cemetery," Duck-Duck said. "We'll see if you're up to par." She sucked down her half of the cupcake and licked her fingers. When she stood to pack up, she was exactly the same height as me. Then she flicked that blond hair with her hand again and skipped down the hallway to the gym.

Most kids joined after-school teams or groups: soccer, drama club, track. Me, each time I had been in a crowd, it had gone wrong. When I was in second grade, I desperately wanted to join the Girl Scouts, but at the first meeting, my mother showed up drunk, and the Scout mother had asked us not to come back.

In my old school, I had been in detention a few times, condemned to the library with other young terrorists. I learned how to do an Internet search for the exact book report I was assigned to write that day. Once when I was just a click away from a perfect report, Sherman Howe caught me behind the library stacks and got as far as a hand in my shirt before I could run. Charlie Peeker squeezed my butt and said he'd tell on me for cheating. As Carmel, I did nothing. As Fishkill, I would have hit them before they got too close. Girls didn't squeeze butts, but after fifth grade, they started to run in dangerous packs. I stayed away from all group gatherings.

In spite of this, I found myself making my way to the gang meeting at the town cemetery where, as Duck-Duck said, all the famous people now "lived." There was the lady poet we'd had to read in sixth grade. There was the politician who ended some kind of war. There was the guy who invented the spiral binding. At least his descendants claimed he had.

I was thinking about how notebooks' spiral bindings tend to unspiral and the pages get all raggy when I noticed that I was being followed by Worm and Frank. Worm's real name was Norm, but Worm made more sense. He was as big as the high-schoolers, and he was fat. No one called him fat, though, because they would have been punched in the eye. Frank was not as big, but he was just as mean. They were puffing on cigarettes and blowing smoke at each other, but I could tell they were aiming for me. Two against one was lousy odds. I might get in a few punches, but then I'd have to run. I was still planning my getaway when they suddenly sprinted, catching up to me and stepping on my heels. There was the hard slice of a boot, and I could feel blood start up in my sock. I flipped around and faced them, fists up.

Suddenly I heard a clear, little voice from above and somewhere behind me. It wasn't just in my head; Worm and Frank heard it too. They started and looked around. Up the cemetery hill on the stone wall, swinging her legs, the afternoon sun on her hair, was Duck-Duck.

"Cut the crap," she said with the clarity of a little lemon bell, all clear and sharp and bright. "Don't you know if you commit a heinous crime when you're a juvenile, it affects your ability to get into the college of your choice? Even if the files are sealed, it's the Internet Age—all hoodlum identities are public. And smoking reduces your sperm count by about eight hundred percent. You will care about that later in life when the doctors test you and you come up deficient. Each inhale makes the little swimmers weaker. You can tell how many have died by taking your pulse. The higher your pulse, the more you're killing."

She jumped off the wall and put her right fingers to her left wrist.

"Count!" she commanded, and to my surprise, and perhaps the surprise of the thugs themselves, Worm and Frank grabbed their wrists and started counting.

"See?" said Duck-Duck. "High already, isn't it? Better go home and lie in a dark room until your count gets back to normal." She swung her pretty blue lunch box and gestured to me. "Come on, Fishy."

I would have protested the nickname, but I was in shock at how quickly my enemies had been neutralized. Duck-Duck was as accurate as a can of Raid, and she hadn't even touched them. The two had dropped their cigarettes and backed off with something that looked very much like fear.

"How'd you do that?" I asked, running after her.

"Oh, it's easy. When boys start thinking about their weenies, they forget everything else," said Duck-Duck as she climbed over the timeless stone wall.

I had never seen a weenie up close. I had never wanted to. I wondered how Duck-Duck knew boys would think about theirs to the exclusion of everything else. It was something to remember.

"You're lucky," she said. "Now you have blood all ready for the blood oath."

I looked down at my heel. Blood had seeped through my sock with the burning sensation of a scab forming. I followed Duck-Duck as she trotted over four cemetery rows. Then she took a quick left turn, and we were under a low quince tree, just behind a refrigerator-size gravestone. It was like a little nest, hidden by dead people.

I looked around and saw only tree, stone, and Duck-Duck. If this was to be a group initiation, everyone else was late or lost. "How many gang members are there?"

"We're low on membership just now," said Duck-Duck. "That makes you all the more important." She spread a pink napkin out on a flat rock. "You know, a blood oath can't be undone. Once you oath, you're oathed for life."

Oathing for life made me nervous, and I wondered why blood would be more permanent than, say, Magic Marker. I didn't want to seem dumb, though, so I said, "Well, sure. I know that."

"So first you take a stick or pencil or something and scrape up some oath blood." She dug in her backpack, handed me a Popsicle stick, and gestured to my heel. "Quick, before it dries up."

The Popsicle stick was a little sticky and just a little orange, as if it used to live inside a Creamsicle. I wondered if there were any more Creamsicles packed away in Duck-Duck's freezer. I sat down on the ground and wiped the stick along the back of my heel where Worm's boot had scraped off skin. It stung and started oozing like a cigarette burn. That was good, according to Duck-Duck. She tore a piece of lined paper from her spiral notebook and laid it down on the grass.

"You want to write your whole name. If you run out of blood, it means you are only partially committed to the cause."

After several minutes of scraping ooze and blood with the Popsicle-stick pen and trying to write with it, I began to wish I had a shorter name. I got as far as FISH when my blood started to dry up. On the paper, it looked reddish black.

"Just do a Y and we will call you oathed," said Duck-Duck. "You have good-quality blood. The high clotting ability corresponds with high loyalty."

Ignoring my stinging heel, I poked and grated until I had enough new blood. Y, I wrote. I wanted my whole name, but the entire back of my foot was burning, and I didn't know how I was going to get my sock clean.

"Fishy," Duck-Duck said, "oathed in blood on this date of September in the Cemetery of Famous People. Put your hand on your heart and swear: 'I, Fishy, do solemnly swear to follow the eloquent rules of the G.R. gang. I do pledge to spread fear and make graffiti of great promise and keep all Grr secrets safe. If captured, I promise to suffer torture silently and to stab myself with a pen before I would ever reveal our secret passwords. I promise to vanquish all enemies to rescue a fellow gang member. With my own red blood, to these oaths, I swear.' "

"I swear."

"You are now oathed for life. Congratulations. Does your heel hurt?"

"Not bad." It felt like knives and needles and fire, but I didn't care.

Duck-Duck zipped up her backpack. "Okay," she said. "Let's go to my house and get a Band-Aid."

We scrambled back over the stone wall, through prickly brush, and across a tiny stream. Duck-Duck trotted ahead of me, picking out invisible holes in the bushes, hopping over logs before I even knew they were lurking. I had back ways too, out through the woods and swamps to my house, but Duck-Duck's ways seemed more adventurous, like we might bump into a unicorn along the way and think it was an ordinary day.

Eventually, we passed through a hedge right into the backyard of a small house. Surrounded by hedges, I had the sudden idea we had popped through to another planet, and the journey through the woods was just there to confuse me. Close to the house, I saw a lady sitting at a picnic table.

At my house, we had a backyard too, but it was full of dead trucks and a rusty refrigerator. This backyard had green grass and soldier-tall hedges all around. It made me worry a little bit about how I'd get away. I always scouted out exits, just in case. There was barely any space between the sides of the house and the hedges. If I had to run, I'd have to go through the house.

Duck-Duck didn't seem to have any worries. She ran up to the picnic-table lady and hugged and kissed her. I'd read books where girls kissed their mothers every morning and every night and sometimes more in between. It seemed like a lot of kissing. I hoped I wasn't supposed to kiss the lady too.

When Duck-Duck and the lady were done hugging and kissing, the lady looked straight at me. She didn't look like a kissing kind of lady. She had short, spiky blond hair and big shoulders. She had blue blue sky eyes that seemed to be making a list of all the dirt spots on my shirt and the hole in the knee of my pants. It was better when grown-ups didn't see me. Fewer bad things happened. Suddenly I was mad that I'd let Duck-Duck lead me here.

"This is Fishkill Carmel," said Duck-Duck. She said it like I was a surprise chocolate chip in her lemon cupcake. She told her mother how Worm and Frank ran after me and sliced my heel open and how my sock was soaked in blood. She didn't say anything about the blood writing. All the while, the lady just kept looking at me.

The lady finally said, "Carmel? I don't know any Carmels."

Now I was sure that coming here was a mistake. I shrugged.

"Do I know your parents?"

I wanted to run back through the hedge. "Probably not. My mom is Keely Jamison. We live on Birge Hill," I added, to make her stop asking questions.

"How old are you?" she said.

"Twelve."

"And it's just you and your mom?"

I started to really dislike how she was staring at me, and I wanted to say, "Fuck you, bitch," but she was Duck-Duck's mother and they probably didn't say *bitch* or *fuck you*.

"Yes," I said. I added my Fishkill sneer and crossed my arms so she couldn't see whatever it was she was looking for.

The fancy paper in the top desk drawer at home said my father was "unknown." *Unknown.* I always wondered how you could not know something like that. I mean, it's not like a baby is a package you get in the mail with no return address. I asked my mother once when I was seven, and all she said was there were worse things than "unknown." At seven, I didn't know what she meant. Now I think I do.

Duck-Duck's mother just raised her eyebrows and said, "Let me take a look at your foot. Chrissy, go get the first-aid kit."

I sat down on the picnic bench, took off my shoe, and peeled off my sock. I wondered who Chrissy was, and then I realized the lady was talking to Duck-Duck. The blood had made the sock stiff, and my heel started bleeding again because the sock had been stuck to the drying blood. New blood, old blood, new blood—it almost made me dizzy looking at it, but blood wouldn't scare Fishkill, so I just acted like I often got trapped at backyard picnic tables with weird, big ladies who had cotton balls and a bottle in their hands, saying, "This is going to sting."

It really did sting, but I was glad that she said it. People always said stuff like "This won't hurt a bit" when really it hurt like hell.

After the Band-Aid, Duck-Duck's mother gave me a new pair of socks and two chocolate-chip cookies and milk. She poured the milk with one hand, which made me think she was really strong, because the milk wasn't in a carton but in a glass bottle. I watched the milk running out of the bottle like a white river from her big hand. White like the socks I wore. I guessed they were Duck-Duck's socks. They were kind of soft and cushy. Mine were always dry and woody because I never got socks new and I wore them till they weren't really socks anymore. The cookies were soft too, with enough chips in them that I got one in each bite.

After I ate a few more cookies, Duck-Duck's mother started looking at her watch and making comments about homework, so I knew she wanted me out. When I left, I went through the house and out the front door. I didn't see much that first time. Just the way the couch leaned up against the wall, like it liked living there.

The next day for lunch, Duck-Duck had a turkey sandwich with mayo and a pickle. I got half the sandwich and half the pickle. I don't think I had ever had a pickle like that, light green and sour, not pucker-up dark. Then we had little cookies with grape jelly squashed in the middle. She called them thumb cookies but they weren't shaped like thumbs. Not my thumb, anyways. Maybe someone with big thumbs like three of mine.

After school we walked to our cemetery quince tree, and Duck-Duck got all businesslike.

"Blood oath was the first trial," said Duck-Duck, eating a leftover cookie and licking her grape-jelly fingers. "Gang graffiti is the second."

She pulled out a can of spray paint from her backpack and shook it up. "You pick a headstone. Then you pick a word to spray on it. Something nasty but very smart," she said.

I hadn't thought of that before. I knew Fishkill should be tough. And nasty, of course. But Fishkill should also be very smart.

"Graffiti is art," Duck-Duck said, "but it's meaner."

I wasn't so sure about art, but I liked mean. I took the spray-paint can from her and walked up and down the rows of dead people. I had to do well on the mean gang graffiti test.

"Don't think about it too much," said Duck-Duck. She had now unwrapped a stick of gum and was rolling it up like a little sleeping bag. "Artists don't think about stuff too much." She popped the gum in her mouth and started flipping it around with her tongue. "It's instinct. Like the way birds make nests."

I came to the lady poet's stone. Last year, the sixth-grade teacher had made us read four of her poems, one after another, and hadn't explained a thing. I pretended I understood them, but afterward I tore the pages out of the book and tossed them in the cafeteria trash. It was lasagna day.

The spray paint was a mean red. I made droplets in the path so it looked like the gravestone had walked, dripping blood, and then died right there. It served the lady poet right, getting stuck under a bloody rock.

"You done?" called Duck-Duck, hopping over the big stone and cutting across the aisle to see. She stood in front of the lady poet, chewing her gum, and read, *"Lesbo."* She raised her eyebrows. "Hmm."

I could tell I had somehow failed the test. I bit my lip.

"What's wrong with it?" I couldn't believe I was asking. Fishkill didn't need a gang to be mean. I could be mean without any help. I should've just shoved the paint can in her face and pulled the trigger. Maybe she'd choke on that peppermint gum that smelled like Christmas or toothpaste. "What's wrong?"

"*Lesbo*'s not an artistic word. It's only mean. You want balance. Don't worry—it takes practice. It's like"—she paused the way the math teacher, Miss Treadway, did when everyone got the wrong answer, and she had to explain again, but slower—"it's like calling someone a piece of poop when really they just have a different kind of library card than you do. See?"

I had no idea what she was talking about.

Poop was a touchy subject. My grandfather used to ration toilet paper. Before each visit to the bathroom, we had to ask. We had to say if it was for a piss or crap. For a piss you got two sheets. For a crap, three.

Duck-Duck cast a critical eye on the blood-drip path. "Nice gravy droppings though."

Gravy? I looked at the grass. "It isn't gravy," I said. "It's blood."

"Blood? Even better."

Maybe I hadn't failed completely.

"The dead rock bled out. See?" I pointed to the drops, like steps to the bloody stone. "It didn't start out dead." I wasn't sure why she needed me to explain that.

"Movement and color. Very artistic," said Duck-Duck. "We could edit it a little, though," and she picked up the spray can again.

First she sprayed red all over my *Lesbo,* and then she dug in her bag and pulled out a white can. In sharp, shining letters she wrote *Dead Rok,* with a thick underline.

Duck-Duck stood back to admire her work. "Very nice. See? You knew what to write. Next time it will come right away. Now we have to pick up all the evidence so no one will suspect us."

We shoved everything into her backpack and escaped through the bushes just as two men with a dog came up the cemetery path.

2

When I was eight, Keely got drunk and ran her junk Escort into a ditch on Guttersnake Road. The cops came all the way up the hill to tell Grandpa.

"Why don't you answer your phone?" they kept asking. "Get the car towed, will you? And someone has to pick up your daughter."

Grandpa only drove to Guttersnake because the cops expected him to. I pretended to be asleep, because otherwise Grandpa would have thrown me in the back of the truck and I would have had to be there and watch the whole thing. When they came back, Keely was bloody and cursing, and Grandpa was punching the walls. I didn't know if Keely was bloody from running off the road or from Grandpa's fists. After that, she didn't have a car anymore and she had to walk everywhere, like I did. If she had been smart, she would have just walked home in the first place.

The next morning, Grandpa was still mad because he had lost his truck keys, and he blamed Keely.

I always thought the name Keely was a whiny misspelling of Kelly. It would be just like Grandpa to misspell a baby girl's name. *Kelly* sounded like a lady newscaster. *Keely* sounded like someone who couldn't get up in the morning even if the alarm clock went off three times. *Keely* sounded like someone who would run her car off the road. She was more a Keely than a Mom. Even when she bought popcorn and shared it with me, she was more like a screwed-up big sister, more a Keely than a Mom. *Keely* fit her.

Duck-Duck's mom had a nice unrusty car with four doors, an open-up back hatch, and cup holders for everyone. I liked looking at the car. I was sure Duck-Duck's mother never ran her car off a road in the middle of the night. The Wednesday after we sprayed gang graffiti, Duck-Duck and I stood in the driveway looking at the bird poop on the back hatch of her mom's car. The car was blue, and the poop was green.

"Do you think birds aim for cars, or do you think it's an accident every time?" asked Duck-Duck. She had thrown her backpack on the front step. I kept mine on.

I thought about the birds sitting in the trees, eating seeds and laughing at us.

"I think it's a kind of bird joke," I said. "'Can you hit the blue car? I bet I can get the window.'"

Duck-Duck laughed. "Hey," she said, "want me to teach you how to open car doors with the power of your mind?"

It wasn't a gang test, she said. It was just regular gang activity.

Something to make sure people would remember to be very scared of us.

She blinked three times and then closed her eyes.

"The power of the brain," she whispered, "hasn't ever been fully tapped. If you concentrate hard enough, locks are no barrier." She started breathing loudly, in, out, in, out.

I didn't know that gangs tapped the power of minds. Gangs spit and spray-painted words on walls. Or at least that's what I thought gangs did. And that was enough. Scary and enough.

"Can't we just use the clicker?" I said. Duck-Duck was holding it in her hand. She started swinging it like a pendulum before the car door.

"It works better this way," she said, but then she hit the button. *Beep-beep, flash-flash,* said the car.

"Hop in," said Duck-Duck. "Would you like to drive?"

My grandfather always drove the green pickup, slimy with rust, and with cruel pointy seat springs. When I was a passenger, I would lie in the bed of the truck, flattened low so the police wouldn't see me. Grandpa said it was illegal to ride back there. He said if they caught me, he would have to let the cops handcuff me and take me to jail. Once I cut my hand on a rusty sheet of metal, and I lay in the back, slamming against the jarring bed of road, bleeding until Grandpa stopped. He was mad because blood got on his new tarp and made a stain he said wouldn't come out. The tailgate didn't stay shut, and at night I dreamed of sliding out onto the road, only to be run over by a police car that had been tailing us. If I could drive, I wouldn't have to ride in the bed of anyone's truck ever again.

"Sure," I said to Duck-Duck. "Do we have enough gas?" Before Keely smashed up her car, she was always running out of gas.

"Yup. I've got Mom's license too. If we get stopped, I'm going to argue that since my mother pays taxes, her license should be a family membership, and I'm her dependent." Duck-Duck adjusted the mirror and handed me the keys. "I'm going to be a lawyer when I grow up."

Grandpa would argue, *I didn't hit her—she hit me* and *Do I look like someone who would do something that stupid?* but his kind of arguing didn't seem to help with the cops. The only license I ever had was the get-free-lunch-because-you're-poor license. I filled out that application because Grandpa wouldn't and Keely said she had a headache.

"They fucking want to know about my money?" Grandpa said. "Why don't they just go piss in a bucket and call it lunch?"

Lunch on a tray seemed like a step up from tomato soup, so later I grabbed the form out of the trash. On the income line, I wrote it messy-like, with too many decimal points. I had no idea what would win me lunch, so I erased and smudged, making a list of numbers that could be mistaken for other numbers, and passed it to the gray lunch lady at the register. Over her little glasses, she gave me a gray lunch-lady look, and I was sure she was going to pass it back, but no—I got a card with lunches in it.

There's always something wrong with it if they give it to you for free.

The Every Tuesday Chicken Fingers were a perfect example. I would imagine chickens with ten breaded fingers, and then I could feel the greasy skin sticking in my teeth and I'd have to stop chewing. Grandpa was so wrong, it was hard to think he might have been right about lunch and the piss in the bucket.

"Hey," said Duck-Duck. "Are you with me? You need to turn the car key." She guided my hand and the key to the ignition and prodded me just a little. "Turn it."

I had to move the seat first because I couldn't see and reach all at the same time. Duck-Duck showed me the levers and the pushers, and I levered and pushed the seat all the way forward and a little bit up.

The first time I turned the key, I held on too long and it gave this wiry rattle that didn't sound like a real car. The second time, I let go quick, and it kept running like a car is supposed to. I was probably a natural driver.

"What now?" Grandpa's truck had three pedals. This car had just two.

"One for go, one for stop," said Duck-Duck. "If you make a mistake, we'll get the best lawyer in town to defend you. That's why I want to be a lawyer. What are you going to be when you grow up?"

This caught me off guard. I couldn't tell her I had never thought about being anything. "I'm going to have my own apartment in the city," I said, "and maybe a car too."

"Well, sure, but what are you going to *do*?" She looked up and down the street. "There isn't anyone coming. Push the go pedal."

I pressed the pedal for go, but the car just whirred and spun and didn't go anywhere.

"You have to take off the E brake," Duck-Duck said.

I had to figure out how to push the button and pull on the E brake lever between the seats. You had to do both at the same time, but once I did, the brake was off and the car rolled backward, but just a little. It took me a second to remember which pedal was stop and which was go, but then I slammed the stop pedal hard and we jerked forward and back and stopped immediately.

"Do it again," said Duck-Duck, "but this time go forward." She rammed the stick between our seats from the *P* position to *D* and said, "Go!"

This time the car rolled forward when I let my foot up. I rolled and rolled and then I remembered I should steer too. I was halfway down the street when I remembered you're supposed to stay on one side of the road and not the other. When I steered to the right, I went over a bit too far and drove up on the corner of someone's lawn where they had pink flowers and ugly plastic statues.

Crunch went the statues. The pink flowers were flattened.

"Cool," said Duck-Duck. "That was just beautiful."

This was fun. I could see why everyone wanted to drive. I was busy thinking of all the places we could go and the lawns we could pulverize when Duck-Duck pointed to the side of the road.

"Can you stop right there?"

I floated over and jammed on the stop pedal, and sure enough, I stopped right where Duck-Duck wanted.

"Now what?" I asked.

"Now we park and put the keys back where they were, and my mother will flip out, looking for her car. Then she'll find it and think she forgot where she parked and wonder whether that means she's losing her marbles like my grandmother did." Duck-Duck had a little smirk that reminded me of a cat hiding under the table just waiting for some bare legs to pass by.

With her short hair and her tough shoulders, I couldn't really imagine Duck-Duck's mother flipping out about anything.

"Park the car. No problem," I said, and I twisted the key back. The car gagged but then it shut up. It was good to know I could drive, I thought as we walked back. It might come in handy later.

"I'm going to be a lawyer and go to court every day. I'll argue cases no one can argue against. Then someday maybe I'll become a judge. My mother says lawyers can become judges later. So what are you going to be?"

That question again.

"I haven't decided yet," I said.

"No problem," said Duck-Duck. "It's good to decide early so you can pick the right college, but you have a little time. At least now you can drive."

Then we walked in the front door of Duck-Duck's house, as if we had just come home from school and were hoping for a peanut-butter-banana sandwich.

3

A couple days after I learned to drive, Duck-Duck invited me to her house to do homework. I wasn't sure if I should go. Each time I missed the school bus, it was a long walk home. After the edge of town, there were no sidewalks, so I had to walk on the gravel shoulder. Also, I was worried Duck-Duck would think I was stupid. I was in the dumb math class, after all. If we only stuck to language arts and reading, I might be able to get by.

Years before I learned to bash boys into the dirt, I learned that reading was a form of self-defense. The alphabet meant nothing until I realized spelling could read minds and predict the future. Exactly halfway through first grade, letters clicked into place and became words. In Grandpa's house, a scribbled note, a phone message, or a piece of mail could mean a night of chaos. An envelope from the Department of Motor Vehicles was almost always a bad thing, as was anything from the courts.

Those notes meant Grandpa cursed and threw beer cans at us. A message from the gun club was good. Maybe I'd get four sheets of toilet paper instead of three. A note from the Health Department was always bad, since it meant Grandpa would have to pay another fine, and then he'd refuse to buy us bread. Reading meant I could identify and disappear school mail, sounding out notes for parent-teacher conferences or memos regarding shots and fluoride swishing. Grandpa was against swishing, so I knew it was something I wanted.

It wasn't until second grade that I found out reading was for fun too. Miss Carew was the pretty librarian. She wore skirts and wound up her hair like an old lady, but somehow it didn't make her look old. She invited me over to her desk and asked my name. The first book she gave me to read was *Charlotte's Web*, even though the other kids were still reading picture books. Later, she asked me what I thought of it, in a way that sounded like she really cared. And even though she never asked, she somehow understood that Keely didn't read to me at night or buy me Nancy Drews. During all-school assembly, the vice principal said we should read more biographies and historical fiction, and less about talking animals and orphans becoming superheroes. I figured the old Nancy Drews counted as historical fiction, since Nancy had no computers or cell phones and she had a housekeeper who baked homemade pies.

In third grade, other girls panned *Harriet the Spy* as dumb, since who carries around a notebook anymore? They all had computers at home and phones in their pockets. I liked the spying part of the book, but I could never figure out why Harriet got so whiny. Harriet had two parents, a nanny, and a cook, and she could keep her notebook inside the house without worrying that someone would tear it to pieces. Maybe having two parents made you soft, unless you lived in pioneer days, and sometimes maybe even then.

In the middle of fourth grade, Miss Carew went away and was replaced by two women who shelved books and stamped cards and didn't ask me what I thought about anything.

Doing English homework with Duck-Duck would be fine, but what if Duck-Duck wanted to do math instead?

"Um, sorry, my mother wants me to clean my room," I mumbled.

"Tell her you'll clean it later. We'll just tell her that education is more important to society's moral foundation than house-keeping. We can call her from my house," said Duck-Duck. "My mom got me a cell phone, but she rigged it so that I can only call her and nine-one-one. She's totally paranoid. She thinks I'll be tricked by some serial killer like on *CSI,* but I'm going to figure out how to unlock it. Meanwhile, we can write notes in code to each other if we have to communicate."

I had never owned a cell phone, so notes in code were fine with me.

"We can tell your mother that homework is best done by the cooperative learning method." She started walking, occasionally giving a little skip, tugging my hand as she headed home. I didn't pull away.

"What's the 'cooperative learning method'?"

"Teachers always come up with new reasons they do stuff. Your mother will just think it's a modern teaching philosophy."

I didn't tell Duck-Duck that my mother would never call anything a philosophy. I wasn't sure I knew what a philosophy was. I was sure my mother didn't. Grandpa would have torn up any philosophy book that came his way. He always went on about how his tax money was stolen by schools and libraries to buy cardboard and paper.

"They're brainwashing you into thinking you're better than everyone else," he sneered. He would tear up any book he saw in the house. Even schoolbooks.

In second grade, I found a hole under a rock at the end of our driveway, on the outside of Grandpa's fence. It was almost as good as a safe. I stashed my lunch pass and my library card there so Grandpa wouldn't know I had them. After he tore up *The Secret of the Old Clock,* I started putting my library books there too, although *Harry Potter* wouldn't fit. I stole a Ziploc plastic bag from the art teacher and put all my things in it and zipped it up so they wouldn't get wet.

I still had my doubts about cooperative homework, but I walked along with Duck-Duck anyway. When we got to her house, we went through the pretty red front door with the gold knocker and handle. The first thing I noticed was the smell of chicken roasting. It made me want to live there, with the chicken in the oven and Duck-Duck. I kind of forgot about Duck-Duck's mother.

There she was, though, in the kitchen. She raised her

eyebrows a little when she saw me but gave us both granola bars and milk. She said we should make sure to do our homework before we played outside. I was glad when she went into the living room and stopped watching us chew.

Duck-Duck's bedroom was like a circus. Or maybe a castle. On the wall were pictures of pink princesses and lions and women writers. She showed me how her bed looked like just one bed at first but underneath it was another one that pulled out and popped up: a second perfect pink bed with ruffles. The pillows were cushy and soft and made you want to lie down and sleep and wake up special and re-carnated.

Re-carnation seemed like a weird word, but last year, the sixth-grade teacher said it meant some people believed you could have a new life, which did make sense. I certainly wanted that. But you'd have to do it right. Like think of how powdered milk is just dry and sticky if you eat it straight. When you add water, it makes milk — but you have to add just the right amount of water. Too little, and it's still thick, like mud; too much, and it tastes like a ghost of milk. If you did it right, re-carnation sounded like a great idea.

When I was Carmel, boys hit me, and I didn't hit back. I ate tomato soup and didn't complain. I thought Social Services could make us normal. Now that I was Fishkill, it was different. Like powered-milk-with-water different. You wouldn't think water was such a big deal. It doesn't have any color or taste. But when I switched my name, I realized it was like that water.

I didn't tell anyone I was re-carnated when I filled out school papers. I just told teachers at the start of seventh grade that my name got typed backward on the old lists and that they should say Fishkill Carmel, not Carmel Fishkill. Schools made mistakes like that all the time in the front office, where they keep track of who you are and if you show up for school in the morning.

I don't know why—maybe it was the promise of those soft pillows—but now I told Duck-Duck: "I was re-carnated," I said.

"Wow, cool, like the Dalai Lama?"

"Umm," I said, "not really." I didn't know what she was talking about. "Things were hard before, so something had to change."

I wasn't sure if that helped, but Duck-Duck seemed to get it. She just pulled out an old-fashioned board game she said would help teach us the skills needed if we ever ended up in a house with a dead body and many suspects.

"That's more important than homework any day," she said.

We must have been in her room a long time, because when we came out, it was dark, and the wind was blowing pebble rain against the windows.

"It's almost hurricane strength," said Duck-Duck's mother. "I'm not sure it's safe to drive right now."

"Oh, good," said Duck-Duck. "We can have a sleepover."

I'd never stayed over at anyone else's house before. My first thought was the chicken in the oven. My second thought was where I would sleep. In the pink under-bed with ruffles?

"You want to call your mother and ask if it's okay?" said Duck-Duck.

"Sure," I said. My hands got a little sweaty, but the roasted chicken was going to be worth it. Duck-Duck handed me the phone, and I punched in the seven numbers.

"Hi, Mom?" I said. "Can I stay at Duck-Duck's tonight? Her mother said I could." I held my breath and listened. Then I handed the phone back. "Mom said it's okay."

Duck-Duck's mother was giving me that adult razor-eye, see-through-you stare. "Let me speak to her."

"Uh, sorry," I said. "She hung up already. She's really busy."

I kept my eyes looking toward the kitchen. I could feel Duck-Duck's mother still staring into the side of my head, but I pretended to ignore her.

"Can I help set the table, Mrs. Farina?" Good girls in books always helped set the table.

Duck-Duck's mother gave a cough-sneeze. "No *Mrs.* here, Fishy. You can call me Molly."

It was funny that she had a name of her own. It was also funny to hear her use Duck-Duck's name for me.

The chicken from the oven had hot little carrots and potatoes baked inside it. Not cut-up carrots and potatoes, but little ones, like they came from tiny-land. Cafeteria chicken was oily and somehow tasted the same, no matter what name it had. Chicken Potpie, Chicken Fricassee, Chicken Stew. It was like a trick to make you think you were eating different food every day. Why couldn't they make chicken like this? I could tell Molly was still eyeing me, but she kept putting more food on my plate, and I kept eating it.

For dessert we had four little vanilla wafers each. I dunked mine in my milk even though Duck-Duck didn't.

The roof of Grandpa's house on Birge Hill had cracks, so when it rained, I never slept good. Rain makes different noises outside and inside. Outside, it's wild and fast. Inside, it's slow drip-drips, making blankets wet and changing bread to glue.

But on Cherry Road, I slept through the storm in Duck-Duck's secret guest bed with the pink ruffles. I dreamed we were on a root-beer river. I could hear the outside water, but I was on a big, dry boat, sailing down the root-beer river past vanilla-wafer islands with leafy carrot trees.

When I woke, the sun was shining again, and Duck-Duck was saying, "It's Saturday! What do you want for breakfast?"

While Duck-Duck was in the bathroom, I looked at her books. She had shelves and shelves of them. Some of them were little-kid picture books. Some were big thick books about lawyers and courts and why we have laws. One book was called *A Beginner's Introduction to Forensics,* whatever that was. She had the entire Harry Potter series. It was like Miss Carew had visited and brought Duck-Duck all my favorite books, plus some.

After a pancake breakfast, with maple syrup that tasted like it could have come from *Little House in the Big Woods,* Duck-Duck's mother picked up her car keys and said, "I'm taking Chrissy to soccer practice, and then I'll drive you home." She didn't ask. She just got her car keys and stood at the door like a prison guard with the only key.

My palms got sweaty. Things didn't go well when grown-ups saw Grandpa's house. Our closest neighbors were a mile away, but they still complained about the old trucks and the dead refrigerator in the yard. Grandpa had put up an ugly fence in front of the driveway so they couldn't see in. He'd picked the cheapest, ugliest fence he could find, and he'd topped it with barbed wire so they would have to look at it every time they drove by. The problem with this was we had to look at it too.

The Social Service ladies didn't like the fence. They didn't like the shed either. When the town had changed the dump rules and you had to put a sticker on each bag of garbage and each sticker cost fifty cents, Grandpa had said the town council members were donkey's asses and no way was he going to pay their salaries with his garbage. The town warned him if he threw it in the river, they would arrest him, so we just tossed the bags into the shed. We kept doing it even after Grandpa died. When you closed the door, it really wasn't that bad, but the ladies thought it was. When they opened the shed door for the first time, the one lady almost threw up. She pretended she had allergies, but I knew she had almost heaved. They were scared of the dead cat in there too. They were always scared of the wrong things.

I tried to find reasons and excuses to keep Molly away from the house, but she raised her eyebrows and folded her arms. Her eyes got squinty again, and she looked even more like a prison guard. She ordered me into the backseat of the car and then clicked the child locks. I took a test push, and sure enough, I couldn't open the door. Parents were weird. Did they think we were going to jump out of a moving car?

We dropped off Duck-Duck, and then Molly said, "Where

to?" like we were out for a little drive and she was the chauffeur. I thought of other houses I could tell her to drive to, but she might decide she had to go in, so I gave up and told her the directions.

In elementary school, I used to get picked up by the school bus at the end of our short driveway, but then they wanted the parents to drop us at the crossroads so the bus could pick us all up in one place. I had to walk fifteen minutes to the crossroads, but I would get there ten minutes early so everyone would just assume that my mom had driven and dropped me off early. It was extra walking, but at least everyone didn't stare at our fence.

It was kind of amazing how quick it took to get home in a car compared with walking. Molly followed my directions. We drove out of town, past a few fields, into the woods, where houses weren't so nice, and in fifteen minutes we were pulling up in front of the fence. For once I was glad it was there, because you couldn't really see the house. Grandpa had blocked off the end of the driveway with a dead trailer, and Keely and I had never unblocked it.

"Thanks!" I said, and rattled the lock to remind her that she was supposed to free her prisoner.

"I'll walk up with you and say hi to your mother," said Molly, and she clicked the locks open.

"Oh, she's not here," I said quickly. "She's working. She works a lot. Sometimes nights, sometimes even on the weekend."

"Oh?" said Molly.

I didn't like how she said that. It made me think like

Grandpa—that people should just mind their own damn business. At least she wasn't getting out of the car.

Molly had turned in her seat to face me. "What does she do for work?"

That was a stumper.

"She's a consultant," I said. Grandpa once said that to the census guy.

I waited for more grilling, but Molly just said, "Have a good weekend. Don't forget your backpack."

It all made me wonder how stupid people really were. Molly obviously wasn't as smart as Duck-Duck. If I had picked someone else's ordinary house to be dropped off at, how would she have known it wasn't mine?

4

When teachers went to teacher school, they must have learned
that when you don't know what to teach, teach about butterflies. It seemed like in every grade, we talked cocoons. I got the
re-carnation part of a butterfly's life, but it had always seemed
to me like they changed in the wrong direction. Butterflies are
pretty and have wings, which is nice, but caterpillars are tougher.
Butterflies are always getting hit by cars and stepped on by shoes.
Caterpillars blend in and hide. They have little suction feet to
hang in the air if they need to. They don't have wings to pull off.
If you go to the trouble of re-carnating, you should get tougher,
not weaker, but still all those teachers were so impressed by the
butterflies. Pretty won't keep you from being hit by the grille of
a truck. Pretty talking won't either.

Duck-Duck didn't get that. She thought she could talk her
way out of anything. It was kind of smart of her, but it was also

kind of dumb. The problem with talking your way out of a fight is that, no matter how good you are at arguing, the other person has to be willing to listen.

When Worm came out of the math room all green and mad from being the dumbest in our dumb class, I could tell he wanted to hit someone. I walked real slow so it wouldn't be me, but Duck-Duck had no warning.

We all knew it was the dumb math class, even though the teachers kept changing the names. Little-kid classes had animal names: the beavers, the raccoons, the chipmunks. Now they just had colors. But who didn't know that Blue Group was teacher code for dumb? It wasn't just dumb either. I once made a list of all the Blue Group kids, and every single one of them except Manny Winter had either dead parents or dirt-poor parents. Manny had parents, but he had a tic and a stutter. He wasn't dumb. He just couldn't answer quick. He sat in the corner and drew engines and maps. Once he helped me with fractions.

Worm knew when he failed the math test that he was too dumb for the dumb group, so he looked around for someone to beat up, something he was very good at.

Out in the schoolyard, Worm ran right up behind Duck-Duck and pushed her from behind. She tripped forward onto the concrete and hit the ground with her face. Worm kicked her backpack into the mud, and then he began kicking her too, he was so mad about being dumb. I started running toward them, willing Duck-Duck to stay down on the ground. She looked so freaked out, like it was the first time anyone had hit her. There was mud on her yellow dress, and her hands and face were all scraped up from the concrete. And then I saw the big tears in those blue eyes too, another mistake.

I charged and hit Worm in the stomach as hard as I could. The stomach is a good target because it hurts like hell. It also doesn't leave a black eye or draw blood, so no teachers can see what happened. Worm doubled over like he was going to puke, and I hit him again so he couldn't catch his breath. I grabbed Duck-Duck by her arm and her backpack and pulled, hoping she wasn't so freaked out that she wouldn't be able to run. I'd seen kids just sit there and cry instead of run. Duck-Duck got up, but she looked bad. She had blood and snot all over her face, and she had this stunned look like people get when they've just seen their cat get run over.

Duck-Duck and I just about got away, but Worm ran over to the gym teacher. People think you're a rat if you tell, but you're worse off if the other guy tells first. Teachers always side with the story they hear first.

The teacher spotted us. "You," he yelled, aiming a sausage finger at me. "Get over here." I stepped in front of Duck-Duck.

"Did you hit him?"

"Yup," I said. "I hit him." Mr. MacNamara wasn't chatty. He never wanted to sit down and talk it through with you like the other teachers did. He never asked why.

"Detention. Now."

First rat outweighed truth. If I argued, I'd get another day of detention.

Duck-Duck didn't seem to know we were screwed. She stepped out from behind me. She had lost the dead-cat look.

"Fishkill was just protecting me," she said. "Norm performed an unprovoked act of aggression." She brushed off her dirty dress and rubbed her dirty cheek and then her nose with her fist.

If Worm or I had done that, we would have been outed as babies and suck-up pretenders. But Duck-Duck didn't even know she was acting like a suck-up baby, and Mr. MacNamara fell for it. He coughed and shuffled his feet. "You *both* get detention," he said, gesturing to me and Worm.

"Fishy was acting in good faith," said Duck-Duck. "The Good Samaritan law states you can't blame a person for ill effects if their intent was to help. Look it up." Blood was smeared across her nose, but she sounded like a grown-up, all logical and patient.

Mr. MacNamara apparently thought so too. "All right," he said. He gave me the evil eye, but all he said was "You're off the hook *this* time. Just walk Miss Farina home." He was still gripping Worm's shoulder, and maybe he sent Worm home too, but I didn't stick around to find out. I quick grabbed Duck-Duck's arm and started moving.

"I gotta teach you how to fight," I said.

When we got past the school field, I turned to Duck-Duck.

"Don't you know to stay on the ground when someone's kicking you?"

Law of the jungle, my grandfather used to say when I came home bloody. He was wrong about that, though, because in the jungle, monkeys have other monkeys and rabbits have other rabbits. Even birds stick up for other birds. No one stuck up for me.

41

Duck-Duck didn't answer me, maybe because she was busy wiping blood and snot off her face.

Duck-Duck's version of the afternoon confused me. She didn't tell her mother about the tears or the mud. Instead, she talked about how huge Worm's feet were and how the words *PinPoint Correctional Facility* were sewn onto his canvas jacket. All I noticed was how his shoe went into her ribs and how he lost his balance when he tried to kick her again.

"You think the jacket means he's a felon?" Duck-Duck asked as Molly cleaned her scrapes.

"He's twelve. I doubt he has a criminal record," said her mother. "Maybe his father works at the prison."

My grandfather worked as a prison guard for thirty years. Keely said Grandpa loved barbed wire because of that. Even after he retired, it was like Grandpa still needed walls and people to hate.

"He kicked me, Mom," said Duck-Duck, and Molly flinched.

"And then Fishy whammed him in the stomach," Duck-Duck reported.

I was pleased, but I took a peek at Molly, since she was probably one of those parents who thought you shouldn't fight back because the eye-for-an-eye thing was wrong. She looked like she was trying not to laugh.

"It's good to have friends," was all she said.

Later, Molly called the school and talked to the teacher and the counselor and the principal and even Worm's father. It was a little weird to see a mother getting involved in kids' business like that, but Duck-Duck didn't seem to mind.

5

"Have you ever been to the ocean?" Duck-Duck asked. "Have you ever seen a whale?" We were camped out in her pink room, doing homework. Outside, it was raining, and the early fall leaves were weighed down with pounding water.

I had seen the ocean once on a third-grade trip to Plymouth Rock. It was much different from the Birge Hill river.

In the spring, the river would flood, merging with the swamps out behind the house, eating little bridges, chewing up sheds. It even killed fish. When I was in third grade, it covered the roads and trapped us on Birge Hill: prisoners for two whole days. After day and night, day and night with Grandpa, Keely grew as gray as the water. I pretended I was Harry Potter and hid under the porch stairs with my raincoat and a can of sardines.

From my hiding spot, the river drowned out the *thump-thump* of Grandpa's bed against the wall.

I once saw a coffin floating downstream. At least that's what it looked like. Maybe it was a planter.

Once I saw Keely walk out into the current up to her waist and just stand there for an hour, staring at the water. I didn't know if she wanted to go farther or if she just forgot to come in.

I'd never seen a whale.

"Sure I have," I said. "They're endangered." That was the kind of thing Duck-Duck would know. I said it so she wouldn't ask me what the whale looked like.

"Exactly," said Duck-Duck. "The Grrs need a socially responsible project. Maybe we should save the whales."

"I thought gangs were supposed to shoot people and make people bleed," I said. "Not save whales." Besides, it wasn't the whales in Salt Run that needed saving.

"How about we make next month Shotgun Month? This month is Socially Responsible Month," said Duck-Duck. "Don't worry. We'll get to everything." She turned on her computer. "How about liberation of animal prisoners?" She double-clicked and started searching.

"Animal prisoners?" PinPoint Correctional, where my grandfather had worked, was a men's prison. Women were sent across the state. I didn't know where they sent animals.

"Pet stores!" said Duck-Duck. With a triumphant click, she brought up a picture of Pet Paradise at the mall.

Keely stopped going to the mall because after her car died, it was too far, and so I'd hardly ever been. Grandpa said we shouldn't go, because the mall was where crackhead teenagers did it on benches.

"Enough bad PR, and the pet-store industry will crumble like a doggy biscuit," said Duck-Duck. "But you have to have a perfect plan or they can sue you for libel, slander, and defamation."

Keely never had plans. Duck-Duck was full of them.

"Step one: deflect responsibility onto the target entity." Duck-Duck cut and pasted the pet-store website logo and then wrote a letter worthy of a twelfth-grade English class.

To the Citizens of Salt Run,
Whereas we, the owners of Pet Paradise,
do acknowledge the grievous error of our ways;
Whereas we acknowledge that we have placed
dogs, cats, mice, guinea pigs, and the occasional
snake into involuntary servitude and cruel slavery;
Whereas we have realized that living, breathing,
feeling beings have rights even though they
happen to not have been born humans;
We resolve to let all animal prisoners in Pet Paradise
go free to good homes on the day of September
the twenty-fifth, that all beings of fur may cease
to be oppressed. A free packet of Kibbles will be
given to the first one hundred visitors.
Yours with regret,
Betty and George Garand
(soon-to-be-former Pet Paradise
slave owners, who have now seen the light)

Duck-Duck printed out the page to proofread. "We can send a copy to all the newspapers. I bet we can figure out how to post it to the pet-store website too. We just have to make sure not to leave any fingerprints, so it can't be traced back to us."

"But the pet store didn't acknowledge any of those *whereases*," I said.

"The beauty of it," said Duck-Duck, "is that it will take ages before people figure out the letter is fake, but by that time, everyone will have accepted that even pet-store owners think pet stores are bad. People will show up for their free Kibbles, and there will be a scene. It's great political theater."

I read it again. "Isn't slavery always cruel?"

"Sometimes you have to spell things out. Lots of people don't read carefully."

This was true.

"Snakes don't have fur," I said, reading it again. "And what about birds?"

"Fair enough," said Duck-Duck, and she added birds and changed the wording to "all beings of feathers, scales, and fur."

In addition to sending it to the newspapers and posting it on the website, we put up flyers. Duck-Duck thumbtacked them to coffee-shop announcement boards along with the girls' soccer schedule. She would slide the pet-store flyer out at the last minute and tack up both, "so if we're being videotaped, it won't be obvious."

The next week, there were two articles in the Sunday paper. One was entitled "Animal Rights Extremists Hack Website" and the other "Confusion at the Mall." Duck-Duck said Molly read the newspaper at breakfast. She thought her mother was looking at her funny afterward, but maybe it was her imagination.

"I don't know why she'd suspect it was me," Duck-Duck complained. "Besides, I didn't even really hack the website. I just posted the letter in the comments section using the company font and logo so it looked like their own writing."

I thought it was kind of cool that Duck-Duck's mother thought her daughter was smart enough to be an extremist. It made me like Molly a little more. I was still worried Molly was suspicious of me because I never invited Duck-Duck to my house.

"Lunch," called Molly from the kitchen. Just hearing her voice made me smell baked chicken, but I tried to act cool. Normal people didn't care so much about what was for lunch.

"What's for lunch?" said Duck-Duck, skipping down the hall with a little hop. I walked behind her. I hoped we looked like extremists.

Molly was ladling out bowls of soup. Even before I saw the red-orange glow, I felt sick to my stomach. I froze in the doorway.

I was back in fourth grade, the year of tomato soup and sardines. Grandpa said he'd gotten a deal, but maybe he just stole them. Cases and cases of canned tomato soup and sardines, stacked in tippy piles in the trash shed. Even after he died, there were still sardines left. The Social Service lady didn't like it that food was in with garbage. I didn't care about that so much—it was all in cans anyways—but she didn't seem to get that that was *all* we ate for a year straight. I'd look at tomato soup and I'd get this chunky feeling in my throat and start to feel like you do when they talk about backed-up sewage flowing into the river. It got so the sound of the can opener made me gag. "What's the difference?" Grandpa would say. "A fruit, a meat—that's all you need to live. Food is fucking food." At school they gave us lessons in food pyramids and talked about grains and vegetables as if they just popped through a mail slot in your refrigerator every day. Each time we peeled another can open, I would think about those pictures of cows and chickens, apples and nuts. I started worrying that my insides would turn red and my poop would smell of fish.

That year, Yodels probably saved my life. I could barely swallow more tomato, and I was afraid I would starve to death if I couldn't eat the soup and sardines anymore.

The first Yodel was left on a cafeteria table by Cruisey Pike. He took off after someone who had swiped his phone, and he never came back. I pulled the Yodel out of its plastic wrap and shoved half of it into my mouth. The sweet chocolate skin hit my teeth first. Next came the chocolate cake. Finally, the cream middle landed softly on my tomato-burned tongue. It was dumb, but I almost cried, it was so good.

The next time, I bought a Yodel three-pack at the corner store. I had found 159 cents of dropped change in the lunch line and some undigested dimes and quarters in the soda machine. I hid the Yodels in my rock box, eating each one slowly. When Grandpa died and the Social Service ladies started coming, we got food stamps, and Mom bought milk and bread. After a while,

I didn't need to eat Yodels so often. I still carried one around with me, though, just in case.

"Fishy?" said Duck-Duck. "You okay? You look like you just saw a ghost."

I took a deep breath to ward off the waves of nausea. I reminded myself that I was in Molly's kitchen, not on Birge Hill. "Sure," I said. "I mean, I'm fine." I could feel sweat pop out on my forehead. I looked away from the red bowls.

"You don't look so fine." Molly was looking at me now too.

I couldn't figure out how to explain myself. Maybe I should say yes, I saw a ghost. It seemed simpler than anything else.

"I don't like tomato soup so much," I said. "It's no biggie. I'll just have saltines."

Something about what I said seemed to worry them even more.

"No problem," said Molly. "I'll make you a sandwich." She gave me that see-through-you look, as if it might actually be a problem but she was doing it anyway.

She made me a peanut-butter-and-jelly sandwich, and no one said anything more about tomato soup, but I got the feeling they were watching to see if I would turn the color of sardines again.

By the end of October, I was spending almost every afternoon at Duck-Duck's. At her house, they opened all school mail together and talked about it, as if everyone had a vote on the field-trip form, as if everyone had a real opinion about the soccer-practice schedule.

When he was still breathing, Grandpa handled all school mail I didn't hide from him. It didn't matter if it was addressed to Keely or me. He opened it with a knife, read a line, and announced his opinion.

"'Reminder: Parent-Teacher meetings,'" he would read. "Tell your teacher, if I wanted to meet her, she'd already have the black eye to remind her."

He'd open another envelope: "'After-school girls' soccer practice.' What's practice gonna do for them? Make them all bull dykes who can kick?"

It got so that I didn't even have to see what was inside the envelope. I could still hear Grandpa's voice. Once he wrote on the meeting-request form under *Preferred Time:* "Never." Under *Other Times Available,* he wrote: "When Hell freezes over."

I made sure that form got lost.

"Is your mom coming to parent-teacher night?" Molly asked me.

She didn't ask about my mother much, but when she did, I kept my head low and my homework pencil moving on my math problems.

"Fishy?" said Duck-Duck. "If your mom's going to the parent meeting, you could come here. We could make cookies and popcorn and tell her we ate chili." She gave her mother a little blue-eyed laugh, and her mother smiled back at her.

"Umm," I said, "probably not. Mom is pretty tired after working so much. She just comes home most nights and goes to bed."

"I thought you said she worked nights," said Molly.

I redid the word problem very slowly so all the percentages added up to one hundred.

"She does. That's why she can't go to parent-teacher meetings," I said. "Sometimes when she has late nights, we go to the diner in the morning," I added, "before I go to school. We get pancakes and syrup and orange juice."

Molly didn't say anything to that, but I could tell I was in trouble. Yet somehow I couldn't keep quiet.

"Last night she made fried chicken," I said. "It's a family recipe. Then I did homework and she corrected it for me."

"That's nice." That was all Molly said, but it sounded off, like she didn't really think it was nice.

"She's a great cook," I said. "She almost won best lemon meringue pie at the county fair one year."

"You'll have to bring us a taste sometime," said Molly.

And still I couldn't shut up.

"She made me a chocolate-raspberry cake for my birthday last year. It had real raspberries inside and it said *Happy Birthday, Fishkill* on top."

"I'll call and ask her if she's going to the meeting," said Molly. "What's your number?"

I redid the word problem. The paper was starting to get holes where I had erased too many times.

Molly was pouring a glass of milk, but I knew she knew I had heard her.

"I'll call her for you," I said, "but I'll have to leave a message. I don't think she's home yet."

I picked up the phone and dialed. "Yup, just the machine," I said after a pause. "Hello, Mom. Molly wants to know if you're going to the parent-teacher meeting. Hope you had a good day at work. See you soon." I hung up.

"Thanks," said Molly.

"No problem," I said.

"It's time I drove you home," she said. "Chrissy and I are visiting friends this evening."

"But we can see each other on Sunday. We're going to the farmers' market," said Duck-Duck. "They have live mushrooms in a terrarium. You can come with us."

"Maybe," said Molly. "Chrissy, why don't you vacuum the living room. I'll just be gone a few minutes."

Molly and I drove to my house in silence. When we got there, Molly stopped in front of the fence and turned off the car. Not a good sign. She got out and walked around to open my door. When I climbed out, she put her hand on my arm, gripping it tightly. I knew she wasn't just being friendly.

She looked me right in the eye and said, "Okay, kiddo, time to be straight with me." I started searching for places to run, but she stood in the way of all of them. "I went back and checked that phone number you called the other night," she said. "It wasn't your mother's number. It was the convenience store."

I thought of saying my mother worked at the convenience store, but that could be disproved. I sucked my front teeth.

Molly kept a grip on my arm and walked us past the fence and the dead trucks. I thought of my backpack, still in the backseat of Molly's car, and I started to panic.

"Should we pretend to knock?" she asked, looking at me

with mean, squinty eyes. I didn't say a word, so Molly went ahead and knocked, and knocked again, and then pushed open the door.

When Molly pulled me inside, it was like I was seeing the house for the first time. I saw it like Duck-Duck, with her beautiful circus-pink bedroom, would see it. I saw it like Molly, with her clean kitchen and oven-full-of-chicken, would see it.

The house I'd lived in my whole life was barely more than a trailer, and very cold. The oil had run out in April, and the propane had petered out before school started. The kitchen smelled of shuttered winter mold, even though it was only October. I had newspapers and magazines tucked in leaky windows for insulation, but condensation had smeared the black ink along the glass. There was a brown, flaky scar on the ceiling above the stove where Keely had burned hot dogs and made a black, smoky cloud. I had tried to clean a little, but grease had built up on the table and along the windowsills, as if the dead driveway trucks had moved in when I wasn't looking.

Grandpa's prized collection was still up on the wall: forty-four license plates from forty-four states, nailed to the wallpapered kitchen walls and up and down the narrow hall. One of the neighbors collected teapots. Grandpa had called her a dimwit.

I had managed to keep the electricity on, paying at the drugstore with change I found under the couch, in a jar behind the cups, in a pocket of an old, forgotten sweater. Despite the lamp, which went on when Molly flipped the switch, the kitchen looked shadowy, almost as if we were underground.

Still gripping my arm, Molly picked up the phone, which

was dead. She opened the refrigerator, which was almost empty. There was a bottle of mustard, some ketchup, and a Yodel, which I kept there to protect it from mice.

In a normal house, there would be bread and milk and orange juice. In a smart-math-class house, there would be chocolate cake and chicken sandwiches just sitting there, waiting for dinnertime.

Suddenly I was jealous of Duck-Duck, who had a pink bedroom and a refrigerator full of food and a bookshelf filled with books. It wasn't her fault she had everything and I had nothing, but it sure felt like it was. What had I done to be stuck in this crap house instead of her?

"How long has your mother been gone?" asked Molly. She didn't look so good in the kitchen light right then. She looked a little like Duck-Duck after Worm had kicked her.

"None of your business," I said. I lifted my arm up, like I was going to wipe tears from my eyes, and felt Molly's grip loosen just a little bit. Then I dropped to the floor, ripping her hand off me. Without standing, I scrabbled backward, out the still-open door. The minute I hit the front step, I jumped up and took off. I could hear Molly running and then calling after me, but she didn't know the dead-truck yard like I did. Soon I was far away.

And then I realized I had just admitted that my mother was gone. Next, Molly would find out my mother was gone because of me.

6

I don't believe in ghosts. Dead people are not scary like live ones. Dead people just watch and listen. They do not drink or tell their children to lie in the dark with noses pressed in rough wood floors. Dead people do not pour whole pots of soup across the kitchen table, leaving steam and waves of slosh and nothing else to eat. Dead people can be trusted to stay in place and let you pass by. It is the live ones who are scary, not the un-live. When Grandpa hit the floor with a heart-attack gasp, he did not wake or turn or beg for help. He did not command or curse. He was just dead. *Were you scared?* the Social Service ladies had asked. *No,* I said. Why should I be? Dead, he was, well, dead. On the floor, losing heat, tensing up, an invisible wire fence around his eyes and muscles. If I had known, I would have wished for it daily. I would have plotted poison or guns. The ladies thought I should mourn or worry, but after a day of jumping when the door slammed, I slept so sound that I realized I'd never really slept before. Imagine sirens and lights and earthquakes shaking. Then think of blue-water calm. That was the difference. The difference was mine for good. Why would I mourn or worry now? I had my sleep. I had my hard name to keep others away from my night sleeps. Fish like water. They sleep with fishy eyes open. Some sleep with both eyes on one side of their head. Down against the water bottom, gravel on my fins, I sleep. I blend, my colors the same as the cemetery rock around me. No one notices me. No one except Duck-Duck.

"What's up, Fishy? Did you sleep here all night?"

It was hard to remember how to speak. It was hard to remember where I was. My knees felt cold, and, for an instant, I thought I was dead too. But why then would Duck-Duck talk to a dead person? And of course I was cold—I'd just spent a night sleeping in a cemetery.

"What are you doing in the cemetery?"

I didn't say anything.

"Did you eat breakfast?" she asked.

I had eaten nothing since the day before. I was dead, or almost dead, so why did I need to eat?

"I have a couple sausage links," she said, pulling out a round Tupperware container from her backpack and peeling off the red top.

I fished one out with my fingers, and Duck-Duck did too.

"Are you going to tell anyone where I am?" I felt like I was talking through water, but it was just fog, and we were just under the cemetery quince tree. I tried to chew.

"Don't be silly. We're oathed, remember? Why are you living in your house alone?"

I didn't say anything. I chewed sausage.

"Where's your mother?"

I looked at her blue eyes and thought of her pretty lunch box and knew she would never think a mom could disappear one morning and never come back.

"If I tell you, are you going to tell your mother?" I said.

"But she sent me to find you. Wouldn't it be good to tell her?" Duck-Duck handed me another sausage. "Okay, I won't tell if you don't want me to. I'd have to stab myself with a pen, remember?" She reached into her pack again and pulled out a grape juice box. She detached the dinky straw and punctured the straw hole in the top and offered me a sip.

"So, you're like Pippi Longstocking?"

It took me a second to figure out what she meant. Miss Carew had lent me those books in second grade. At first all I could remember about them was pancakes and a horse. Then I remembered: Pippi's father was gone. Pippi's mother was dead.

"No, I'm not like Pippi," I said. "I don't have a horse."

"That's really bad logic," said Duck-Duck. "Where's your mother?"

And then, my feet still cold from being dead all night, I told her.

Sometimes I think I am a zoo animal born into the wrong cage: a small monkey living with lions, a turtle contemplating the ways of snakes.

If I lived with the monkeys, the other monkeys would save me bananas and peanut butter and pick nits off my curly tail. I would learn the secret monkey ways—how to swing on vines, how to hang upside down while carrying a monkey baby under my monkey arm, how to sleep in the trees, how to drink milk from coconuts.

Instead, I'm a monkey watching lions bite to kill, knowing that my teeth are way too small to do the same. I don't like eating dead things; I'd rather have a flower or a nut. I hide in the bushes so I'm not mistaken for lunch. But after living with the lions, they have rubbed off on me too much, and now the other monkeys think I'm weird—not a lion, but not a normal monkey either.

When the Social Service ladies showed up after Grandpa died, they didn't get it. They thought a little paint and a cooked vegetable or two would make us a normal family. They lectured a lot, trying to make me nice like them. They treated me as if I were six years old and a bit dumb, even though I was the one who had lived in that house, not them. They said Grandpa had hurt Keely really bad and that was why she didn't make cookies like other mothers. She was so young when she had me, they said, that she didn't know how to be a grown-up mother. And she never learned, I added in my head. They'd only heard a few stories. There were a lot more.

But really, what would I know about other mothers? Even if she made chocolate-chip cookies, she would still be a lion and I would be a monkey born into the lion's cage. The Social Service ladies said that when I turned sixteen, I could be an emancipated minor. I didn't care what name they used—it meant I would be free. I wrote a list of what I needed: a new name, a lunch box, a wallet, and a key. The key was for the apartment I would have in the city.

But in the meantime, I was still stuck on Birge Hill with Keely.

After Grandpa died, Keely and I didn't fight. We didn't talk, even, unless the Social ladies forced us to. She would go out. I would come home. She would come home. I would go out. Even when she was still here, she wasn't really here. A lion and a monkey.

She had a Walmart job for a little while. She would go to work and come back late. Unless she knew the Social Service ladies were coming. Then she'd come home early and leave a little food in the refrigerator. After six months of Walmart, and milk and bread in the fridge, the ladies closed our case and stopped coming. After that, Keely left less and less in the fridge. I didn't really understand. What did she do with the food-stamp money? You couldn't buy anything but food with it. You couldn't buy beer or cigarettes. You couldn't even buy soap or toilet paper. Once I wanted a toothbrush, but it wouldn't buy that either.

I started storing up Yodels again, like I did during the soup-and-sardine year. When Keely was asleep, I would go through her pockets. She must have hid the SNAP food-stamp card somewhere, because I never found it. I would take what little change she had and imagine her cashing her paycheck and buying dinner at the diner: hamburgers, french fries, milk shakes, apple pie.

Once she left me a small can of tomato juice. I would've thought it was a sick joke, if Keely ever made jokes.

School ended in the middle of June. That meant no more school lunches. I survived a week of summer vacation on saltines and a tiny jar of peanut butter.

Then the next week, Keely came home in the middle of the day. She was fired from Walmart. Who gets fired from Walmart?

"What'd you get fired for?" I asked, but Keely just walked down the little hill to the rocks near the river. She stood on a big rock right at the edge. The water churned below her.

"The Social Service ladies said you had to buy milk and bread and Yodels every day," I said, following her. I made up the Yodels part, but I figured she wouldn't remember anyways. The ladies always said to her, "Don't you remember what we talked about last week?" and Keely almost never did. Me, I memorized everything, because in the beginning I thought the ladies were teaching us how to be normal.

"We'll have to economize," Keely said, and she stared at the rushing water like it was a TV show or something.

Standing there, hearing her say "economize" like we had anything to give up, it was like the first time I realized I was always hungry. I'd stolen food, but I'd never once said out loud, "I am hungry." And being Carmel meant I had never fought back.

"You barely buy a box of cereal a week," I said to Keely. "What the hell do you do with it all? Your paycheck? The SNAP card?"

She looked away from the river long enough to open her

wallet to show me there was no cash in it. "You don't understand how much it costs just to keep the electricity on." I could see the SNAP card, though. It was funny how the government thought calling food stamps SNAP would make poor people feel better about taking free food. I could imagine some lady in an office thinking, "SNAP, what a good name. It sounds so up and peppy." Me, every time I heard SNAP, I would think, "Food—gone in a SNAP."

"Give me the food card," I said, trying to pull the card out of the wallet. But she just tucked the card in her pocket and spit in the river.

Grandpa used to spit in the soup and tell us we were only worth spit.

"You're as bad as Grandpa," I said. "I wish you were dead too. Then at least I would get the food card."

Keely looked panicked, like she remembered the *thunk* Grandpa made when he hit the floor. I jammed my hand into her pocket and tried to pull out the card. Her hip was bone against my palm. I closed my fingers over the card and started to pull it out, over her hip.

She clawed the card out of my hand, but I was still there, fighting her for it.

"Give me the card, dead lady," I said. I knew it was mean, but I couldn't stop myself. "Dead," I said again. "Like dead meat. Like the dead cat in the shed. Like Grandpa dead."

When I said "Grandpa," she jerked like I'd stabbed her. She might have had tears in her eyes, but I didn't care. And then everything sped up, as if I had hit the fast-forward button on a slow movie.

Keely jerked back and stumbled, and then, like a wheel or a rock, she fell into the river. The riverbank dropped off sharply into deep, dark water.

I could have reached out. I could have looked for a branch or stick.

I could have run for help. I could have yelled.

But I just watched. Keely sank into the dark, and then she was gone. I never saw her come up.

I told Duck-Duck all this.

"So you see," I said, "I'm a fugitive. I killed her."

"Boy," said Duck-Duck. "Pippi Longstocking has nothing on you."

Somehow she didn't seem horrified. I didn't know why. I was pretty sure she didn't know any murderers. I was pretty sure she had never killed anyone herself. Anyone with any sense would have run the other way.

"As your legal counsel," continued Duck-Duck, "I would advise you to never admit to something you haven't been accused of yet. You didn't kill her. We'll tell the court she disappeared."

"Well, she did disappear. She disappeared over the bank of the river because of me, and now she's dead."

"Was the body recovered? Is there proof?" said Duck-Duck.

"No, but wouldn't it be all bashed up?" I could see pieces of Keely floating down the dark river, getting stuck in boat engines, showing up in fish guts. My stomach clenched.

"People used to go over Niagara Falls in wooden barrels," said Duck-Duck. "This isn't even half a Niagara."

"She didn't have a barrel. She never came up again. She's dead." I was getting pissed. Duck-Duck wasn't there. Why couldn't she just believe me? She always wanted to talk about things that didn't need talking about. "Never mind. I shouldn't have told you."

"No, no," said Duck-Duck. "It's important for counsel to get a full picture of circumstances before taking on a client."

"I don't need counsel," I said. "I need a bus ticket. If your mother figures out I've got no grown-up, she'll tell the school, and they'll find out what happened, and they'll put me in jail." I started to sweat. I had to get moving. Fast.

"Jail? What exactly do you think you did?" said Duck-Duck.

"I wished she was dead, and then it happened." How much clearer could I put it?

Duck-Duck sucked on the juice-box straw thoughtfully. "Thought doesn't equal action," she said.

"I told her she was a dead lady," I said, "and then she was. She could barely swim, and no one can hold their breath that long."

"Talk is cheap," said Duck-Duck. "My mother says that sometimes. Besides, I think we can beat the rap when we go to trial. I watch a lot of crime shows. It's hard to prove things."

"Forget trials—I need a damn bus ticket to get out of town."

"If we tell my mother what happened," she said again, "she could probably help."

"Screw that, Duck-Duck. She's a grown-up. Grown-ups don't help. They only make things worse."

We sat there a minute, Duck-Duck making empty sucking sounds with the straw. I wished we had another juice box. Maybe I shouldn't have said that about her mother.

I should have seen the cop coming. He appeared so quick, he must have sneaked up on us. I couldn't run. He was standing on my foot. How did he find me so quickly?

My mother had a regular relationship with the town cops. She got picked up for drinking without a paper bag. She got picked up for hitting the Slow Children sign after she left the beer-and-spicy-peanut bar. When Grandpa was around, the neighbors would complain about the front yard or about all the yelling, and one of the town cops would show up and talk Grandpa down, or warn him he couldn't burn trash, or give him a ticket for having too many dead trucks in the yard.

I thought I knew all the cops in Salt Run, but I didn't know this one. He looked young and too eager. Any cop who was stalking kids in a cemetery probably didn't have much else to do. It was good he was new, though. He didn't know who I was.

"Ha!" he said, still standing on my foot. He couldn't stand on me and Duck-Duck at the same time, but he looked like he wanted to. It didn't matter, though. Duck-Duck didn't know enough to run.

"I'm guessing you're the kids who desecrated the gravestone," he said. He looked really pleased with himself. "You're coming with me. The Historical Society has been on us to figure this out."

I kept sending Duck-Duck mental messages to run, but she

looked almost happy, like she'd been waiting hours for this guy to appear.

"Good morning, Officer," she said. "What evidence do you have? You're using bad logic if you have no evidence and you think you can get a conviction."

"Jesus Christ, kid, I haven't arrested you yet. Just stand up and come with me." The cop grabbed both of us by an arm, hauled us to our feet, and shoved us toward the gate. "We're just going to have a little chat."

"We're minors," said Duck-Duck as he pushed us toward his car. "You have to get approval from the Supreme Court before you interrogate minors."

"Don't worry, kid. As soon as we get to the station, I'm calling your mothers. That's as Supreme as we get around here," and he pushed us into the back of the cop car and slammed the door.

I was screwed. They would send me to an orphanage or to jail. My stomach cramped. Maybe I could ask to go to the bathroom and climb out a window at the police station. I started thinking of what I didn't have with me for my escape. My backpack, my Yodels. The heat in the car was nice, though, after being in a cemetery all night.

When we got to the police station, there was only one other cop, and he was on the phone. He looked vaguely familiar. Almost all the cops in Salt Run were part-time. I guessed if there were others on duty, they were out doing important things, not arresting kids for spray-painting old gravestones.

"We demand to be released on our own recognizance," said Duck-Duck. "We aren't a flight risk. We can't even drive yet."

"You have to wait for court to say that," said the cop. "Plus, you have to wait till you're arrested. What's your mother's name?"

"I plead the Fifth," said Duck-Duck. She wouldn't sit down where the cop was pointing but stood facing him. "It's not Mom's fault she's related to me."

"Kid, you have watched way too much *Law and Order.* Sit down and tell me your mother's name."

Duck-Duck sat down and made a big show of writing her telephone number and name. To me she whispered, "That's all you have to give them, you know. Your name, your age, and your telephone number."

I was worried about even this, but so far the cop hadn't said a word to me. He seemed to have had enough to think about just dealing with Duck-Duck.

The cop picked up Duck-Duck's number and walked away. I looked around for escape routes until he came back with two Cokes.

All I had had to eat that morning was two sausage links and a little grape juice. My mouth was still sticky with cemetery dirt and night spit.

"Don't touch it," Duck-Duck hissed at me. "They do that just to get your fingerprints and DNA."

"What if I open it with a napkin?"

"Then you have to eat the napkin, or they take that too," whispered Duck-Duck.

I figured I'd rather have the Coke and eat a napkin than not have the Coke. I opened my can with the napkin and poured some into my mouth, trying not to touch the can with my lips. I spilled some on the table, but mostly it went in. The can was damp with condensation, which seeped into the napkin. It would be a lot of work to get DNA off a Coke can, and there were only two policemen. Cops were busy. They always said, "Don't waste my time," when my mother called them to the house, and "Why am I here again?" when they came back for the third time that night.

"Okay, now you, kid." The cop was talking to me. "What's your mother's name and phone?"

In fourth grade, I had a math teacher who didn't like noise. Despite our reputation as the worst-behaved, noisiest class in ten years, Miss Benson insisted that if our minds were quiet, our mouths would be quiet too. She taught us to sit down, put our hands on the desk with the pointer finger and thumb touching, and quiet our minds. When she tapped her table and said, "Calm minds, calm minds," we were supposed to close our eyes too, but that was just dumb. You'd have to be stupid to close your eyes in the middle of the day with the worst kids in ten years sitting right behind you.

I didn't close my eyes at the police station, but I put my hands on the table, pinched my pointer fingers and thumbs together, and thought of Miss Benson.

"Kid, you deaf?" said the cop.

"She's meditating," said Duck-Duck. "You should try it. You wouldn't get so snappy. Her mother is out of town, getting rejuvenated. Fishy is staying with us. When my mother comes, she'll tell you."

"Is that paint on your jacket, kid?" He pulled my sleeve up a little. "No wonder you're not talking."

"Oh. My. God," said Duck-Duck. "That is such circumstantial evidence. You should be ashamed of yourself."

I was still thinking about Calm Mind and Miss Benson when it occurred to me: Duck-Duck had just lied. Not about the circumstantial stuff but about my mother. And she did it like a pro. Not one stutter, not one extra pause.

My feeling about lying was that it was probably wrong. Grandpa did it a lot. The cops would come, and Grandpa would say my mother had walked into a door, or that *she* hit *him,* or that all that the neighbors had heard was the TV. It always made me feel sick because I knew if the cops kept asking questions, eventually they would try to ask me, and I'd have to lie too.

But Duck-Duck lying didn't make me feel sick. It was a nice lie, not a mean-blame lie, so maybe lying wasn't all bad? Maybe it was more like *Little House on the Prairie.* Miss Carew had said it was the story of the writer growing up, but it probably didn't happen exactly like that, or it would be called an autobiography. So *Little House* wasn't exactly true, but you wouldn't call the author a liar either. I didn't want to go to prison, but I couldn't climb out a window when Duck-Duck had just lied for me.

Calm Mind took a lot of work. Just as I was thinking I couldn't stay quiet any longer, Molly showed up. When Molly started talking to the cop, first she looked worried, then she looked mad, then she made nasty eyes at Duck-Duck and me. She looked at us quick, so the cop didn't notice, but we saw.

Duck-Duck made a squinty-eye look back at her. I looked at the floor. All those blue-eyed messages were confusing. I didn't know what they meant for my chances of getting out of there. Molly didn't know Duck-Duck had lied about me staying with them. What if the cop asked her, and Molly said she'd never seen me before in her life? Maybe she was one of those parents who thought life experience was important, and she would leave us here overnight, which would give the cops time to figure out who I was and go looking for my mother. Maybe Molly would say *her* Duck-Duck was a *good* girl and blame everything on me. Even after all that Calm Mind stuff, this almost made me cry. Fishkill was never supposed to cry. Never.

Finally, the cop said, "Okay, kids, your mom and I have negotiated a deal."

"We are representing ourselves," said Duck-Duck. "We don't need outside counsel."

"Too late," said the cop. "Mom and I have decided that if you both promise never to do it again and do a community service cleanup job, we'll just keep this between us. Okay? The Historical Society really just wants to know it won't happen again and wants the stones cleaned up."

Duck-Duck opened her mouth to speak, but the cop cut her off. "Ma'am, Miss Jail-House-Lawyer is about to file a class-action suit, but since the other one is staying with you, I figure you can take care of it for both of them. Do we all have a deal?"

"Yes, we most certainly do," said Molly. "Don't we, girls?" And she gave Duck-Duck and me, but mostly Duck-Duck, a nasty blue-lightning look. And to my surprise, despite the fact there was no good evidence and a lot of bad logic, Duck-Duck tucked in her chin, looked real mad, and didn't say a word.

Molly didn't deny I lived with them. She didn't even blink. Maybe she and Duck-Duck did have telepathic eye-talk. Molly herded us into her car, and we were free. Or at least Duck-Duck was free. Me, I wasn't so sure.

"How could you let him do that to us?" Duck-Duck said to Molly as soon as we were out of the parking lot. "We never even confessed." She crossed her arms and glared into the rearview mirror.

"Mom Court has less burden of proof," said Molly. "He knows, I know, you know. That's good enough. We're lucky he's not pushing it. This afternoon you both are becoming best friends with a can of paint remover. Plus you're grounded for a week."

The weird thing was, after we got home and had real breakfast and got ready to go out and do the community a service, Molly and Duck-Duck still hugged and kissed like all those nasty eyes had never happened.

7

Molly bought us spray bottles of paint remover, little scrapers, washcloths, and rubber gloves. She put water in buckets and drove us to the famous people cemetery.

"I am going food shopping. I will be back in two hours. Every single drop of paint had better be gone by then, or you aren't going to see free time for a month." She sounded mean, but then she handed us a snack, a bag of what looked like potato chips. Duck-Duck gave her squinty eyes, but then she followed that with the kiss-kiss thing again. The two of them really confused me.

"And you," Molly said to me, "if I get the whole story straight up when we get home, you can stay with us for a while." Even though she sounded strict, I didn't think she looked like she was sorry she had bailed me out along with Duck-Duck. After telling Duck-Duck the whole story, it didn't seem so hard to have to tell Molly. She hadn't ratted me out when she had the chance. I had my backpack again. I found it in her car, just where I'd left it. I didn't feel so dead anymore.

After Molly left, we went back to the quince tree.

"Let's not do it right away," said Duck-Duck. "Grrs don't take orders. Besides, we have to recover from our brush with the law first." She pulled herself up on a big gravestone, and I handed up her backpack. The snack turned out to be salted sunflower seeds.

"I hope Mom doesn't ground us through Halloween. I thought we could go trick-or-treating together. Even if she does, though, we could still celebrate Day of the Dead."

"What's Day of the Dead?" I asked. I could think of things I wanted it to mean, but I'd probably be wrong.

"My mother had a patient who was from Mexico. Where he was from, they do Day of the Dead instead of Halloween. It seems like a better holiday than Halloween." Duck-Duck swung her legs and spit out a sunflower shell. I wondered if I dropped a salted sunflower seed would it grow sunflowers later. In the spring. After the salt washed off.

"You're supposed to leave food and drink for the dead. And flowers too, I think. And you talk to them. I don't think you have to speak Spanish. It sounds cooler than just running around asking for candy. Anyone you want to leave food for?"

"Nope," I said. "Did the patient from Mexico die?"

"Yeah."

"Of what?"

"I think he had cancer. My mom's a nurse. She works in a hospital."

The first-aid kit made sense now. No one else I knew kept a little box of bandages.

"Even if we're not Mexican, maybe we could leave the lady poet something," I said. I felt a little bad that I had made her rock all bloody-looking. I wanted to leave her something good. I opened my backpack. "You think she'd like a Yodel?"

"Sure, and a juice box." Duck-Duck pulled out a cranberry juice box. "We should open it for her. These boxes probably aren't easy to open if you're dead." She popped the top with the straw.

She jumped down, and we went over and laid the Yodel and the juice box in front of the lady poet.

"Now you should talk to her," said Duck-Duck.

I looked at the stone with our gang words glowing white and red. "What should I say?"

"It probably doesn't matter a lot. She's probably just happy someone came to say hi and left her a juice box."

I looked at the stone. Maybe she liked the paint. Maybe she had been bored with gray stone and missed her white dresses and red flowers. Maybe she would be sorry to see the paint go. I knelt down and pushed the straw a little deeper into the juice box. On the top was the expiration date, which hadn't come yet. The food my mother used to bring home from the Walmart trash had dates that had already happened. I wondered how long a juice box lasted. The poet lady had an expiration date carved on her stone, but she only found it out when she died. I thought it was funny that a juice box would know how long it had left but a person wouldn't.

"I'm sorry you died," I said to the lady poet. "I hope you liked the paint." I wanted to ask her if she missed being alive, but it seemed a bit rude.

"Maybe she's never had a Yodel before," said Duck-Duck. "She died a long time ago. Maybe even before Yodels were invented."

"I hope you like the Yodel too," I said. The Yodel looked good. "You think she would mind sharing?" I asked Duck-Duck.

"My mother says it's good to break bread with people. That probably means Yodels too." Duck-Duck broke us both off a piece of Yodel and put the third piece down again. "To lady poets and Grrs." She raised her Yodel and then popped it into her pink mouth. I ate mine too. Maybe the lady poet was just a little less lonely after Duck-Duck's toast and a third of a Yodel.

We spent the rest of the afternoon trying to get red and white paint off the gravestone. I didn't think any more about bus tickets or what would happen when Molly picked us up.

Molly came to get us at four o'clock. She examined the lady poet's stone, front and back, taking a little walk around the cemetery as if we might have sprayed something else while we were there. Then we all got in the car, and, except for the fact that Duck-Duck was grounded and probably I was too, that was the end of it. Molly had gone food shopping and brought us two yellow apples. And on the way home, Molly and Duck-Duck's conversation was about what type of tomato sauce was right for whole-wheat spaghetti. Mushroom? Basil? It was kind of nice, but I wondered if something was wrong with their memories. Maybe they didn't hold grudges because they couldn't remember what to be mad about. Grandpa would have gone on for days about having to pick us up at the police station and how much gas cost. Keely wouldn't have spoken to me for a week.

Whole-wheat spaghetti turned out to be okay but not quite as good as white. The sauce had chunks of tomato and mushroom, with whole pieces of parsley—like a garden in a pot. Duck-Duck grated two kinds of cheese, and we sprinkled it over each plate before we ate.

After dinner, Molly made herself a cup of tea and gestured for me to sit down.

"Okay, kid, tell me the deal."

It was easier to tell Molly than it had been to tell Duck-Duck. It was as if after I had done all the work to make it into words once, the next time I could just use the words again and it wasn't as painful.

This time, the story came out a little different. I told Molly how I saw Keely go under, down into the yellow rush of water. I said how at first I froze, staring at the spot as if it were a door that after closing, would open again if I waited long enough. Then how I ran along the riverbank, fighting brush and mud, hoping I would catch her before she washed away to the mountains of Mongolia. I said I ran for miles, searching the water, but I never caught sight of even a hand.

Molly didn't say anything. She just listened. I stopped.

"When did that happen?" she asked.

"June," I said. "Just after school ended."

"So you were alone all summer?"

Duck-Duck started to interrupt, but Molly shushed her.

"Let Fishkill talk," she said, and Duck-Duck made a zipping motion over her mouth. "Tell us about the summer," Molly said to me.

I hadn't made words for that part yet.

It was a long summer of lies, but it didn't feel wrong. For the first time, I was alone on Birge Hill, alone in the world. It was a summer of one, and I liked it. The lies were to try and keep it that way.

People say *summer,* and they think picnics and beach and fun. My summer wasn't like that. I would walk across town and up the hill with my backpack. I would smile and lie and tell the nosy church ladies my mom was sick, or working, or had a new job. I would put as much food as I could in my backpack and walk home. They usually gave out cans. Cans of soup. Cans of baked beans. They gave me powdered milk and powdered Jell-O. Nothing I could eat on the way home. By the time I got home, the backpack would be made of rocks, and I would be hot and hungrier than ever.

I watched the mail for school letters. Anything that needed signing, I signed. I kept a pile, since I had no stamps. At the end of the summer, I walked them up to the school office and gave them to the front-desk people.

It was signing the papers and filling in names that made me

realize I could just sign a different name and that name would become me. I realized I could re-carnate, just like that, and never let anyone hit me again.

Molly had a funny look on her face after I told her the story. I was afraid she had changed her mind about me staying with them, since she knew I was a criminal now. Then I thought that maybe she wasn't used to kids talking so much, but I remembered Duck-Duck talked all the time, and Molly seemed okay with that.

"What about food stamps?" said Molly suddenly. "Why didn't you have food stamps last summer?"

"Mom took the card with her into the river."

"I see," she said, and paused. "Okay. You can stay with us in Chrissy's room. We file a missing-person report tomorrow."

That's when I knew I'd made a mistake. I had been taken in by the garden-in-the-pot spaghetti. Molly was just a grown-up, and grown-ups always made things worse. I looked around for my backpack.

Molly gave me that squinty look she was always giving Duck-Duck. "No more running. Why don't you want to go to the police?"

Duck-Duck piped up: "She thinks they're going to say she's a murderer and put her in jail without bail."

I hadn't thought of the bail part, but I was sure it was true.

I looked Molly straight in the eye. "If you are going to the cops," I said, "I'm going to run away first chance I get." I don't know why I thought threatening would work, but I hoped it would. "It's been months and months," I said. "It won't matter if we wait another month or so. You can tell them I lied to you and said my parents were on vacation."

Molly looked at me, and Duck-Duck looked at her. I folded my arms and looked back.

"Okay," Molly finally said. "Not tomorrow. But we have to tell them soon, you know."

"Yeah," I said. "Just not now." I didn't want to say it, but seeing the cops that morning still had me shaky in my stomach.

Duck-Duck got up from the table. "Never mind Pippi Longstocking," she said. "Harry Potter is a wimp compared to you."

"I agree," said Molly.

I woke the next morning to the sound of the shower, and even though I was in Duck-Duck's house, for a minute I thought it was Grandpa. Grandpa would slam the bathroom door shut and use up all the hot water while he yelled and cursed at no one. The curses were slurred by water and rage, the targets unclear. Sometimes I'd hear him imitate us — my mother and me. Falsetto conversations that he always won. *Bitches,* he would yell, *filthy bitches.* All the hot water gone, he would emerge still edgy with fury. Water is supposed to put out fire, but perhaps that kind of flame is waterproof.

On Cherry Road, Duck-Duck and Molly had two bathrooms, so if one person was pooping, the other person didn't have to go outside behind the shed. On Cherry Road, one bathroom had a shower with a curved glass door, and the other had a lion tub. It stood up on patient, clawed feet, so you knew it would never run away while you were sitting in the water. In Grandpa's house, the bottom of the shower was shallow and dirty, nothing you would ever want to sit in. The Cherry Road lion tub had high sides, and, after you climbed up the little step, the water was deep and hot and smelled like lavender. Nothing on Birge Hill smelled like flowers, especially not the bathroom.

Keely and I seldom showered, but I knew that other people washed with soap and water every morning and every night. I only learned that because in second grade Patrick Hinkel sat in front of me, and he was even dirtier than I was. The teacher came up to his desk one time and told him that in second grade, everyone showered or took a bath with soap, shampoo, and baby powder before they came to school. She spoke quietly, but everyone within ten feet of Patrick shut up so we could hear her. After that, the boys called him Baby Powder Patrick, and I tried to at least wash my face and hands every morning.

On Cherry Road, they had a special time at night for baths. No one talked about baby powder, though. I always wondered if the teacher made up that part just to embarrass Patrick.

Another surprise about living with Duck-Duck and Molly was their garbage habits. Grandpa burned half the trash and shoved the rest into the shed. He even tried to burn tin cans. Molly and Duck-Duck had complicated rules that said you had to look at each piece of garbage, think about where it came from, what it was made of, and where it might want to go next. It was a bit like the TV news interviews Molly watched at night.

> **Me:** So, tell me, sir, what brought you to this point in your life?
>
> **Garbage:** Well, Fishkill, it's been a long road, but before the Albany newspaper and the Dalton paper mill, I was a simple tree, minding my own business.
>
> **Me:** Wow, quite a story. What's your next destination?
>
> **Garbage:** The blue bin to the right of the stove. I want to become one with other newspapers. My ride leaves Saturday morning.

Each apple core, each tin can had its own home. Duck-Duck said it had to do with keeping the earth cool, and even though it was a lot of work, I made sure to memorize the different bin colors. One piece of spoiled lettuce in the wrong bin seemed to be terribly upsetting to both of them, and I wanted them to know I appreciated that they were willing to harbor a fugitive.

Tooth-brushing at Duck-Duck's was different too. In second grade, they passed out toothbrushes with little tubes of striped-blue-and-white toothpaste. I used the toothbrush for two years straight, until the bristles got completely flattened to the plastic stick and bumped over each tooth like when you ran your finger over the spiral binding of a notebook. I didn't think it mattered, though, because I thought when I grew up, I would have no teeth. Grandpa had a fake set that he soaked in water at night. Keely had teeth of her own, but only a few; the rest were missing. After a while, I realized teachers, even the old ones, still had real teeth. Then I realized it was usually the kids with bad sneakers and free-lunch cards who had parents with bad teeth. So they only pulled out poor people's teeth. I figured that was because they couldn't afford all the toothbrushes, paste, and floss the health teacher said you needed. Or maybe it was so the rich people would know who the poor people were.

Molly didn't have fake teeth. In the lion-tub bathroom, there was a drawer with thirty different tiny toothpastes and at least ten new toothbrushes, all still wrapped in plastic. Molly said I could pick whichever brush I wanted, and I looked at every single one before I picked.

When I started staying at Duck-Duck's, I had one pair of jeans, two T-shirts, a few pairs of underwear, and a couple of not-quite-matching socks. My sneakers had holes in the toes and rubber crumbling off the heels. Duck-Duck said this was dangerous because other gangs could track us by a bread-crumb trail of sneaker dust leading them to our hideout.

"See if there's anything of yours you can give her," Molly told Duck-Duck.

"You don't have to give me anything," I said to Duck-Duck as we went upstairs. "That's not fair of her. You need clothes too."

"Mom thinks I have too many," said Duck-Duck. "And she hates shopping for clothes. It's like she's scared of malls or something. Occasionally, I manage to convince her to buy something online."

She opened her closet, and I blinked. I'd never seen such a full closet. It was stuffed with shirts and dresses and jackets. Down at the bottom were rows and rows of sweet little shoes.

Once a year, my mother would give me ten or twenty dollars and drop me off at Goodwill. Most of the clothes were okay, but the sneakers were never right—either too big or too small. I always wished for the kind runners had. Bright-white with blue tread. Or the ones with shiny lights in the soles. I used to dream about those shiny lights.

"If your mother hates shopping, where'd you get all this?"

"My aunt Patty goes shopping with me," said Duck-Duck. "She says a girl has to develop her own sense of style."

I wondered if I had any sense of style.

"We can play beauty pageant. What do you want to try on?"

Duck-Duck was almost exactly my size, but the weird part was, the clothes that looked so perfect on her made me feel like a freak. A monkey in a dress. A monkey-lion with a purse.

"No dresses," I said. "I don't think that's my style."

Duck-Duck held outfits up to me and tilted her head back and forth. She'd squint and say, "As Aunt Patty would say, we're not going to the royal wedding in that one." She pulled open her chest of drawers, and there were more clothes. I wondered if she could even wear it all in a year.

"Don't worry," she said. "Personal style is developed over time. When Aunt Patty comes to visit, she can take us both to the mall. She promised to take me to New York City at Christmastime too, to see the department-store windows." She giggled. "Mom said she would rather be lying in her grave than go to Macy's in Manhattan at Christmastime. Aunt Patty said Mom would be lying in her grave naked, since she wouldn't have bought any clothes for the occasion. Then Mom told her that closed-casket funerals were more tasteful anyway."

Duck-Duck picked out a pair of green jeans and several T-shirts for me. "You can start with these." I tried on a bunch of her sneakers, but the toes were crampy. "We'll tell Mom. She'll just have to suck it up and take us to the mall."

I couldn't decide if I was happy about this or not. Grandpa always used to say that charity was rich people's way of pissing on you, but it felt nice to think of Molly buying me shoes.

"If she hates malls, it wouldn't be nice to force her," I said. "I can wait for Aunt Patty. The other gangs don't seem to have figured out yet that the sneaker crumbs are mine."

Almost every Saturday, Duck-Duck had soccer. She asked if I wanted to go too, but tons of kids running around kicking one another didn't sound like fun to me. So on Saturdays, Molly and I would drop Duck-Duck off and then go food shopping. Luckily Molly didn't hate food shopping.

On Birge Hill, we never had a shopping day. Sometimes Grandpa would buy huge pallets of something, like the tomato soup or the sardines. Otherwise, he or Keely would go out in the afternoon and buy a single jar of instant coffee, or a six-pack of beer and a roll of toilet paper. Sometimes Mom would walk all the way to the convenience store and buy Doritos. And Red Bull for the morning after she had drunk her six-pack.

Molly made a list every Saturday morning.

"What do you want for dinner tonight?" she would ask at breakfast. "What do you want tomorrow?" She would take suggestions and make lists for the whole week. One list for the vegetable-and-fruit store, one for the regular supermarket, one for the store with fancy food I'd never seen anywhere else before.

At first I couldn't figure it out. Why spend an entire day running around town buying food that you would just eat up in a meal or two? Why go to three stores when you could go to one? But then I started to like it. We would go to the vegetable-and-fruit store, and Molly would poke around and pick a forest of broccoli and ask if I thought it looked good. Some looked like miniature trees, fresh from the mountains. Others looked more like after-Christmas trees people put out in the street when they got too yellow and old. There were baskets of ten kinds of apples, and all of them looked just a little different. We picked out pink ones and red ones and made sure to pick the big crunchy ones Duck-Duck liked. It was a lot of responsibility, remembering who liked what and what went in each recipe. Like lasagna wasn't just one ingredient—it was wavy noodles and three different cheeses and real tomatoes and canned tomatoes and about five other things that went in with tomatoes. It was like pieces of a puzzle made a different picture after you cooked them into place.

Molly wrote lists, but every week she let me pick out one thing that wasn't on the list. The first time, I picked a mango. I had never seen a mango before, and even though Molly said it wasn't quite ripe and we would have to put it on the windowsill in the sun before we could cut it open, I took it home. Eating it was like putting a warm beach into my mouth. The next week, I picked clams. They were still alive, the fish man said, just breathing really quietly. I wondered about eating something still alive, but it seemed better to eat something that had recently been breathing than something that had been dead for years and years, like those sardines. We brought the clams home, and Molly steamed them until they were dead and taught us how to crack them open. We melted butter and dipped each one in. I decided no amount of butter could ever make a sardine taste like those clams: strong but sweet, like I imagined the ocean should taste.

One Saturday morning when Duck-Duck had an away game, Molly and I stopped at the bakery and ate lemon cookies at a black metal table. Molly stirred milk into her coffee and started talking.

"Your mother," she said, "she's a missing person. We can't just keep pretending she doesn't exist."

Me, I was okay with pretending she didn't exist. At least I thought I was. When I did think about her, I could hear the roar of the river in my ears, and I had to breathe a lot before I stopped sweating. I had been with Molly and Duck-Duck for a couple of weeks. I'd been hoping Molly would forget about telling the cops.

"Can we wait a little longer?" I said. "If she's not dead, maybe she went on a vacation and forgot to tell me."

"Why don't I think that's what happened?" said Molly. She almost gave me the blue-eyed squinty look she gave Duck-Duck, but then she stopped.

"You can't do that squinty-eye thing with me," I said. "I don't have blue eyes, so I don't know the code."

"Code?" said Molly.

"That wink-wink-squint thing you and Duck-Duck do. Dirt-brown eyes don't understand that kind of talk."

"You? Dirt-brown eyes? Where'd you get that idea?" She looked at me, amused. "You're my green-eyed girl."

I almost choked on my lemon cookie. For a second, I couldn't swallow. Then I wanted to cry, which was stupid.

"Green?" was the only thing I could think of to say.

"Sure, like the lake green," said Molly, and she smiled at me.

I wanted to ask what she meant by "my girl," but it was way too dumb a question. Maybe she just meant it to be funny or cute. If I had had a real mother, maybe I could have these squint conversations and get the jokes and not be embarrassed to ask a grown-up lady if she liked me or not. But I didn't ask. Maybe Duck-Duck would know.

"And they never found a body," said Molly.

"No body, no," I said. This was stupid. If Keely's body had shown up, the cops would already know I'd killed her, and we wouldn't be having this conversation.

When we got home, Molly started going on about cops again.

"It's time to talk to the police," said Molly. "Maybe they found a body but they couldn't identify it because you didn't report her missing."

We were back to the missing-person talk again. The thing was, I wasn't missing her.

"Can you talk to them but keep me out of jail?" I finally said.

"Fishy, it was an accident. You're not going to jail," said Molly, and she picked up her phone.

I didn't believe that for a second. I felt like I was going to puke. I went to the bathroom and shut the door. I ran the water a lot so I couldn't hear anything. Then I changed my mind and opened the door just a hair.

Molly was on the phone with the police.

"She's recovering from trauma, sir," Molly said. "She probably has PTSD. It's not surprising she didn't report it."

Who knew what "PTSD" was? It sounded like bug spray, or the name of one of those crime shows Duck-Duck liked so much. Molly was a good talker, though. Maybe I wouldn't end up in jail for long.

I heard Molly say good-bye. I flushed twice so she'd know I'd been busy. Then I came out to the kitchen.

"We're going down to the station," said Molly. "They want your mother's name and description so they can run her through their database. Maybe she turned up somewhere."

She was careful not say "turned up dead somewhere."

We got in the car and put on our seat belts. Keely never used seat belts. She said they made her feel tied down. That was the point, I said. She would never admit it, but it was just one of Grandpa's thoughts moved to Keely's brain. Grandpa said no pampered government pig was going to tell him what he could do in his own truck. Freedom to drive, freedom to die. No seat belts wasn't how he died, though.

Molly had different rules. Seat belts weren't a choice; they were the law. Molly wouldn't even turn on the engine till she heard all the *click-clicks*. And if a buckle just happened to unclick while you were driving, Molly would pull over to the side and wait. "Click up," she would say. She was hard to fool.

We didn't talk on the drive down to the police station. When we got there, Molly and the cop filled out a bunch of papers. They asked me questions, and I tried to answer: Keely's hair color, eye color, age, weight.

"Brown, dirt-brown, twenty-seven." Molly's eyebrows went up at that, but she didn't say anything. "I dunno, skinny but not really skinny?"

The same young cop who arrested us in the cemetery started going on about the Department of Social Services when another cop came in. Grandpa always called him Bub, but I think his name was Greg. I knew him; he knew me.

"Hey, Sam," he said to the young cop. "She's old man Jamison's kid's kid. She must be one tough cookie. I would have gone wacko in that house. If this lady says she'll keep her, let her stay. It's Saturday. The Department can deal on Monday." He didn't talk to me, since adults always talk about kids like they're not in the room.

Sam got his back up. "The *law* says"—and he went on to say what the law said about minors and protective services and calling DSS immediately.

"Sure, sure," said the old cop. "Do what you got to do. I'm just telling you . . ."

Sam waved his hand to shoo Bub away. He started looking

around his desk for the phone number for DSS. Then he got on the phone and left messages for people.

Molly told him we were going to wait for as long as it took. "Don't worry," she said to me. "It's just a lot of bureaucracy. Everything will work out."

Here I was in the police station again. Here Molly was in the police station again. She probably hadn't ever been in a police station before she met me. They were going to call the Department for Children with No Mothers and send me away for good.

I couldn't run away right now. They probably had bars and locks on even the bathroom windows. If the bathroom had windows. There was a desk at the front with a woman who probably had a gun. Even if I ran as fast as I could, I wouldn't be able to get out quick enough. And they had police cars to chase me. And dogs. I didn't even have a bike.

Molly gave me quarters to put in the soda machine, and I bought a Coke for me and a ginger ale for her. While I was there, I checked for windows in the bathroom. I was right. There were none.

Both of us had finished our sodas before someone from Social Services called Officer Sam back. I tried to hear what he was saying, but then I started to sweat and decided I wasn't going to listen. Wherever he sent me, I would run away.

I paced around the station room, clutching the empty Coke can, making it crunch with each step. I tried not to listen to the phone call.

I still overheard the cop say "protective services."

Protective services sounded like a zoo. A zoo for children with dead mothers and no fathers. We'd be kept in cages, and people would stare at us behind the bars, throwing peanuts at us and laughing. There would be no Yodels. There would be no Duck-Duck. I almost started to cry, but I kept circling around the station, knocking my soda can against any metal I saw. *Clink, bang, twack.*

Molly looked like she was going to ask me to stop, but then she didn't.

"Are you related to Ms. Farina and her daughter?" the cop asked me. He held the phone to his chest like we were sharing a secret or something.

I wanted to say, "Yes, she's my aunt," but I didn't.

"No," said Molly. "We are not blood relations. Just very close friends. She and my daughter are in school together."

The cop went back to talking on the phone, and then he hung up.

"A caseworker is coming to pick her up. The kid can't stay with you, since there's no kinship bond. You could apply to be a foster parent and, after six months or so, maybe the Department would place the kid with you."

He kept calling me *the kid*. Maybe because I didn't answer him about the blood relations. I realized I hadn't spoken since they asked what my mother looked like. Maybe he thought I had lost the ability to speak. I started to say I could talk and I didn't want to leave Molly's house, but the young cop had already walked away and now we were waiting for the caseworker.

"You might have to go for a night or two," said Molly. "But only if I can't convince them otherwise."

In the beginning, she had said, "Don't worry," and

"Everything will work out." Now a caseworker was coming to take me away. If Molly didn't think she could convince them, I was screwed.

I didn't have any money with me. I had spent Molly's quarters on soda. I didn't have my backpack or even one Yodel. I went back to the bathroom.

When I came out, Officer Greg saw me.

"Hey," he said, walking over to the bathroom door.

"Umm," I said.

"I knew your grandpa," he said.

"Lucky you." I was immediately sorry I had opened my mouth. Duck-Duck would have known never to say something that could label her a behavior problem. Especially to someone with a gun.

Officer Greg laughed. "Yeah, that's about right." He looked me over like he was trying to see if I had washed my hair that morning. "You want to stay with Ms. Farina?"

"Yes!" I said, trying to look decisive and trustworthy.

"I'll try to put in a good word for you. Sometimes they'll do what the kid really wants, especially if you're older." Then he gave me a fake little salute and went off with his gun.

I went back into the bathroom to rest. I didn't know why, but my heart was going *bang-bang* up and down in my chest, and my stomach had started to hurt.

At noon, Molly opened her purse and gave me a peanut-butter sandwich. I hadn't even seen her put it in there that morning. Where I was going I probably would never get another peanut-butter sandwich ever again.

It took a long time for the caseworker to show up. When she finally arrived, she was just another Social Service lady like the ones who used to visit me and Keely after my grandfather died. She had a gray suit and a gray briefcase. She didn't want to be here. I could tell by the way she kept stretching her neck side to side and cracking her knuckles. "I'm Mrs. Jones, the caseworker on call."

She put a pile of papers on the table. Molly pulled out a bunch of papers from her purse. They both started talking at once.

I kept walking around the station, around each desk, around each chair. I found a dime on the floor. I pretended I had to tie my shoe and picked it up.

"Older kids are harder to place. Especially when there are special needs involved," said the caseworker lady to Molly.

I kept walking, and I hummed a little so I couldn't hear words, but out of the side of my eye I watched them. It was like one of Duck-Duck's crime shows without the sound. Then I listened a little before my stomach made me stop.

> **Molly:** What family are you going to place Fishkill with?
> **Mrs. Jones:** Well, I'm working on that.
> **Molly:** So, where are you taking her tonight?
> **Mrs. Jones:** She'll be in the Department's custody.

Custody sounded like jail. There was no way I should get in a car with this woman. Who knew where she would take me?

Molly: Taking into account the trauma she has already experienced, I don't believe it would be a good idea to disrupt her again. She's been going to the same school as my daughter. Enrolling her somewhere else seems unproductive.

Mrs. Jones: Hmmmmph.

The lady looked pissy. At the word *disrupt,* she kind of twitched. "You aren't an approved foster home, and I doubt there's any exceptions in this case, but I'll call my supervisor. Maybe she will give you an emergency twenty-four-hour stay, since it will be hard to find an appropriate placement that quickly. I'm promising nothing," she said, like she was doing Molly a huge favor.

Foster home. You didn't need to read many books to know this was bad. I decided I would act like the cheerful, plucky orphans who kept up a good front even though the food was horrible. I would have to smile a lot. This would make them think I was going cheerfully along with their plans, and then I would run.

The caseworker's boss called back. Molly gave me some raisins she took out of her purse. She seemed to have everything in there.

"Okay, fine, fine."

The lady talked to the boss for a while, and then Molly got on the phone and said something magical that made the lady smile and pull more papers out of her bag.

"Okay, sounds good," she said to the phone, and hung up.

"Okay *what?*" I said.

"You can stay with Ms. Farina for now. We are considering your existing relationship with her and the fact that she has
some basic training. Although"—she turned to Molly—"your
certification has expired, and you'll have to take the training
again. We're making a special exception for you. It is a *temporary*
placement, though."

"Huh?" I said, and looked at Molly.

Molly almost looked embarrassed. "I took the foster parent
training a few years ago, but I never used it."

I wondered what Duck-Duck would have thought of a little
brother or sister.

There were lots of papers to sign. Molly had to give the
police her fingerprints again for another background check. I
wondered if people's fingerprints changed, the way their faces
did. Duck-Duck would know.

We were also required to have home visits, starting the next
day. This struck me as kind of funny. If Social Services let me
stay with Keely after they saw Birge Hill, surely they would be
thrilled when they saw Molly's backyard and picnic table. When
they saw a clean refrigerator with a total of at least ten meals in
it, they would be overjoyed that they didn't have to come back
again and again.

Molly was signed up for the training class to learn how to
be a mother, even though she had been to it before. I almost
laughed at that too. Keely was the one who needed a class, and
they were sending Molly, who knew how to make chicken with
little carrots and had telepathic eye-talk with a daughter who
was probably smarter than all of these ladies put together.

The caseworker was already packing up her bag. She was trying to get away as quickly as possible now that she had an okay from her boss.

"We'll continue to investigate to see if there are any other blood relatives in the picture," she said.

I thought about Keely and Grandpa. Blood relatives were a bad thing. I knew they wouldn't find anyone else, and that was a good thing. At least I was going to get to stay with Molly and Duck-Duck.

The cops wanted to grill me more about Keely, but we had to go pick up Duck-Duck from soccer.

"We'll come back tomorrow," said Molly.

Duck-Duck was furious when she found out we'd gone to the police station without her.

"You answered all those questions without legal counsel?" she said. "They could have taken Fishy hostage and thrown her into solitary confinement. What were you thinking?" she said to her mother.

"If we got into any trouble, we would have called you for bail," said Molly.

"*If* you got into trouble?" said Duck-Duck. "*If*? Who knows what they're doing right this minute, now that they have all that information and no guarantee of a fair trial."

"Uh-huh," said Molly, and she kissed Duck-Duck on the nose.

The two of them really confused me, but I was glad Duck-Duck had my back. I was worried too.

◆ ◆ ◆

The next day, when we went back to the police station, Duck-Duck insisted that she come along. Officers Sam and Greg listened to more of my story and wrote notes, but none of their questions really made sense to me.

"Did she come home after she fell into the water?" Officer Sam said.

"No," I said as patiently as I could. "She fell in, and then I never saw her again."

"Did she have any friends or family you think she could be staying with?"

Molly was watching me like she watched Duck-Duck, with those squinty blue eyes, so I had to try to say no without sounding sarcastic.

"Did she take her credit cards? Her cell phone?"

I explained that Keely had neither. She didn't have a bank account either, which was their next question.

Molly had forbidden Duck-Duck to talk, so Duck-Duck wrote a whole list of what the cops should be doing and questions they should be asking. She made a big show of silently handing it to her mother. Molly read the list.

"Can you search the system for any unidentified bodies that may have been picked up downstream from Birge Hill?" Molly asked.

Apparently this kind of search took time, not like on television, where they rattled the computer for two seconds and out popped half a dozen lost or drowned ladies in their twenties who fit Keely's description.

"Did she have any e-mail accounts?" they asked.

With no credit card, no e-mail account, no bank account, and no cell phone, there wasn't much to run down in the computer. Duck-Duck rolled her eyes.

When we got back in the car, Duck-Duck had a lot to say.

"Even if the body is decomposed," said Duck-Duck, "you can use dental records to identify it. They need dental records. Don't they ever watch TV?"

"Where do you get this stuff?" I asked. All I could think of was teeth, separated out from their head, clacking up and down the river, looking for Keely.

"She watches crime shows when I'm not home," said Molly. "Even though there's a three-hours-a-week television rule."

"You have absolutely no proof of that," said Duck-Duck, rolling her eyes again. "You could be sued for libel."

I started thinking about being an orphan. In books, orphan kids spent most of their time looking for families. Those story kids never seemed to realize that there were things far worse than being an orphan.

Every few days, Molly checked in with Sam and Greg. I wondered how many drowned bodies there were out there and how many didn't have names.

One day they found a body on the highway. At first they thought it was a woman, but then they realized it wasn't.

"Bright, aren't they?" said Duck-Duck. "Why don't they just let us follow up all the leads? They can take care of parking tickets."

Molly gave her a look that said she'd better stop being so

snarky. I was getting better at reading the Molly/Duck-Duck code.

"They're spending a lot of time on this," said Molly. "I'm sure they're trying their best."

"Uh-huh," said Duck-Duck, and she tossed her apple core into the right can for apple cores.

"Stop being a pill," said Molly.

I kept quiet. I wasn't sure whose side I was on.

8

A week after we went to the police station, I had a pop quiz in math.

"We're having the quiz today because so many people did poorly on the last one," said Miss Treadway. She was one of those young ones who graduated from college and came straight here specially to teach poor people. Maybe she thought she could change us, but after only two months of trying to change us, we changed her. She thought we should be grateful, and when we weren't, she wanted revenge. For Miss Treadway, revenge was often a pop quiz.

"We had a few Bs but mostly Cs," she said. "And one F." And I swear she looked right at Worm.

Worm thought so too, because he spit on his desk and made loud fake-puking sounds. He was sitting way in the back near the window with the view of the bus lot.

Miss Treadway passed out the quiz and placed one directly on Worm's desk spit. "Why don't we try a little harder this time?" she said. "We don't want to stay back again, do we?"

I was facing the board, but my spine went into full alert. All through the quiz, I could feel Worm's fury crackling from the back of the room. Angry and sad are very close, though.

A few minutes later she looked up from her desk. "Norman, since you're all done with the quiz, tell us the answer to number three."

Everyone turned to look at him. His paper was blank, with a damp patch in the middle where the spit had been. Instead of spitting some more or laughing in her face, Worm turned so red, we knew he felt like dirt. Miss Treadway didn't seem to care. This was payback for all the times Worm had spit on her tests or talked trash during class.

"Why don't you write the answer up on the board, Norm, where we all can see it."

I didn't know why she was doing that, rubbing it in. Treating mean people like dirt didn't make them nicer; it just made them meaner. Finally Worm dragged himself up to the blackboard. Somewhere between his desk and the board, he turned from a shit-mean bully into a humiliated fat kid who wanted to cry. And then, just before he did, the bell rang and he ran out of the room, leaving his books and his backpack behind.

I made sure he didn't see me, but when I left class, I picked up his stuff and put it in front of his locker, tucking his math papers into his textbooks so they wouldn't fall out.

◆ ◆ ◆

Duck-Duck was in the hard, smart math class.

"Where'd you go to school before?" I asked. Duck-Duck pulled out two Nutella sandwiches for our lunch. She said it was like peanut butter, but to me it tasted like candy.

"Mom and I homeschooled up to sixth grade, when we lived in Albany with Ellen."

I'd heard about homeschooling. It sounded like Hell, a big Hell with barbed wire where prisoners couldn't see one another and they were locked up for eighteen years with no contact with the outside world.

"Did you hate it?" I said.

"No," said Duck-Duck, "it was fun. But then Ellen left, sort of like a divorce, and we had to move, and I had to go to regular school because Mom had to work." She started rummaging around in her blue lunch box and then pulled out a tiny box of raisins. Peeling up the top piece of sandwich bread, she laid out four rows of raisins across her field of Nutella. Then she closed it up and took a bite.

I couldn't imagine Molly married. She seemed too tough and smart for that.

"Divorced from who?" I asked.

"Divorced from Ellen," said Duck-Duck patiently. "She left, and Mom flipped out for a while. She cried a lot. Now she says the finances are tricky, but it's going to be all right."

That's when it clicked: Molly and Ellen had been "sort of" married to *each other*. "Who's your father?"

"Sperm bank," said Duck-Duck. "Donor number two-nine-five-five-six."

That was even weirder than having *Unknown* on your birth certificate.

"So, you don't even know who he was?" I said.

"I know that he was six feet tall with blue eyes and brown hair. He went to an Ivy League college, and he was a lawyer." She finished up her raisin-Nutella lunch.

Maybe knowing your father's donor number was enough to keep you out of the dumb math class. Maybe having two mothers kept you smart.

"So, does Ellen visit?" I'd been hanging out at Duck-Duck's for a while, and I hadn't seen any divorced second mothers wandering around Cherry Road.

"No, not much. We talk on the phone sometimes," said Duck-Duck. "She wasn't really my mother, you know. She was Mom's girlfriend. She moved in when I was eight. She's nice, but I don't have any of her genes. My genes come from Mom and number two-nine-five-five-six. His sperm gave me good lawyer genes. That's why I'm so logical."

"Wow," I said. "I wish I had good genes."

Duck-Duck stopped wiping crumbs into her hand and looked at me. "What makes you think you don't have good genes?"

I thought of Grandpa and his hitting stick. I thought of Keely and her beer. "All the genes I know about are bad genes," I said. "The genes I don't know about probably suck too." I'd bet that if you lined up a bunch of guys, starting with the town perv and ending up with the mayor, Keely would choose the perv.

"Sometimes people get a little bad luck, and it just looks like it's bad genes," suggested Duck-Duck.

"You never met Grandpa," I said.

"Just because he had sucky genes doesn't mean you're sucky too," she said. "It's like making cupcakes. All the ingredients could make different things, but only one specific combo makes a cupcake. The whole is more than its parts."

If I were in the smart math class with one and a half mothers and a sperm bank, I would have been able to come up with that too.

"Let's hope so," I said. If I couldn't be a cupcake, I wouldn't mind being at least a Yodel.

Every night before we went to bed, Molly and Duck-Duck hugged and kissed and recited some silly kids' poem about bedbugs and peanuts. I would stay in the bathroom until they were done and then just wave good night to Molly from the stairs. Then Duck-Duck and I would go to sleep in her circus bedroom.

That night, after the bug poem, I lay in the pink bed and thought about Molly being sort of married to and sort of divorced from a woman. Grandpa had said women like that were man-hating bull dykes. I understood the man-hating part; Grandpa was a man and anyone with even reasonably good genes hated him. I'd never really thought about the bull-dyke part, though. Kids called one another fags and pansies and lesbo-queers, but that was mostly just to be stupid-mean, like calling one another freaks and nerds. I had never really thought about whether it was a bad thing to be a dyke or not. I wasn't even sure if I had ever met a real one before. Everyone said that Miss Thompson, the middle school volleyball coach, was a lesbian, but that was probably just jealousy. Miss Thompson could spike a ball twice as far as any student, even the boys.

That night, under the pink covers, I decided dykes, lesbo-queers, and lesbians all fell under the Opposite Rule.

In kindergarten, I once told Nellie Robbins that storytime was for sissies. I was repeating what Grandpa had said when I asked him to take me to Saturday storytime at the library.

Nellie looked at me like I was nuts.

"Who told you that?" she asked.

"My grandpa."

"Your grandpa is a dumbo," said Nellie, and she ate her entire peanut-butter cookie in three bites. I had been hoping she would share.

Even though she moved to California in second grade, I thought about Nellie a lot. When Grandpa growled noisy opinions, Nellie Robbins would pop into my head, and I would think, "That's dumb. It's really the opposite." Eventually it became just the Opposite Rule. Whatever Grandpa thought, the opposite was true.

Ice cream, storytime, library cards, seat belts, fluoride, and garbage pickup were all good. I could tell because Grandpa hated them.

I added lesbians to the list.

I lay in bed, wondering what Ellen looked like, and why Molly and Ellen got the divorce. I wondered if Ellen could make cupcakes, and if she did, what kind they would be, and then I fell asleep.

◆ ◆ ◆

The day after our gene conversation, Duck-Duck started helping me with my math homework. She decided I shouldn't be in the dumb class.

"It just takes a little concentration," she said. "Just like law."

So, first she corrected my homework. And then she made me do the next lesson, the one ahead of the teacher. She even skipped soccer practice one day to make sure we were on schedule.

"If we catch you up, next year we could be in the same math class," she said. "You still have a lot of time, but college-prep classes want you to be at the top of your game."

When she explained word problems, they didn't seem all that bad anymore. Every day, I did an extra lesson, and pretty soon we hit the end of the book.

"How am I going to tell Miss Treadway I need to be in a new class?" I said.

"We'll have to draw up a legal document. With signatures and everything. You'll have to take a test too, I'm sure. They won't take our word for it, but legal paperwork always helps." We were lying on her bed with our books propped up with pillows. The sun coming in the windows, even though it was November, made it feel like a September afternoon. "Write it up," she said.

I had never written a legal document, but if I had finished the math book, maybe I could be a lawyer too. I tore a piece of paper out of my notebook and thought for a second.

I wrote, "This paper promises that Fishkill Carmel finished the Blue Group math book and is totally ready to go on to the next group now and not wait for next year." I drew two lines for our signatures, like they did on the free-lunch form. Underneath the lines, I printed my name and then hers. I rolled over in the bed and showed her the paper.

"That's not the right spelling," said Duck-Duck. "Remember? I told you, it's D-U-K-D-U-K."

I knew I should spell it her way. But I couldn't let go of the image of wild ducks flying in the fall—brown against blue—high above the dirt roads near Birge Hill.

"It's prettier with the *c*'s," I said, and then I blushed. I didn't know why.

Duck-Duck didn't answer, but she looked at the paper again. "Okay," she said. "We shouldn't really use our gang names, but maybe just this once." She didn't look mad or offended. She actually looked a little pleased. Maybe she liked taking risks.

"Why doesn't your mother call you Duck-Duck?" I asked.

"She says I already have a perfectly good name. Chrissy. Doesn't that sound like a laundry detergent? Chriissssy." She hissed the *s*'s loudly, and you could just hear the soap bubbles.

I started laughing. "Chrrriissssy." She was right.

"Chrrrrissssy," she said, giggling, and she poked me.

"Chrrrris-ss-sy," I said between gaspy breaths. I was laughing so hard, I couldn't talk straight. Her little fingers were poking me between my ribs, making me twitch and hop and giggle. I grabbed at her pink fingers, but they were too quick for me. She tickled me so bad I almost fell off the bed. She stopped, but I still lay there giggling about soap bubbles and how her hands felt like liquid with candy edges, and all of a sudden she was just looking at me with her blue, blue eyes.

"We could kiss," she said. "Like they do in the movies. You know?"

I had never seen a girl-kissing movie, but I hadn't seen many movies. "Sure," I said. "Chrissssy."

She giggled, and to prove I'd seen kissing movies, I leaned over and kissed her on her pink mouth. She gave a little hiccup, like she wasn't done giggling, but she kissed me right back, with the soap bubbles in my belly and the candy on my tongue. Her fingers on my ribs felt like really they were down there, you know, between my legs, but I wasn't going to tell her that. Lying on the bed, I was sure I was going to pop from all those bubbles.

"You should open your mouth," she said. "It's called French kissing."

I was going to ask why French, but when I opened my mouth to ask, she put her soft little tongue in my mouth, and I knew why. Speaking French sounded like talking with someone else's tongue in your mouth as well as your own, and now it felt like her tongue was down there too. I didn't want to say anything about that. It was hard enough just breathing.

We kissed some more and French-giggled, and I think we fell asleep, because then Molly was calling us to get up and come to dinner. I could smell melting cheese and tomato sauce.

9

Unlike Birge Hill, Duck-Duck's house was close to school. If we called Molly and told her we were doing homework at the library, we could go to the cemetery or the store, or spy on the teachers through the office windows. Social Services insisted that Molly know where I was at all times.

"Mom just has to *believe* she knows," said Duck-Duck. "That way she'll never have to lie under oath."

Teacher-spying had been our plan the afternoon we saw a bunch of the boys running out back of school toward the rear entrance of the bus garage. There were at least four. One of them was Worm.

"Let's follow them," said Duck-Duck. "If something is going down, we should find out."

I thought this was a horrible idea, but Duck-Duck ran after them, keeping low in the grass, running up to the bus-garage wall, and creeping around the side. I reluctantly followed.

Duck-Duck and I plastered ourselves against the metal siding of the garage near the front doors and peeked around the corner. We saw four boys: Worm, Frank, and two others who I knew brought bologna sandwiches for lunch every day. At first it was confusing; it seemed like everyone was hitting everyone else. Then I sorted out that three of them were all hitting the fourth, Worm. Even Frank, who was supposed to be Worm's buddy. They pinned Worm up against the wall and two of them tried to hold him there while the other one punched him in the face, but they couldn't do it. Worm was like a bear holding off foxes, an elephant fighting dogs. The dogs bit him and jumped up to scratch, but he would bat one away and then another, even as the others managed to pull his pants down and kick him in the balls. Three against one. Despite the bloody heel Worm had given me, despite how he treated Duck-Duck, I found myself cringing each time they landed a punch in his gut, and then silently cheering him on when he twisted Frank's arm behind his back.

"It's like rooting for the Mouse King in *The Nutcracker*," whispered Duck-Duck.

I'd never seen *The Nutcracker*, but I thought I knew what she meant.

"We should call for help," she said.

I knew she was right, but the problem with calling for help was that it made you involved, almost as guilty as the attackers. Plus, Frank and his boys would know we had ratted on them, and then they would be our problem too, not just Worm's.

"Hold on," I said. I slid around the corner and ran back to

the front. The garage doors were all open, so if I wasn't careful, they would see me at the front through the rear doors. I sneaked along the inside of the garage and worked my way back to the fire alarm, making sure I was never in view of the fight. I jammed the alarm lever down and then ducked as the alarm screamed and the three attackers ran for it, through the garage, right past me toward the school.

I crept back to Duck-Duck and we watched Worm try to pull his pants up. Adults were pouring in, but we were invisible, hunkered down in the grass. Worm's face was bloody, and he was limping, but he still cursed the teacher who arrived first to help him and wouldn't touch the vice principal, who reached to take his hand.

"What are they going to do now?" whispered Duck-Duck. "Call an ambulance?"

"Naw," I said. "He's conscious, and he can walk. They'll take him to the nurse's office and call his father."

We cut a big circle around the playing field and beat all the adults and Worm back to the school. We ducked into our spy place, in the bushes under the window, and waited. Sure enough, ten minutes later, a huge man drove up in a Jeep and went into the school, his head grazing the top of the door frame. He looked mad and scared, even though he was as big as a tractor. An elephant tractor. Elephant tractors probably didn't like their baby tractors being beat on.

"You know," said Duck-Duck, "if Worm plays football in high school, all his problems will be solved."

"How do you mean?" I said.

"Everyone will like him for what they hate him for now," she said. "He's big and mean, and he doesn't care if he gets hurt." She added, "And they tend to be more lenient about academics for top football players. He'll be a lot happier in ninth grade, if he can make it there."

She was probably right. It was too bad the middle school didn't have a football team.

We watched Worm's father almost carry him to the Jeep. On the way, he dropped Worm's backpack. After installing Worm in the rear seat, he walked back to get it. He had on a prison-guard jacket and was moving like it had been him who had been beaten up. Without thinking much about it, I stepped out from our spy position.

"Hey," I said, and the giant man turned.

"It took three of them to take him down," I said. "I just thought you should know."

He smiled at me, just a little. "Yeah," he said.

"Make sure he tries out for football in high school," called Duck-Duck. "It would be a pity to waste such potential."

Worm was out of school for three days. When he came back, he had a blue Velcro arm cast and everyone avoided him like he had cooties. Before, he had one nasty friend. Now, it seemed, he had no friends at all.

If boys were bad, girls were worse. If you had a boy fight, he would hit you in the face and maybe you would have a black eye for a day or two. If a girl was after you, you might never know until everyone in school had already seen the locker-room picture she snapped of your ass. Girls were invisible enemies.

When I was in first grade, I had a best friend for a month. I only knew I had a best friend because one day Darsa Peterman told me, "If anyone asks, we're best friends." For a month we ate lunch together every day. We sat together in music class when you had to share the recorders and tambourines. I even loaned her my one colored pencil. At the end of that month, Darsa got invited to Wanda Scurtley's birthday party, and she never needed to talk to me again. She never gave me back my pencil either. I moped a little — I was only seven, after all — but later I just took it as a good lesson. Girls were more dangerous than boys. I didn't need a best friend.

Darsa became one of the popular girls with pretty lunch boxes who smiled over their white-bread sandwiches and ran in a pack like wolves. Darsa was the head wolf; the other girls, her doggy attendants. When they saw me in the halls, they called me Fishbreath and fanned their noses as if overcome by stench.

I hadn't worried about Darsa or her wolf pack in a long time, until Molly and I went to pick up Duck-Duck at soccer practice and I saw that Darsa had joined the team.

"She's got a great block tackle," Duck-Duck was telling Molly. "You should have seen her at the last game."

Duck-Duck had only been in real school since September. Why hadn't she asked me about Darsa? I could have told her about more than just block tackles. Half the girls in school had been burned by Darsa.

But I didn't say anything. I was quiet, since in Molly's house they didn't keep grudges the way Grandpa did. And besides, it would have looked like I was jealous, which I wasn't.

Since that time we kissed like in the movies, Duck-Duck hadn't mentioned it at all. Sometimes I would look at her fingers and feel bubbles, but she acted like everything was the same as it had been before. Maybe it was. I wasn't sure.

Homeschooling might have helped with hard math, but it didn't help with understanding wolf packs. While Molly was cooking dinner, I tried to explain them to Duck-Duck, scientific-like so she wouldn't think I was bad-mouthing anyone or being illogical, but would understand my warning.

"Girls adhere to the M&M theory," I said.

"M&M theory?"

"Yeah," I said, "it goes like this: If you're a popular kid—if you have a nice lunch box and good sneakers and good block tackles and everyone talks to you—you're inside the M&M bag with all the other M&Ms. If you're someone everyone ignores or picks on—if you have bad sneakers or you're in the slow math class—you're outside the bag, on the counter, all boring and stale."

"Can you be out on the counter and then get back in the bag?" asked Duck-Duck.

"There's only one tear at the top of the bag," I explained. "So it's possible for an M&M to fall out, but it's really hard for it to fall back in."

"It must be lonely on the counter," Duck-Duck said.

Now I felt bad. "Yeah, but it's crowded in the bag. And if it gets hot, you're stuck all glued together and you can't breathe. It's better to be on the counter."

"Free the M&Ms," said Duck-Duck, pulling out the plates to set the table. "That would be a good secret password."

I didn't know if Duck-Duck really got my point. It didn't seem like she understood what a wolf pack could do.

10

Salt Run cops were used to a town where everyone was home in their kitchen by six, provided they didn't work the night shift and weren't the type to go drinking till eleven. If you needed to arrest someone who wasn't home, you just went to their boss and told them to call you when they got there. Our cops weren't used to missing persons who might or might not be dead.

Duck-Duck said if we lived in a big *Law & Order* city, the cops would have tracked Keely's DNA, hacked into surveillance systems, and searched databases bigger than ten libraries. Because we lived in Salt Run, it was just Officer Sam and Officer Greg looking into the "disappearance of a mother of one." They had to call the state cops in to help. I secretly agreed with Duck-Duck that they had no clue.

Three weeks after we reported Keely as a missing person, the cops came to the door. Molly had just pulled the vegetarian shepherd's pie out of the oven when we heard the gold knocker against the door. I knew it wasn't good news, or they would have called on the phone. Then I wasn't sure what would be good news and what would be bad news. Then I felt guilty that I didn't know.

"I'm really sorry to have to tell you this," said Officer Sam, with his cop hat in his hand.

He did look sorry. Maybe he was sorry he was missing dinner.

"They found a body in Carrieville that matched the description of your mother. It had been in the water for a long time, so the time line seems about right too."

"Did you do a dental match?" asked Duck-Duck.

The cop didn't look at her. He kept looking at me. He hadn't known Grandpa, but maybe Officer Greg had filled him in, because they both looked real sorry for me. "Ms. Jamison had no dental records that we could find," he said. "The one dentist who had any knowledge of Ms. Jamison didn't have any X-rays on file. All he had in his notes was that she would probably require a partial set of dentures soon. That fit the description of the body."

He kept using the words *the body* as if the body wasn't actually a person, which I guess it wasn't anymore. Would you still be a person if you weren't alive? Maybe you would be if afterward you were buried with a name and a stone like the lady poet.

"Does she have a face?" said Duck-Duck.

"Christine Farina!" said Molly. "Stop being so insensitive!"

"Mom!" Duck-Duck waved her hand at Molly. "I'm not being insensitive. You should watch more TV. They could be totally wrong, and Fishkill will be all upset her mom is dead when really she's not. Fishy needs a good lawyer."

"You don't have to be rude to be a good lawyer," said Molly, but then she looked at the cops too. "Well?" she said to Officer Greg.

Greg looked mortified. "No face, ma'am," he said. "The body was found two months ago. Since there was no matching missing-person report and no one claimed the body, it was released for cremation and buried in the Carrieville General Population cemetery. We're really sorry."

General Population probably meant poor. *Special Population* probably meant rich.

Duck-Duck was stubborn. "What about DNA? Surely someone took a sample? You could compare it to Fishkill's to see if they are related." She looked at her mother. "They do it on *CSI* all the time."

"You're right, miss," said Officer Greg. "We can do that. If we take Fishkill's sample, we can send it off to the lab to be compared. We can swab her cheek and send it away to be tested."

It was weird that the inside of my cheek might have a bit of Keely in it, but I let them swab it with the Q-tip, which they then dropped into a vial.

"Make sure you label it correctly," said Duck-Duck.

The cops glanced at Molly, who glared at Duck-Duck. Then they looked at the shepherd's pie.

"That sure looks tasty," said Greg. "Just like my late wife used to make."

I wondered why he would be thinking about his wife just

117

now. Maybe she didn't have a face when she died either. Or maybe he didn't like talking about dead bodies any more than I did.

"We'll send the sample off and let you know what they find, but the rest of the details do match exactly," said Officer Greg. "We're really sorry," he said one last time.

It was weird, but I didn't feel sorry. I didn't feel sad or happy either.

Molly thanked them for all their hard work, and they said they wished they could have done more, ma'am, and then they went out to their cop car and drove away without turning on the blue lights. We sat down to dinner and didn't talk about bodies anymore. For dessert, Molly brought out the chocolate-cherry ice cream she hadn't let us eat the night before, and she even let me have seconds. Duck-Duck gave me sprinkles to put on top. Before I went to bed, Molly hugged and kissed me, the way she hugged and kissed Duck-Duck every night. I wasn't sure if I liked the hugging and kissing or not.

"We'll make sure you stay with us," she said.

Then Duck-Duck and I went to sleep in Duck-Duck's pink room with the two frilly beds.

11

Grandpa used to say that paying a kid to do housework was double theft. Parents already had to support them for years and years, and then they were expected to pay a kid extra to mow the lawn? In his mind, Mom was still paying off the ride he gave her up the Taconic Parkway from New York City.

"Go milk a dead cow," he said whenever Keely asked for money.

I never asked for money.

We were supposed to get $225 for Grandpa when he died, but Social Security said that, because he died in February and Keely went ahead and deposited his March check, we actually owed *them* money. So we basically had to pay money for him to be dead. I thought it was worth it, but Keely whined and complained until Social Security finally gave up and said they wouldn't make us pay back the March check, but we still didn't get the $225 either.

When the Social Service ladies came to Birge Hill after Grandpa died, they thought we would be upset if parts of him went to scientists for research before the rest of him went to the cemetery. I wasn't upset. I said it was fine, that maybe the scientists could figure out why he was so mean.

On Cherry Road, Duck-Duck got an allowance every week, not exactly for anything she did, although she was supposed to wash the dishes and keep the recycling bins neat and correct, but apparently she got money just for being a daughter. When I started living on Cherry Road, Molly started giving me money too. I wanted to ask if it was because she didn't want me stealing money from her purse, something she might have thought, although she never said it.

Every time Molly gave me money, I stashed it away. Since I didn't have the rock box anymore, I put it in the toe of my old blue sock and pushed the sock into the springs of the pop-up bed. I didn't need to buy more Yodels since Molly gave us lunch every day, plus dinner and breakfast. But if Molly decided she didn't want me to stay with them anymore, I'd need to be able to take care of myself. I wondered if I would get $225 for Keely or if I'd need to show them a body.

"Would you like to have a funeral?" asked Molly the morning after Officer Greg and Officer Sam's visit. "They seemed pretty sure it was her. When they get the DNA tests back, we could have a memorial service." We had just finished eating pancakes and bacon. Duck-Duck was in her bedroom under orders to clean her room.

I wasn't sure what they did at funerals. I had seen the funeral home with long black cars and people in suits waiting patiently for everyone to drive the right way. No one at Birge Hill owned a suit.

"No," I said. "I don't think so."

"Or you could take a walk in a place that was special to her," said Molly, "and think about the things you'll miss about her."

I knew for sure that normal kids would say they missed their mothers. Normal kids would cry and sniffle and want a funeral with big cars.

"It's okay," I said. "She didn't have anyplace special."

Then I remembered the river. The river, taking away Keely, taking her face. The face without Keely. My stomach crunched up like a soda can getting stomped.

"It's not your fault," said Molly, as if she could hear me crunching. "There wasn't anything you could have done. Even though she was so young, she lived a hard life."

"Yeah," I said, "because she lived most of it with Grandpa."

Molly stopped clearing the table and sat down opposite me. I had licked the maple syrup off my plate until it looked clean. Except if you touched it, it was still sticky.

"Sometimes when someone dies," she said, "you don't have to have a funeral with lots of people around. You can just think of what was good about the person and how you want to remember them." She wiped the crumbs in front of her, but she didn't sweep them into her other hand. "When my mother died, I was mad because she had said a lot of mean things to me, but I remembered how she always called people when they were sick and asked if they needed anything. Somehow that little thing stuck in my mind. I decided I would do that too—just my way of remembering her. You could try something like that if you want to."

"And you became a nurse," I said. My stomach was un-crunching.

"So I did," said Molly, and she smiled at me.

It was lucky she didn't ask what I was going to remember about Keely, because all I could think of just then were things I didn't want: she was a drunk, a pushover, a wimp. Molly wouldn't comprehend there could be a mother who wouldn't stand up for her kid.

"I'll think about it," I said, and then we washed the dishes, and I put the maple syrup in the refrigerator door next to the organic mayonnaise. I was sure Keely had never had organic mayonnaise within ten miles of her mouth, let alone in her refrigerator.

That night I dreamed the river spoke. It didn't speak in words or thoughts. It spoke in white air and black waves. Screaming and dark, it inhaled, and Keely fell in, sucked down into the river's throat. I screamed at her to fight, to swim, but my words came out as thin squeaks of wind. I ran along the riverbank, looking and hoping, and suddenly there she was, rising out of the river's rusty gullet. I grabbed her by the wrist, but just as I made contact, Grandpa suddenly pushed me from behind and I fell in too. Keely sank down between the red rocks, and I was sucked in after her as Grandpa laughed.

◆ ◆ ◆

In the morning I asked Molly, "What does it mean if you dream about somebody?"

"Somebody?" she said.

Somehow she knew I meant Keely. It bothered me how she knew so much. It almost felt like she was digging around in my brain.

"Yeah," I said. "Somebody."

Molly was hurrying because she had to be at work and we had to be at school, but she stopped for a second. Then I felt bad because I was being snotty and she was being helpful.

"Sometimes," said Molly, "dreams about someone who's died can be our way of visiting them one last time." She raised her eyebrows in a little question.

I shrugged.

"Or," she added, "sometimes it can just be us trying to process the feelings we had about them when they were alive."

I shouldn't have asked. Dreams were just dreams. Some were bad, and some were nicer. Kind of like the weather.

That afternoon, instead of walking home with Duck-Duck, I went to the river. I didn't go all the way to Birge Hill, but I walked to where the river ran after it twisted down through town. I watched the white water churning and spinning. The sky was drizzling a cold gray rain.

I threw a pebble into the water and watched it disappear, and then I threw another. I threw a whole fistful of pebbles, and still I didn't feel right.

Maybe if I had been nice to Keely when she got fired from Walmart, we could have started over. Maybe we could have gone to the supermarket and bought bread and milk, and she would have felt better and she would have gone out to look for another job.

"I'm sorry, Mom," I whispered. "I'm sorry I didn't catch you."

I listened for an answer, but all I could hear was water—rushing water—and wind.

The next weekend, when Molly and I picked up Duck-Duck from soccer practice, I spotted Darsa. She was tall and had bigger breasts than some high-school girls. She ran like an antelope on the range: an antelope with magazine-model legs and a cool haircut. She loped; she jumped; she back-switched in midair. I could see why Duck-Duck was impressed.

"Isn't she great?" said Duck-Duck after practice.

"Umm," I said. I could feel Molly looking at me. Or maybe she was just thinking at me really loud.

I didn't want to ask in front of Molly if we were going to hang out in the cemetery. When we got back home it seemed we were, because Duck-Duck took the apples Molly gave her and put them in her pack. Then she did the secret-password knock.

I actually didn't know it was a secret-password knock until she told me.

"Swear on your oath blood you won't tell anyone," she said.

"Tell anyone what?"

"The secret-password knock, stupid," said Duck-Duck.

"I swear," I said. "What do you need a secret-password knock for?"

"If you are kidnapped by the enemy, silly. Or swallowed by zombies."

"Of course," I said, even though there was no way a secret-password knock would help in the belly of a zombie, and we went out. I wondered if Duck-Duck talked to the girls on the soccer team about secret-password knocks, and if she did, what they thought of it. They probably wouldn't be so buddy-buddy with her if she told them.

When we got to the cemetery lookout spot, we set up camp. We lay under the bushes, which used to be green and then red but now were brown. We crunched our apples, watching down the hill for other gangs' spies. You could tell other gangs, Duck-Duck said, by their different-color lunch boxes. I didn't have a lunch box. Not yet, anyways. It was still on my list. Molly had been putting my lunch in Duck-Duck's box.

We also counted Priuses because Duck-Duck said she wanted her mother to buy one. She said that in a Prius, you could get a little TV screen of behind you that would aid your ability to stay alert to espionage. Very important if you operated outside the law.

Then I saw the green pickup.

"Shit," I whispered, and shoved Duck-Duck down to the ground.

"Is it gang spies?" Duck-Duck asked, her mouth in the wood chips.

"Shhh," I hissed, suddenly sweating, my hands digging into the dirt. Again in my mind I was at the river, watching Keely fall in, watching her grab for my hand but then, like she changed her mind, let go. She didn't scream, like people should do when they fall. She didn't struggle, like people should do when they don't want to die. She just smiled a little, like she had planned this all along and was laughing at me.

But here was the green truck, the pickup that had disappeared before she did. I thought she had sold it for junk or that it had disintegrated into mean little green particles, like metal crumbs of Grandpa. The passenger door was rusted half off, and the windows weren't windows anymore, just duct-taped plastic. No one but Keely would still be driving that truck. I heard a scary, panting breath, and I realized it was mine.

12

"It's my mother," I whispered.

The pickup stopped by the side of the road, and the door opened. Half of me wanted to throw myself down the hill toward her. The other half was ready to run into an open grave if she spotted me, but the cemetery bushes bent low around us, and she never looked up. Duck-Duck sat up a little. I couldn't get my hands to stop shaking.

"She doesn't look dead," Duck-Duck whispered.

And she didn't. She was wearing new tight jeans and black sunglasses. She got out, went around to the passenger side, opened the door, and poured the contents of her purse out onto the ripped seat. She seemed to be looking for something. We watched her sort small objects until she picked one up and applied it to her lips. Keely had never used makeup. She tried using the side mirror, and, not satisfied, climbed back into the truck to use the rearview mirror, blotting the corners of her mouth and wiping her teeth.

"Why's she wiping her teeth?" hissed Duck-Duck.

"Maybe when you come back from being dead, there's green stuff in your mouth." There was something bizarre about putting on lipstick when your car was a junk pickup.

"I don't think she's dead," said Duck-Duck, a little louder.

"Well, duh," I said, and then I was sorry. I jabbed Duck-Duck in the ribs so she would know I didn't mean it nasty. "Dead people don't need red lips."

After the lipstick, Keely pulled out a plastic cup with a lid, and a black-and-yellow cardboard canister. She scooped stuff from the canister into the cup and went around to the back of the truck, where she had a gallon of water. She poured the water into the cup, screwed on the lid, and shook up the contents. She closed her eyes and took a big gulp.

"What's she doing?" Duck-Duck tried to get a better view. I pushed her down again. "What's in the cup?"

"I have no idea."

After my mother drank most of whatever was in the cup, she did the lipstick thing and the mirror thing again. She smoked a cigarette, and again, more lipstick. Then she pushed everything back into the purse and shut the passenger door. For a second, she glanced up in our direction, and I froze, but her eyes didn't focus on me or even on the bushes. She got into the pickup and drove away, the cracked muffler beating our ears until the truck disappeared over the hill. Then the street was quiet and empty.

"What the hell am I going to do now?" I said.

We ran home as quickly as we could. Maybe we were running because Keely could show up and take me back to Birge Hill at any moment. Maybe we were running because it wasn't every day you saw a dead person walking around. It was hard not to run fast when you were thinking about zombies.

"I have something to tell you," Molly said when we burst in through the door.

"We have something to tell *you*," Duck-Duck said, and just went ahead and told Molly about the green truck and about Keely coming back from the dead.

"Maybe she's a zombie. But I don't know if zombies use lipstick, unless it's to pretend they aren't zombies," said Duck-Duck.

"No zombie," said Molly. "The cops got the DNA report back. That body they found isn't a match. Also, the cops traced Keely's SNAP card. It was used several times since Keely's disappearance."

"Were there video cameras where the card was used? It could have been someone else," said Duck-Duck. "You could get proof."

Molly laughed. "Didn't the two of you just get proof? She's alive. A positive ID, as you would say."

◆ ◆ ◆

There were a limited number of places you could hide a green truck in the town of Salt Run, and two days after Keely came back from the dead, Officer Greg called Molly to tell her he had spotted the truck on a dirt road on the north side of town. Keely had been sitting on the tailgate, drinking a shake, when he came up to her. I wondered why Keely hadn't gone back to Birge Hill. I could think of a few reasons why she wouldn't want to, but wasn't it better than living in a truck?

"We're talking to her at the station," Officer Greg said. "Social Services is coming down too."

"Are they going to charge her with abandonment?" asked Duck-Duck after Molly hung up.

"I don't know. Why don't we pick the movie we want to watch tonight?" said Molly.

"They should put her in jail for forgetting she had a kid. What about the courts? Are they going to make her prove she's really the mother?"

Molly gave Duck-Duck one of those sideways blue-lightning looks. "I'm sure she didn't forget she had a kid, Chrissy. But we don't know anything yet."

"Are they going to track her movements in the last five months to see if she was running drugs?"

"Enough," said Molly. "We'll see what the police say when they call again. Why don't you stop worrying about it right now and pick a movie."

Now that Keely was back, I thought I would see her walking in Molly's front door at any time, but several days went by, and no

Keely. It made me nervous, not knowing if she had decided to be dead again or not. Finally, I asked Molly to call.

"Maybe they put her in the slammer for wasting state and city funds to locate a not-missing person," said Duck-Duck.

I knew Duck-Duck was just being logical, but sometimes I wished she would keep her logic to herself.

Molly called Mrs. Jones and held the phone away from her ear a bit so I could hear too.

"We met up with her and set an intake appointment for the next day, but she never showed. I had given her some forms to fill out, and she never returned them. I had the officers leave a note on her car telling her that her SNAP card could be renewed if she came to see me, but she hasn't come. She doesn't have a cell phone, and she's living in a truck. We're too under-staffed to have to keep tracking her down." The lady sounded frustrated.

I knew asking Keely to fill out a form was useless. If I forced her, I could sometimes get her to sign on a dotted line, but fill out an entire form? I'd never seen her even try.

"Tell them if she shows up again, to have her fill out the forms in the office," I said. "Otherwise it will never happen."

Molly raised an eyebrow and relayed my advice.

After a few more days, Mrs. Jones called us to report that Keely had finally showed up at their office, and they had begun a comprehensive assessment related to visitation, custody, and financial responsibility. I knew this meant me. The first thing Keely was supposed to do was go to group therapy once a week at the Family Center and visit the Social Service ladies once every two weeks in their office. Then we were supposed to start family therapy, just the two of us.

"She's allowed an initial supervised visit," said Molly. "Do you want to see her?"

I was surprised by the question. I had assumed that whatever the cops and the ladies decided was what I had to do.

"I guess," I said. "Maybe she'll tell me where she's been."

"I'd like to know too," said Duck-Duck.

"Fishkill can ask," said Molly, "not you." And she called the lady back.

The next Saturday morning, Molly dropped me off at the Family Center.

"Call if you need me," she said.

I had to give her credit. If it had been me, I would have wanted to listen in.

A new Social Service lady led me to a seat in a room connected to her office and then she got Keely, who came in and sat down too. Keely put her bag on the floor. She had on the same tight jeans as when Duck-Duck and I saw her from the cemetery, and her lipstick was very red. Her eyes weren't blurry, the way they got when she'd been drinking; they were steady and almost pretty. It was like a famous person's grave had been dug up and the person had been alive the whole time, drinking beer and watching soap operas down there in the hole of dirt.

"You look good," said my mother. "How's school?"

That's what strangers asked. *What grade are you in now? What subject do you like best?*

Keely pulled a small plastic bag from her jacket pocket. She measured two tablespoons of off-white powder from it into her plastic drink cup, which she held between her knees, poured in water from a canteen, put the lid on, and shook the cup with both hands.

"It's a protein shake," she said. "Want a taste? These have changed my life."

Molly thought it was important to break bread with people, so I took a sip. It tasted like tomato soup, but maybe that was just my imagination.

"It has all the essential vitamins and minerals you need to live a serene life." She took another gulp. She clicked her teeth together and swished the shake.

"Where'd you go?" I said.

For the first time, Mom looked a little glazed, the way she did after a six-pack and a bag of Doritos. Maybe protein shakes didn't change her as much as she thought. Maybe a serene life was beyond the reach of a powdered drink.

"I took a ride to Reno," she said, like you would say, *I went to the diner.*

"But I saw you fall in the river," I said, "and you never came up." I wished Duck-Duck were there. She would know the right questions to ask. Her hands wouldn't be sweaty for no reason.

Keely didn't answer right away. "I thought if I stayed down long enough, I would move on," she finally said. "But then my head came up, and I was still breathing." She swallowed more shake. "I thought, 'Hey, that didn't work, but I can still move on, just in a different direction.' So I walked out to the road, and there was my ride, the Reno Man himself." She clicked her teeth.

All the time I lived with her, Mom never kept her mouth still. She clicked in the day, she ground in the night. She chewed gum, and she spit tobacco. It probably got really noisy in there, inside her head. It sure was noisy out here.

"Did he have a name — the Reno Man?"

"No. Well, he did, but he didn't really take me to Reno like he said he would."

I wasn't surprised.

"Where did he take you?" The conversation was like one of those word problems. Lots of words, lots of problems, not a lot of story.

"We ended up in Lorain, Ohio. I should have gone on to Nevada." Keely swallowed more shake.

"What did you do in Lorain, Ohio?" I said.

Keely smiled. It was a weird smile, like the smile of someone who was just learning how to smile and had gotten it a little wrong. "I found Auga-L," she said, "and the Four Freedoms."

I wished again for Duck-Duck. Surely she would be able to get my mother to answer questions in English. My social studies teacher told us that the United Nations had interpreters who spoke every language in the world, and they all sat there with headphones, making sure everyone understood everyone else. I could have used one of those right then.

"What's the *L* stand for?" I asked.

"Auga-L," said Keely, "makes my shakes, but they also make

my life. You just apply the mission statement to your personal choices and you start to see changes. Immediately."

"Huh?" This made even less sense. Also, she hadn't answered the *L* question.

"Every time you have a problem, you think of the Four Freedoms: Cleaner, Concentrated, Secure, and Free—C.C.S.F.—and an answer will come to you."

"Let's go back to the part about the river," I said.

"So," said Molly when she came to pick me up, "did you catch up with your mother?"

"No," I said. "I think I'm more behind than when I thought she was dead."

"Being dead is definitely simpler," Molly agreed.

I told Molly how Keely had tried to sell me a carton of shake mix.

"She says she learned the Four Freedoms and how to be a balanced person." I gave Molly a look so she would know that was a fairy story if ever there was one.

"Why do you think she's not balanced?" Molly didn't ask like she disbelieved me, just like she was curious to know.

"You didn't live with her all those years. No way she's better."

"You don't think people can change? She's still so young."

"All she eats is protein shakes," I said. After surviving the tomato soup year, why would Keely do that to herself? "She won't even eat apples. She says their energy is too acidic. Duck-Duck would call that bad logic."

Molly laughed. "She would." Molly seemed used to me

saying Duck-Duck, even though she still called her Chrissy. "Give your mother a little time. She's only just back from wherever she went."

"If I could only figure out where that was," I said.

The next Monday, Duck-Duck stayed after school without me. "I have extra soccer practice with Darsa," she said. "We're almost good enough to transfer to a Division One team. Then, when we go to college, everyone will be offering us great recruitment deals."

It was funny. Before Duck-Duck, I wasn't lonely. Maybe I might not have had someone to do homework with, but I didn't have a big jagged shell in my chest like a broken egg either. It was really stupid, but I felt like crying all afternoon, and Fishkill wasn't supposed to ever cry. Maybe I was getting sick.

Duck-Duck stayed after school the next day too.

"You sure practice a lot," I said when she got home.

"Discipline is really important," she said. "You wouldn't understand, since you don't do sports."

How do you fight back against that?

In the backyard, I tried to kick the ball the way Duck-Duck did, but all it did was roll off into the corner and get stuck in the leaves. Even if I practiced all day, I would never catch up to Darsa.

Duck-Duck was staying after school several times a week. I pretended I didn't notice. I did notice Darsa's best friend, second-wolf-in-command, Brittany, was now not-in-command. That left the best-friend spot open.

"Maybe you should be careful," I had said to Duck-Duck one day when she came home late. "Darsa isn't necessarily as great as she seems."

"What do you mean?" she had said. "You think I should be like you and never talk to anyone?"

My stomach got all tight, and after that I shut up.

At the next meeting with Social Services, there were two new ladies. They said Mrs. Jones had left and that she'd taken a new job. The new Social Service ladies sat me down in their office and asked me hundreds of questions about Birge Hill.

"Maybe they think it was part of a drug ring," said Duck-Duck. It was the first thing she'd said that wasn't about Darsa since she'd come home late again from soccer.

They hadn't asked about drugs; they kept grilling me about Keely and Grandpa.

They asked about food and doctors and shots. They asked about school and money and electric bills. I wasn't sure why they were asking me. Now that they had Keely, they could ask her. One lady kept asking me questions, but she really wanted to ask other questions, not the questions she was actually asking. I could tell because she had a piece of paper in front of her, and she kept her finger as a placeholder. She moved her eyes down the paper but never moved that finger. It was like the one thing on her list she never got around to.

"Did you have your own bedroom?" she asked.

I would have laughed, but that would have upset her more. Obviously, this lady had never visited Birge Hill. I slept on a cot in the corner of the living room. Keely had a closet for a room, the size of Molly's pantry. Grandpa had the bedroom. After he died, it still felt like any moment Grandpa would stamp in with his stick. Mom must have felt the same way, because she never moved her bed out of the closet. We started leaving empty soda bottles and Red Bull cans in Grandpa's room, stacking them high before we redeemed them.

"I wish the ladies would stop being so nosy. Sometimes I just want to forget stuff, but it's hard if someone keeps bugging you," I said to Duck-Duck. We were sitting in the living room, doing homework.

After Grandpa died, the Social Service ladies used to write lists and post them on the refrigerator. One list for me, one list for Mom. My list would say things like *Go to school every day* and *Clean your room.* Mom's list would say *Make lunch for Carmel, Write shopping list, Go to therapy.* The next week, the ladies would come back, and my list would be all checked off, and Mom would say, "Oh, I forgot." They kept prying into what she did and what Grandpa had done and she just clammed up.

After a while, if Mom kept cereal and bread in the house and didn't drink more beer than milk, the ladies let it be. Maybe they didn't really want to know what Grandpa had done and why he did it either.

"Hello?" Duck-Duck was saying. "Did you hear what I said?" She was waving her hand in front of my face.

"Yeah," I said. "I just forgot where I was for a second."

"Maybe," said Duck-Duck, "Keely can't read. Maybe that's why she won't fill out any of those forms."

"Huh?" My brain kind of froze and then went into go-back mode, like on Duck-Duck's TV when you missed what someone said and you pressed go-back and then they said it again. I saw Mom not checking off lists, not signing school papers, not reading the principal's letters, getting fired from Walmart for not following the rules. Written rules, lists of rules.

It all made sense if she couldn't read.

"Shit," I said, not caring that I was swearing in Molly's house. "I never thought of that. How could I have missed it?"

"I guess she faked it. It would be really hard to not read," said Duck-Duck. "It would almost be like not having a memory. Or only having part of one. Mom says she's lost without her list. If you couldn't read, you'd have to spend your whole day faking it, even to your daughter."

There were soup cans and road signs and newspapers and letters. There were e-mails and electric bills and candy-bar wrappers.

"You're right," I said, although I couldn't really imagine it. Reading was like eating to me. Who needs to learn to eat? "Maybe that's why she drinks those shakes."

"Why?" said Duck-Duck.

"So she doesn't have to go shopping or read labels or even remember a list. She just makes another shake. Just add water."

"If I couldn't read, I'd have a better memory, since I'd have to use it all the time," said Duck-Duck.

"Not if you lived with Grandpa," I said. "He gave you a lot to forget. Keely got more practice at forgetting than remembering. No wonder she never finished high school. It wasn't just that she got pregnant. She couldn't read." I tapped the eraser end of my pencil on the table. It made a smacking sound. "Why did I never figure that out?"

Duck-Duck looked at me. "Maybe," she said, "you didn't think it was possible to be a grown-up and not be able to read."

That night, I dreamed of words, all the words I'd ever read, floating down the river. Whenever I tried to grab a good one— *Banana, Turquoise, Alabama*—it slipped out of my hands and got swept away in the swirling current.

It was beginning to get really cold outside. Not just fall cold, but winter cold. At Birge Hill, Grandpa used to wait until the thermometer hit freezing to turn on the heat. If the pipes froze, he would have to pay money. Before that, we could just suck it up.

"Put on a coat," he would say. "You think I have millions to pour into heat?"

At Cherry Road, they didn't even talk about heating the house. The heat just went on automatically when it was cold outside. We would come in from the yard and it would be bright and warm in the kitchen, and it would smell like apple cider or hot chocolate, or maybe just peanut-butter toast.

In books, winter was fun. Kids went sledding and ice-skating and had races with dogs. Sometimes there were bad accidents and girls ended up falling on the ice, but everyone was sorry and tried to make it up to them. Duck-Duck and Molly seemed to think winter was fun too. Even though it hadn't snowed yet, they pulled the sled out from the garage and tried on ice skates to make sure they still fit.

We were looking through the box of skates to see if any would fit me when Duck-Duck said, "You look all pissy. Don't you like skating? It's not like we're forcing you or anything."

"I'm not pissy," I said. I'd never gone skating, but I was sure I would like it. I tried to think of why I might look pissy. "I keep worrying about my mother." When I said it, I realized I had been worried ever since she came back to life.

"Worried that she'll leave again?" asked Duck-Duck. She tossed a pair of skates out of the box into the too-small pile.

"Crap, no. Worried she's going to flip out. Worried she's going to stalk me. Worried she's going to run naked through town. I don't know." I guessed maybe I *was* feeling a little pissy. "Worried."

"Maybe we should spy on her," said Duck-Duck, "like when cops stake out a suspect. Who knows what happened after she fell in the river? We don't even really know where she went."

Spying together sounded nice. Like it was totally normal. Like Darsa and soccer didn't exist. Like Duck-Duck didn't hang out with Darsa more and more at school and somehow not even see me when she passed me in the halls. I wanted spying together to be normal again. Maybe we could even find something out about my mother.

"We have to take quiet provisions with us," said Duck-Duck. "Nothing that will alert the suspect to the fact that she is being watched. No apples. No potato chips. No sunflower seeds." She tied up her blond ponytail tight and stuck it in her jacket collar, like spies do.

We caught up with Keely in the Main Street Convenience

Store. We slipped into the potato chip aisle and then circled around back when she was in the beer aisle. When she came up to the register, I was sure she would have a six-pack, but she only bought a box of tissues, a pack of gum, and a can of motor oil.

"I guess the truck is leaking oil again," I whispered.

Next Keely walked out to the pickup, which was parked in the lot. We slipped out too, peering around the store corner as she stacked and restacked the packages in the truck bed. She stacked everything along the cab wall. Then she laid a tarp over the boxes and tucked it in underneath.

"If she drives off, we'll lose her," hissed Duck-Duck.

But she didn't drive off. Through the whole afternoon, Keely didn't drive at all. She'd walk off and then come back to the truck and fuss with the boxes. She went to the Social Security office and to the Family Center, where group therapy was supposed to happen, but she just walked around it and never went in.

"Is she spying on someone too?" whispered Duck-Duck.

"Naw," I said, "she's just avoiding group. Now she can say she intended to go, but, for some reason she will make up on the spot, she never got there. That's what she did when they wanted her to go to counseling after Grandpa died."

After group would have been over, Keely finally went inside. The Family Center was a funny building. It used to be the Salt Run bowling alley, but then they put up a bunch of walls and made offices for Social Service ladies and a big room for supervised visitation. The building's windows were old and rickety.

Outside it was cold. I had on an old winter jacket of Duck-Duck's. It was pink with fake fur on the collar. It wasn't my favorite color, but the fur felt nice on my chin. In the Family Center, though, the heat must have been on high, because everyone with an office window had it open as far as it would go.

We watched Keely walk in the front door. Through the glass doors, I saw her go past the receptionist and down the right hallway, which meant she was going to the Social Service lady.

Duck-Duck and I crawled along the right side of the building until I thought we were far enough down, and then we peeked into the windows until we found the right one.

"The cameras can't see us," whispered Duck-Duck. "See how they're aimed for the sidewalk?"

I looked up, and sure enough, at each corner of the building, there were cameras straining for pictures of the sidewalk, the parking lot, the front door. The Family Center ladies were a suspicious bunch. We plastered ourselves against the wall and gave quick peeks through the window at the lady sitting at her desk with her back to us.

Keely must have been banging on the Social Service lady's door, because the lady slammed the phone down, threw up her hands, and stood up.

"Maybe she has a gun," murmured Duck-Duck.

Keely didn't have a gun, but she came in, plunked herself down in a chair, and started complaining. Through the open window, we heard every word she said.

"Lady, I have rights" was the first thing Keely said. "You've got a lot of nerve telling me I can't see my daughter."

"That's not what we discussed last time," said the lady. "Do you remember our agreement?"

"Screw your agreement," said Keely. "She's my blood. She should do what I say."

This sounded a lot like Grandpa. Except for the blood part. Grandpa would have been glad to un-blood us if he could have.

"We agreed," said the lady, obviously not for the first time, "that there were certain conditions that had to be met before you could have more than minimal visitation rights."

"What right do you have," said Keely, "to tell me what I can and can't do? You're just a lady behind a desk."

This wasn't much of a comeback. Grandpa would have said something with much more sting to it. He would have called her a pregnant sow. Or maybe a neutered paper-pusher with a bladder problem.

The lady cleared her throat. "The primary benefit of visitation is for the child. The goal is frequent and meaningful supervised visitation. Did you go to group therapy today?" she said.

I knew the answer to that one, but Keely ignored her.

"Some goon has to watch us the whole time?" said Keely. "As soon as I can, I'm taking Carmel to Arizona, away from all of you wack jobs. Cleaner, Concentrated, Secure, and Free. Think about how it applies to *you*," she said, and she banged out the office door and tromped down the hall.

In a way, I was impressed. For years, Keely never talked back to anyone. I hoped the Social Service lady appreciated that.

In a way, it made me nervous. If Keely ever cleaned up her act, she might drag me to Arizona. I clutched the fur on the collar of my jacket.

"Arizona?" I whispered to Duck-Duck. "You think she'd really do that?"

We followed Keely back to the truck. This time she poured in the oil and started it up. Green smoke streamed out of the tailpipe as she drove off.

"Kind of like the Wicked Witch of the West," said Duck-Duck. "No offense."

"None taken," I said, and we both giggled so hard we had to stop in the convenience store and buy a Yodel to calm ourselves down.

13

After school the next day, Duck-Duck suggested we bake cookies. She took a stack of Molly's cookbooks off the shelf, a pile so
high she almost couldn't see past her arms. We laid them out on
the kitchen table; the pictures of shiny food made me hungry for
dishes I'd never even heard of before. "We can make whatever
kind of cookie you want," said Duck-Duck. "Just look it up." She
flipped to the index of the biggest book.

It seemed kind of nuts to think you could make chocolate-
chip cookies at home. How would you get them all round,
chippy, and brown only on the bottom? But Duck-Duck assured
me she did it all the time.

For about a week after Grandpa died, Keely had made a go
at being a real mother. She did laundry; she bought toilet paper;
she washed dishes. On the third day, she tried to make red velvet
cupcakes from a mix. Not many people are capable of ruining

a cake mix, but somehow Keely did it. The cupcakes were dry and crumbly, sucking moisture out of your tongue the instant you bit in. They reminded me of charcoal, with just a whiff of lighter fluid.

"What did you put in this?" I said, trying not to sound too mean.

"I think they wanted milk or water or something, but I put in sugar-free Red Bull instead. Don't you like it?"

You'd think I would have caught on to the reading thing then, but somehow it didn't cross my mind.

"You put in Red Bull?"

"Haven't you ever had red velvet cake?" she asked.

I hadn't, but whatever made red velvet cake red, it definitely wasn't Red Bull.

"It seemed a little dry. I was thinking of putting in some beer, but I ran out," said Keely.

That was the last time Keely ever tried to bake anything.

"There's a recipe for everything in the whole world," Duck-Duck said. "If it's not in a book, it's on the Internet. Come on, we can have cooking class."

I'd never thought about it before, but there were probably people all over the world wanting cookies every minute of the day.

"What kind should we make?" asked Duck-Duck, flipping the pages of the big book.

"Banana," I said, "with chocolate chips." That would be the kind of cookie that monkeys would like. Wolf packs, on the other hand, probably ate raw-meat cookies with crunchy ground-up bones in place of nuts and drizzled blood for icing. It made me mad that I felt so grateful Duck-Duck was behaving normally. When we were home, Duck-Duck acted like she had never avoided me in the lunchroom or spent every afternoon with Darsa. I wanted to stay mad at her, but all I could feel was this pathetic gratitude that she wanted to make cookies.

We looked through the endless index, and Duck-Duck was right: there were banana cookies — but with walnuts, not chocolate chips.

"Don't worry," said Duck-Duck. "We can swap out the walnuts for chocolate chips. One should not be confined by words on a page." She started clearing the table. "It's not creative to follow recipes exactly."

Recipes were like word problems, said Duck-Duck. You had to read through the whole thing first so you knew what was coming.

"If you can read, you can cook," she said.

That was definitely comforting. As long as I could read, I was set for life.

"The only reason I ever wanted to be a Girl Scout was because of the cookies," I said while we were cleaning up the spilled flour and the egg I had dropped into the silverware drawer. "I told my mother I wanted to go camping, but it wasn't true."

"This is better," said Duck-Duck. "You can have all the cookies you want without that organizational bureaucracy."

We preheated the oven and then watched through the window as the batter turned golden-brown and the chips melted into little chocolate pools. When they were done, all the bottoms were brown, not black. They were perfect.

"You think we could make Yodels at home too?" I asked.

"You can bake anything at home. Just Google the recipe," said Duck-Duck. "Not tomorrow, though, I have soccer practice. Oh, that reminds me, we should pick up some Lemon Energy. It's so much better than lemonade."

Lemon Energy was a sports drink, apparently the kind marathon runners drank at the Olympics. Darsa now drank it, which was why Duck-Duck had started drinking it. Darsa also ate energy bars. Duck-Duck had brought one home a few days ago. It tasted more like stale crackers than anything healthy, but Duck-Duck said it was good because it had scientific research behind it. With anyone else, Duck-Duck would have called that bad logic. With Darsa, it was like she forgot all about reason and proof. It made my stomach hurt.

I wanted to make a joke about Darsa and her Lemon Energy and Keely and her Auga-L shakes, but I didn't. It was the kind of joke Duck-Duck would have thought was funny before but maybe not now. Yesterday I couldn't even find her at lunch. I spent the whole time looking for her and finally found her outside playing soccer when she was supposed to be inside eating lunch.

I didn't get soccer. I didn't get lemon drinks. My stomach started hurting a lot.

The next day while I was at my locker, I spotted Duck-Duck halfway down the hall. I called, but she didn't turn around. Had she heard me or not? When I got to the lunchroom, Duck-Duck was sitting with the wolf pack.

I knew I couldn't sit with the wolves. Head wolf Darsa made the rules, and it was an unbreakable rule that you couldn't sit with Darsa unless Darsa invited you to sit with her. Once, a new girl sat down there by mistake, and she spent the rest of the month sitting with the boys because no one in the wolf pack would risk pissing off Darsa.

I went and hid in the bathroom for a long time.

While Duck-Duck went to after-school soccer practice, Molly picked me up. We bought fruit smoothies and brought them home and watched *Harry Potter and the Sorcerer's Stone* together.

"You okay?" asked Molly.

"Yeah, sure," I said.

"Want to talk about it?"

"Talk about what?" There was no way I was going to tell her what happened at lunch.

That night I was sick. First, I didn't want to eat dinner. Then I felt puke waves, and then I was throwing up in Molly's nice clean toilet. Molly heard me, and the amazing thing was that she came in and held my forehead while I was puking. I never imagined anyone would get so close to another person's puke. It was nice of her, keeping my face from dipping too close to the gross toilet water. Afterward, she cleaned up everything too, like it wasn't me who had made the mess.

"You just rest," she said. "In a little while, I'll get you a Popsicle. Maybe you caught a virus."

The Popsicle was cold and wet, and after I sucked it all down, I somehow fell asleep. When I woke up, I didn't feel like puking anymore.

Duck-Duck was already in the kitchen when I made my way down to breakfast. I could hear her and Molly talking.

"She was sick last night," Molly told her.

I heard the rustle of cereal boxes and the *thunk* of the refrigerator door.

"She probably has jungle fever," said Duck-Duck.

"When you hear hoofbeats, think of horses, not zebras," Molly said.

"What's that supposed to mean?"

"It means the most likely and commonsense conclusion is usually the right conclusion. The commonsense conclusion in this case would be the flu, not jungle fever. If you heard hooves, the logical conclusion would be horses, not zebras," said Molly.

"Unless you live in Africa," said Duck-Duck.

Then I realized my mistake. If I hadn't been living in this exotic new land of Africa with Duck-Duck and Molly, I would be able to just start over and pretend Duck-Duck didn't exist. I could totally avoid her in the lunchroom. I could leave school by the back door so I wouldn't see her walking home. I could disappear and never have to think of zebras again.

But I was living on Cherry Road. Even if I avoided Duck-Duck all day, even if she stayed for extra soccer, I still had to see her at night. I still had to see her in the morning eating cereal.

I still had to pretend in front of Molly that Duck-Duck hadn't turned into a Darsa wolf-girl.

I started having more sympathy for Harriet in *Harriet the Spy*. Even if she did have two parents, a nanny, and a cook, she had lost her best friends, and no words could fix that.

14

A few days later, when Keely showed up at Cherry Road, she didn't even knock. She just walked right in. "My *casa* is your *casa*," she said, as if that made it okay.

That was stupid, since it wasn't her *casa* in the first place. It was Molly's. Keely learned the word *casa* from the Spanish-speaking gas-station guy. She used it so people would think she knew Spanish.

"Hi," I said. "Whatever."

I had no idea Keely even knew where Molly's house was. We had always met at the Family Center. That was the rule. She definitely wasn't supposed to be here, but if I said so, she might get upset and take me to Arizona. Or maybe Mexico.

I looked at the clock. Molly had gone to pick up Duck-Duck from soccer practice and wouldn't be back for a while.

Keely sat down at Molly's table, pulled out a bag of tobacco and some dirty rolling papers, and spit on her fingers. Grandpa used to roll tobacco on the kitchen table, scattering dust and leaves to get wicked up by your sardines. Mom had moved on to a cheaper brand, but she still rolled just like he did.

"It's all natural," she said. "Harvested by Native Americans who fast while they say smoke prayers so that the energy is just right."

Spitting at Molly's clean table sure didn't seem just right. I would have to wipe it down before Molly and Duck-Duck got home.

"Got anything to eat?" Keely said.

I knew she could smell cookies. Those Auga-L shake people couldn't make up their minds. Apples were bad, but cookies were okay? I crossed my arms and looked at my mother.

"Why'd you take the SNAP card with you?" I asked. "What was I supposed to eat?"

"I didn't take it on purpose. I was on my way to Reno, and I found the card. I thought about mailing it back, but you always were very resourceful and independent. I figured you'd be okay." She finished rolling her cigarette and then lit it on Molly's stove. She took a puff and blew smoke into the room. I realized I should have banned the cigarettes, but it felt too late now.

"You got anything to eat?" she asked again.

No way was one of my and Duck-Duck's cookies getting mixed up with rolling papers and smoke prayer energy.

"Nope," I said. "All out."

"I wasn't worried about you," Keely went on, as if I hadn't said anything. "I knew the elements would take care of you."

I thought about my summer of carrying backpacks of canned baked beans all the way across town. I thought about stealing strawberries from neighborhood gardens and the occasional Yodel.

"What a shit-poor excuse," I said. "There were no 'elements' taking care of me. I took care of me."

Keely fiddled with her tobacco. "Cleaner, Concentrated, Secure, and Free, as everyone who knows Auga-L would say," she said. "Think of how it applies to *you*. I figured if I left, the Department ladies would come back and set you on the right track better than I could anyway."

I was stumped. Nothing stuck to her. She was like Jell-O, words just slipping through and out the other side without making a dent.

"Didn't you feel guilty, even a little bit?" I asked.

Keely got this serious look on her face. But it was a practiced look. When the Social Service ladies first started coming around after Grandpa died, she would look bored, or mad, or just blank. She hadn't quite mastered the serious look. Now she could look like she had given an idea a lot of thought. It was a lot like the lipstick she'd started wearing. Her hair and eyes were still dirt-brown, but now she wore lipstick, and she could put on a new serious look.

"I only ran away one other time." She blew out smoke. "I was pregnant and I thought it was my last chance to get away. I mean, who would have a baby while living with someone like Pop?"

I had to give her credit for that one. I never knew she had even thought about it, even once. Then I realized she hadn't answered my question. Maybe there were so many things she couldn't answer that she didn't even try anymore.

"I left with my boyfriend, Jack," she said. "We'd been going out for a few months, and he said he wanted to go make it big in New York City. I couldn't think of anywhere else. New York would be a good place to have a kid. That's where Sesame Street is." She clicked her teeth.

That's what happened when you didn't read books: you decided where to live on the basis of one TV show—a *kids'* show. Didn't she know *Law & Order* happened in New York City too? Duck-Duck was forever telling me about *Law & Order* plots with people who got killed for money or because they used bad logic, or worse.

Keely click-clacked her teeth. "For a couple months, I thought we had it made," she said, "but then Jack held up a Seven-Eleven, and he got caught. I had no money for an apartment and no job. I was too young to drive. All I had was two packs of Tic Tacs. I had to call Pop to come get me." She gave this little sigh-sniff, but she didn't really sound sad. She sounded like she was reading a newspaper article reporting the facts.

"Pop left me on the streets for weeks before he finally drove down to get me. He told me I was a fat slut and that I looked like a cow and no wonder Jack left me. Pop just hit me, threw me into the backseat of the borrowed Ford, and started driving. That was the one nice thing he did—not make me ride in the bed of the pickup. Then, just as we left the city, my water broke. I begged him to stop at a hospital. All the way up the Taconic Parkway, I yelled and screamed, but he said, 'Hey, you wanted me to pick you up. Well, here I am, so now we're going home.' I kept begging, and he said, 'Shut up, bitch. Who else would save your worthless ass?' When the baby came out, it almost fell off the seat. It was bluish and I thought it was dead, but then it started to cry." She ground her cigarette butt into a saucer. "Pop told me I was gonna have to work off the money it would take to redo the seat cushions."

She talked about "the baby" as if it were someone, some thing, neither of us had ever met, when actually it was *me*. It was weird she was telling me this now, when what she should have been telling me was what happened in the river.

"Next time, smoke outside," I said. I was too stunned to say anything else.

Keely just shrugged and stood up. She gave one last look around the kitchen, maybe looking for those cookies, and wandered out the door without even saying good-bye.

I wondered if she ever really connected me with "the baby." Or "the baby" with me. It occurred to me that no one else would ever believe this story: a father picking up his pregnant fifteen-year-old daughter and then, after calling her names, forcing her to give birth in the backseat of a moving car? I was the only person who would ever believe it, because I was the only other person alive who knew Grandpa like she did. Those Social Service ladies probably thought she made shit like that up.

I wiped away Keely's cigarette ashes and opened the door to air out the kitchen. I never told Molly about Keely's visit.

15

Grandpa's rules had changed every day. And every day it was Keely's and my job to guess what the rules were. Be quiet. Don't be quiet. Set the table. Don't set the table. Answer the door. Don't answer the door.

At the beginning of every school year, teachers talked a lot about Rules and the Real World. They went on about how we weren't babies anymore; if we didn't learn to follow the rules, what did we think was going to happen when we got to high school? They had rules for eating and not eating, for peeing and not peeing, for talking and not talking. *Don't think the real world is this easy!* they said. Don't run, but don't be late. Don't wear short dresses. Don't wear long earrings. They had rules about swearing and teasing and back talk. They had rules about bikes and skates and scooters. They banned cell phones and knives and cigarettes. It was all online too, in case you forgot.

Once I almost got detention for sitting down and shutting up when we were supposed to be standing up and talking. When I told Duck-Duck about that, she called it a *travesty of justice*. I thought I would say that to the principal the next time he accused me of disobedience/defiance, which was forbidden according to page fifty-two of the *Salt Run Middle School Code of Conduct*.

Molly would have made a good lawyer. I think even Duck-Duck was impressed. Molly talked to the lawyers, she talked to the Social Service ladies, she talked to the police, and they all came up with rules. Keely was my mother, so she had a claim on me, they said, but not if she didn't clean up her act. *How do we know you won't disappear again?* they asked Keely. This was something Molly had said. *We need to see that you can provide a good home,* they said. Molly also had said this. *Good home* meant cooking and cleaning and going to parent-teacher conferences and group therapy. The Social Service ladies laid down rules. Fishkill stays with Molly and Duck-Duck, they said, until Mom cleans up her act. This meant no-drinking rules and clean-pee-test rules. This meant getting a job, even if it was just McDonald's, and keeping it for six months. This meant showing up for group therapy with other screwed-up mothers every Friday at ten o'clock in the morning. It meant family therapy with me and one of the Social Service ladies.

I would have added a test to see if she could learn how to make a peanut-butter sandwich and if she could buy milk, bread, and Yodels without being reminded, but Molly didn't say this, so the ladies didn't either.

In general, I was relieved, because six months was a lot of time, and it would be next to impossible for Keely to keep going to therapy for that long. Maybe she would get bored and move to California. Maybe she would fall into the river again, this time without any help. I felt guilty when I thought that, but I couldn't take it back. Even inside my brain.

Keely made a big fuss and put on a lot of lipstick for the meetings with Social Services, but she wasn't a good lawyer like Molly was. Keely said she didn't drink anymore. She went on about the Four Freedoms, and the ladies looked at one another and took more notes, like they were going to add another rule to the list, but they didn't.

Keely had trouble with rules. She had the hardest time following the group-therapy rule. The first meeting she missed because she forgot to turn on her new alarm clock. The second meeting, she showed up late, and they had already locked the door.

"You've got to get here at ten o'clock sharp," the front-desk woman said, "or they close the group. Everyone has to feel safe, you know. How can anyone feel safe if people just come and go whenever they want?"

The third group meeting, Keely actually made it inside the room, but then she went out to the bathroom and never made it back in.

"She stayed for affirmations," said the group leader, "but walked out while Debra was talking about her son's tonsillectomy."

Each time, the Social Service ladies would chase Keely down and explain the rules again. They would talk about "family reunification" and about "living up to your part of the bargain." I could never be sure if Keely forgot or if she just had no intention of living up to any part of any bargain.

Once a week we had supervised time together in the Family Center. There were rules about that too. Keely had to show up on time. She had to call if she was going to cancel or if she was going to be late. We had to stay in the Social Service lady's office or the Family Center visitor room, where they could keep an eye on us. We had to sign in and sign out.

"What do they think we're going to do?" complained Keely. "Watch dirty movies?"

Even if we had wanted to watch movies, the television channels in the visitor room were controlled by the front-desk ladies, who would change the channels if you asked, but certainly would have said no if something looked too interesting. The TV sound was always turned up so high that you had to yell to hear each other. It was usually turned to cartoons or soap operas. Once it was on *Law & Order,* but then a five-year-old boy came in, and they turned it back to cartoons.

I decided to use all this free time to confront her.

"Look at this story in *TV Guide,*" I said, shoving the magazine at her. "You think that's true?"

"Sure," she said, shrugging and pushing the magazine back to me. "If they wrote it, it's true."

Then I picked up the Auga-L shake box, which she always

carried with her. "Look at this shake label," I said. "Don't you spell *low-fat* with a hyphen?"

Keely just shrugged again and didn't even glance at the box.

"Here," I said, "right near the comments about Serenity."

She made like she was looking and then said, "I don't have my reading glasses."

"You can't read, can you?" I said.

She pretended she didn't hear me and started rummaging in her purse.

"You never could."

She stopped, her hands drooping into her bag. I suddenly felt bad. What was the point of making her admit it, anyway? But I couldn't help myself.

"How'd you get through high school if you couldn't read?"

"I don't know," she said. "I only made it through tenth grade, anyway. They gave me Ds so I'd pass. I could draw real good, though."

"I could teach you," I said. "It's not really all that hard."

Keely stood and walked to the window. "Nah, it's too late. I don't need it anyways." And she put on her coat and went out, as if for a smoke. I watched cartoons for twenty minutes, but she never came back.

"How was your visit?" Molly asked when she picked me up.

"Fine," I said. "What's for dinner?"

Keely and I had to go to family therapy together every week as well. Keely talked and complained, and the Social Service lady therapist analyzed, and every once in a while she said, "Fishkill, do you have any feelings about this?" and I said, "No, not really," or "Naw," or just shrugged.

"This is *your* therapy session too," the Social Service lady said.

"Uh-huh," I replied. She couldn't force me to talk.

It wasn't until the second meeting that I found out this particular Social Service lady had gone to school with Keely.

Her name was Candy. She didn't look like a Candy. If she did, she would have had red hair, worked in a bakery, and iced cakes for a living. Instead, she looked like a Social Service lady, complete with a gray suit, a clipboard, and many lists.

Keely and I were in the waiting room when that news finally came out.

"Candy acts like she's hot stuff," Keely said, "but she's no better than me. We grew up together."

"Really?" I said. "You were friends?"

Keely shrugged. "Kinda. We went to elementary and middle school together. We went to high school together too, but I didn't see her much, and then I was gone after tenth grade."

I guessed why she didn't see her much. Same as now, the dumb kids and the smart kids never saw one another unless they played sports. Keely definitely would have been one of the dumb kids, and I doubted she played sports.

"What was Mom like when she was little?" I asked Candy during one of Keely's frequent bathroom visits. The Social Service ladies got upset if I called my mother Keely.

Candy looked at me and set her face to friendly remembering.

"She was pretty quiet. She could draw really well, though."

That's what Keely had said, but I'd never seen her even pick up a crayon.

"What did she draw?" If Candy had answered beer bottles, I might have believed her.

"Flowers," said Candy, "and portraits."

"That's a crock," I said. She definitely had Keely confused with someone else.

"Don't curse," said Candy.

I hadn't even realized *crock* was a curse word.

It was hard not to say bad words. They had so much more power than regular words. The rules for curse words were complicated, though. Grandpa didn't blink if anyone said *hell*. Teachers choked if I even said, *What the hey*.

Fuck was really bad. *Screw* was a little better. Most of the time. For most people.

Grandpa liked curses, but he could wreak havoc without using any of those words, real or made-up. Animal dung and a scary anatomical reference could do it every time. I almost admired him for it.

I invented bad words in my head. Twisted tough words that made people gasp and choke. *Stickack* your momma. *Gazz* you. My favorite invention was *You ant-eating piece of piss pie*. I saved it as my secret weapon.

"Sorry," I said to Candy.

"Apology accepted," Candy said. "Next time, think before you speak." She started packing up her clipboard and her pens. "Next time we should talk about plans for Christmas."

"Sure," I said out loud. But in my head I silently added, *You ant-eating piece of piss pie.* The words had a nice ring.

Christmas was coming, and this seemed to worry Duck-Duck and Molly.

"It's our first Christmas here in the new place, and we'll be alone," explained Duck-Duck.

"What do you mean 'alone'?" I said. How were they alone if they had each other? Or was she trying to give me a hint—that they'd be alone without me? That I needed to go away and give them their special day? It was hard to find a place to hang out on Christmas. Everything was closed. Even the library. Plus it was cold outside.

Maybe Duck-Duck really did want me to go away. She seemed to want a double life. It was as if that same week she hadn't giggled when Darsa fanned her nose and said I smelled like fish. I wondered why Duck-Duck didn't get confused about whether she was at home or at school and whether she should be mean when she was being nice, or nice when she was being mean.

"Why are you acting like Darsa is so smart?" I finally said to her. "She's just being mean."

"Don't be so sensitive," said Duck-Duck. "She's just being funny. She has a developed sense of irony."

I guessed my sense of irony wasn't developed enough. Maybe you needed homeschooling for that.

I tried to get my brain back into the Christmas spirit.

"It's our first Christmas since Ellen left," said Duck-Duck, "and Aunt Patty has to work this year, so she can't come. What do you usually do for Christmas?"

"Well," I said, "Grandpa usually went hunting."

This was a nice way of saying he took his shotgun outside and shot cans, trees, birds, and basically anything that moved. Keely and I stayed in the house all day because it was too dangerous to leave. After hours of shooting holes in things, Grandpa would come inside and drink rum mixed with a little eggnog, and we would try to go out. Sometimes he let us; sometimes he didn't.

"You think you got an invitation to Christmas dinner?" he would say. "No one in Salt Run wants to eat with you ugly bitches."

The day before Christmas, the Social Service ladies called Molly and told her that Keely had requested a Christmas visit, and would Molly drop me off at the Family Center at ten the next morning? The Family Center apparently was where everyone who had supervised visits did Christmas.

"I'm sure it will make your mother very happy," said Molly.

I didn't tell her that I couldn't think of a single time I'd ever seen my mother happy.

Christmas morning on Cherry Road was warm and friendly, just like in storybooks. There wasn't any snow yet, but there was a pretty tree, hot chocolate, and presents for everyone, even me. This was a surprise. As we sorted out the wrapped boxes, I realized I should have gotten Molly and Duck-Duck presents too.

"Crap," I said out loud, and they both turned.

"Sorry," I said. "I didn't get you guys anything."

"Don't worry," said Duck-Duck. "There's plenty."

Plenty. What a thought.

Christmas presents for Duck-Duck meant big books about women lawyers, a new blue dress, and candy in a box. There were also bright-red mittens that fit Duck-Duck perfectly. There was a little computer that Duck-Duck turned on the minute she opened the box.

I opened my gifts slowly, since I'd never had Christmas presents before, unless you counted the box of crayons my second-grade teacher gave everybody in the class, and the Hershey's Kisses my fifth-grade English teacher passed out the last day before break.

The first gift I opened was a cookie cookbook. Instead of a written table of contents, it had a list of pictures of all the cookies: round ones, square ones, cookies shaped like cigars, cookies with jam. Looking through that book was like being inside a bakery.

I also got four pairs of socks, a pair of green mittens, and a long scarf with green tassels. I got a box of candy too. Each piece looked like a fruit or a vegetable. They were so pretty, I wasn't sure whether I wanted to eat them or save them forever.

Getting presents was a little weird. I mean, it was nice, because I'd never gotten presents before, but I also found myself wishing that I'd gotten the red mittens instead of Duck-Duck. I imagined what I would do with a little computer if I had one.

It was weird, like finally getting a present wasn't good enough; it had to be a better present.

At nine o'clock, Aunt Patty called on the computer. She was in Paris for work, so she wouldn't be able to take Duck-Duck to New York City to shop. Aunt Patty waved to me, and I waved back. She had sent presents, but somehow they hadn't gotten to us even though Aunt Patty swore she sent them in plenty of time for Christmas.

"You can open them on New Year's," said Aunt Patty. "Love to you all!"

I wondered about that. She had never met me, so was she really sending me love, or was it just a thing you said, like *See you later* or *Thanks so much*?

At ten o'clock, Molly dropped me at the Family Center.

"Merry Christmas," she said. "Say hi to your mother for me."

I found Keely sitting on a metal folding chair in the far corner of a room full of screaming kids.

"Welcome to Hell," she said.

I couldn't believe the number of people in Salt Run who required supervision. Maybe they were visiting from other towns because other towns had no supervisors?

"Molly says hi."

"Whoop-de-doo," she said. "I bet Molly doesn't have to spend the day with fifty screaming brats."

The more Keely went to therapy, the more she reminded me of Grandpa and his curses.

"I brought you something," she said.

Before I could feel bad for not getting her a present, Keely pulled out a vanilla shake and a small booklet.

"Merry Christmas," she said.

The shake, apparently, we were supposed to share. The booklet was the Auga-L product manual.

"Gosh, thanks," I said. Keely never picked up on sarcasm.

"I thought you could read about the Auga-L Principles," she said. "Then you will understand why they are so important. You were always good at the reading thing."

"It's a little noisy in here for reading," I said. On the other hand, what else was there to do? The clock said 10:05. Molly was coming back at noon. "Okay, I'll read it if you tell me where you were for five months after you fell in the river."

Keely handed me the pamphlet but showed no signs of disclosing anything. I began to read.

"'Auga-L, the Serenity Company,'" I read aloud. "How can a company be selling serenity? It sounds like bad logic."

"Keep reading. Just take it in. Make your mind an open vessel." She took a few deep breaths. Was she relaxing, or just trying not to hit me? It was hard to tell.

"Uh-huh." I kept reading: "'New and Improved Shake of the Century. Bringing patterns of peace and prosperity to your person.'"

Not even the lady poet in the famous people cemetery talked like this, but I didn't say that to Keely. She seemed almost happy.

"'With each swallow, REMEMBER: Every time you have

a problem, think of the Four Freedoms: Cleaner, Concentrated, Secure, and Free—C.C.S.F.—and an answer will come to you.'"

Remember was written in fancy pink script so you wouldn't forget.

"'Ingest this freedom and spread the good news to all that you meet.'" I guessed this was what Keely was doing, spreading the news. I did wish she wasn't spreading it so thick on Christmas, though. "'In our go-go-go lives, we often wish for the simple life. Drink our nonglycemic, higher-protein, low-fat shake, and you too will say, Simple, Simple, Simple.'"

"Simple, Simple, Simple," chanted Keely.

"I have to pee," I said. I got up and pushed my way through groups of people to the other side of the room. At the ladies' room, there was a line of little girls and their mothers, and I took my place behind a little girl holding a big cookie shaped like a reindeer.

"Where'd you get the cookie?" I asked.

She pointed to the back corner of the room, and I could see a table with soda and plates.

"Why are you here?" I asked her.

"I'm being supervised, stupid," she said. "Because it's Christmas." She took a big bite from the reindeer and chewed with her mouth open. Her hair was tied with a pink hair clip, but some was falling down in front of her eyes. When she chewed, a few hairs went in and out of her mouth.

"Are you here with your mom?"

"With my pop." She chewed off her reindeer's head and started in on the feet. "Mom said he was in jail for stealing and for diddling, and that's why I have to be supervised." She pushed the little girl in front of her in line, who shoved her back. "Why don't they have more potties here?"

"Good question," I said. I didn't mind the lines. The longer the lines, the longer I would have away from Miss Simple.

"Do you live in Salt Run?"

"Mom lives in Albany. Dad used to live in PinPoint, but now he lives in half a house in Salt Run. I guess that's why I can't visit, since maybe it doesn't have enough potties for everyone."

It took me a second to piece this together. "Half a house"— a halfway house. Then the little girl got her turn to use the toilet. I watched as the women and girls came out of the stalls. Everyone's skin looked gray and pasty, but maybe it was just the light.

When I came out of the bathroom, I went and stood in line for Christmas cookies and apple juice.

After drinking the last of my juice, I went back to Keely. She immediately pointed to the pamphlet. "What do you think? Doesn't it just make you feel . . ." She paused.

"Simple?"

"Yes, exactly."

"Yup," I said. "Not much plot, though."

When Molly came to pick me up at noon, I almost ran out the door.

"Here's my ride," I said. "Merry Christmas."

Keely started to say something, but I was already out of the building and jerking open the car door.

"Go, go, go!" I said to Molly.

◆ ◆ ◆

When we got back to Cherry Road, I discovered that Duck-Duck had gone to the soccer field to practice kicks with Darsa, just the two of them.

"She'll be back in an hour," said Molly. "Since there's no snow yet, they're getting it in while they can. Darsa got new cleats for Christmas."

I had been dying for visitation to finish. Now I wished I was still there.

16

The house on Birge Hill was so small, you always knew exactly where everyone else was. You could hear doors opening and closing. You could hear breath where there shouldn't be breath. Breath lingered as sound, as heat, hovering in the air above you. In a way, this was good, because you weren't easily caught off guard. It meant you were always ready.

I moved through school halls with that same keen alertness, sensing trouble and moving away from it, speeding past wild packs of jocks, populars, and nerds before they even saw my shadow. If I was sloppy and got noticed, the wolves would descend.

"Hey, freak," they would call.

"Hey, weird girl," they would growl.

Fag, fat, slut—their insults were strangely unimaginative compared to Grandpa's curses. I could have outnamed them, outcursed them, in a second if I had tried.

For me, evading the wolves was simply a way of life, a tactical move I did with a cool that came with long practice. But other girls let their hearts break open in the hall for everyone to witness. We could almost see the blood.

When they called her a slut, Frannie Synolds ran to the bathroom and put her finger down her throat.

One time Patsy Smart started banging her forehead against her locker hard, like a fist on a rock. As I walked by, I could hear her mumbling, "Freakhead, freakhead, freakhead," over and over again.

I was packless, and I was curse-proof. I had also learned how important it was to be invisible, especially important before I learned to fight back. I was almost as good as Harry Potter.

When Duck-Duck started ignoring me and sitting with the wolf-girls, being invisible didn't feel like such a good trick anymore. It made me feel sad instead of magic. It made me worry about what would happen when my birthday came around. The wolves always had big parties where they invited everyone except people they wanted to make feel bad. I knew I wasn't going to have a party. I was invisible and had no one to invite.

For weeks, Keely had been asking the Social Service ladies if she could take me to the Auga-L convention. We'd had one unsupervised visit, where we were allowed to go the drugstore and back, but this was different. It was bigger, longer. Plus it was half an hour away.

"It will be a good experience for her," said Keely. "She'll learn about serenity."

"So it's a religious organization?" asked Candy.

Keely didn't answer that one, but she handed out Auga-L pamphlets to Candy and anyone else who would take one. Finally Candy and the other Social Service ladies said okay.

"But you have to bring her back in the evening," they said. "It's not an overnight visit. Baby steps, you know."

Keely was so excited, it almost made me think she liked the idea of working up to an overnight stay. "You won't be sorry," she kept saying to me.

I had never been to a convention before, so I was definitely curious. I figured it would be like the Olympics or a football game, with people sitting on bleachers with binoculars. Maybe it would be like a circus, with popcorn and cotton candy and tigers jumping through rings of fire. What made it even more exciting was that it was going to happen on my birthday.

"Are you sure you want to go on your birthday?" said Molly. "We could have a party here if you wanted."

I knew she was just being nice, but she probably didn't know that Duck-Duck was my only friend, and even she was turning out to be a wolf-girl.

"Naw," I said. "I'll just go with Keely to the convention. They'll probably have cake there too."

January fifteenth was a Saturday, so I was going to miss shopping with Molly, but I wasn't thinking about that when Keely came to pick me up in the green truck.

"See you later," I called to Molly and Duck-Duck. It felt like a normal thing I was doing, going out with my mother on my birthday. Going somewhere they couldn't go. Maybe they even wished they could come too.

The heat in the green truck was broken, so my feet were frozen by the time we got there. It turned out a convention wasn't a big party in a football stadium or even a concert hall. It was only twenty ladies in a living room, drinking shakes. There were a couple men, but I was the only kid.

"Carmel!" said the lady who lived there. "I've heard so much about you! Your mother talks about you constantly. I'm Barbara, Barb for short. I'm sure your mother has told you about me."

I didn't want to say *No, I've never heard of you,* so I shook her hand and kind of smiled.

"Your mother says you play the piano. You'll have to play us a song before you leave."

At first I thought Barb had started talking to someone else.

"Excuse me?"

"Your mother said you play like a prodigy. You'll have to show us."

She definitely had me mixed up with some other lady and her kid, since I was sure the word *prodigy* had never come out of Keely's mouth. I fake-smiled again and didn't say anything.

Keely didn't seem to be listening to Barb's story about my musical skills. She was on the other side of the room, picking up pamphlets and pretending to read them. I slid up behind her.

"What the hell?" I whispered. "Why are you telling people I can play the piano?"

Keely took a step back from the table she was admiring and

ignored my question. "Look at that poster. Now you know I'm not the only one who believes in Auga-L."

I looked at the picture and saw smiling ladies in black and yellow, holding up black and yellow canisters that said *Auga-L* in big type. They looked totally satisfied, like they knew for sure all their daughters could play the piano like prodigies and didn't have to lie about it.

Then, before I could ask Keely again about piano lies, or kick her because that was probably the only way to get her attention, Barb rang a little bell and called out, "Come on, girls, let's start."

They weren't all girls, since two were men. One acted like he might be the husband of one of the ladies sitting on the couch. He sat with his arm around her back. His arm was so long, his hand reached around to her left breast. He would squeeze with the ends of his fingers when he thought no one was looking.

The other man was little with glasses, and he sat, gripping pamphlets, on a kitchen chair in the back. He didn't look at anyone except Barb. Maybe he wanted to be squeezing *her* breast but was sitting too far away.

"We are all here because . . ." said Barb loudly, drawing out the *because* since not everyone was sitting down yet. "Because we have a lifestyle we believe in, and we have a product that makes our lifestyle. What is that lifestyle?" she called out to her audience.

"Auga-L!" her visitors yelled, looking very happy with themselves.

Barb asked, "What is your goal in life?"

Keely screamed, "Simple, Simple, Simple!" But apparently

the answer was "Cleaner, Concentrated, Secure, and Free." Still, the women smiled at Keely.

I didn't answer any of the questions. Barb obviously already knew the answers. I kept quiet and tried to sink into the couch cushions whenever Keely yelled too loudly.

Then Barb showed a little movie. It had people with big houses talking about how, when they failed at everything else, Auga-L had saved their lives. Saving their lives meant it gave them big houses and something to eat every night that didn't need cooking. I wondered what Molly, with her shelf of cookbooks and her whole-wheat spaghetti, would think of this.

At the end of the convention, they had a little call-and-response chant. You didn't need to know the response, because Barb gave it to us before we said it.

"Give me a *C*," Barb sang out, and the guests answered, "*C*!"

"Give me another *C*!"

"*C*!"

"Give me an *S*!"

"*S*!"

Give me an *F*!"

"*F*!"

"What does it spell?"

That was kind of funny. It didn't spell anything, but that didn't stop everyone from chanting "C!C!S!F!" Even Keely, who couldn't read or spell.

I had been hoping for party food, but all they had was shakes. They had flavors other than the vanilla Keely always got, but Keely said the founder had created vanilla first, so that was the most original. I tasted the strawberry, but it didn't really taste much different from the vanilla. Just pink.

When we left, another woman, who had bought twenty-four cartons of shake mix, came up to us and tried to hug me, even though she was holding the box of twenty-four cartons.

"Carmel, you little darling. Did you learn a lot about Auga-L?"

"Sure," I said. "But what does the *L* stand for?"

The woman just laughed and hugged someone else.

"Don't you feel so serene?" Keely sighed as we got into the green truck.

"Umm," I said.

"Simple, Simple, Simple," said Keely, and we drove off.

Keely dropped me at the Family Center. She gave me a carton of shake mix and told me to drink one shake for every meal. I decided I'd drop it in the garbage-that-goes-to-the-dump bin when I got home. I didn't think shakes were biodegradable or recyclable.

"Did you have a good time?" asked Molly. She was waiting in the car. She looked like she had been baking. There was chocolate on her wrist.

"It was okay," I said.

"Did you have cake?"

I was about to lie and say yes, when I remembered Keely's piano lies. "No," I said. "No cake." Not even a Yodel.

"I figured I'd make one just in case," said Molly. "It came out of the oven right before I left the house."

For some reason, this made me sad instead of happy.

"What kind?" I asked. Then I realized that was rude. "I mean, thank you."

"Chocolate with raspberry filling. You can help me with the raspberry."

"Did Duck-Duck help you bake it?" I asked.

"No, she went over to Darsa's house, but she'll be home soon."

That made the chocolate not sound so good, but when we got home, we iced the cake with chocolate on the top and raspberry in the middle. After Duck-Duck got back and we all had dinner, Molly and Duck-Duck lit cake candles and sang.

"Happy birthday, Fishkill," said Molly. "I'm so glad you're with us to celebrate your thirteenth birthday."

That sounded weird. So old. Thirteen sounded too old to have to drink shakes. Thirteen sounded so final.

I started thinking about Birge Hill. I had lived there almost all of my thirteen years. It wasn't like I wanted to be back there, but it seemed like everyone had a place where they really belonged except me. Keely and me.

When Keely first reappeared, the ladies and the police and whoever else had an opinion said Keely had no shot at getting custody if she didn't have a stable address. I thought the stable part was funny, but no one else seemed to.

"Stable?" I said. "Horses? Get it?"

They didn't.

The ladies said Keely couldn't live in her car, or wherever

it was she spent her nights, if she wanted a child to live with her. First, they found her a long-term hotel to stay in while she was looking for something more long-term and more stable. I thought that was kind of funny too. Why call a hotel *long-term* if it wasn't? I never went inside, since most of our visits were supervised in the office, but I did see the outside. The roof looked like gray cardboard, and the apartments were stacked like boxes of Kleenex at the store: big and rectangular but easy to tip if you knocked it just a little. I thought about Keely in her Kleenex hotel when the wind blew hard. Maybe that was why it wasn't long-term; it could blow away, and they wouldn't know where she had gone. They were all very big on knowing where everyone was. I wondered why they didn't let Keely move back to Birge Hill, but maybe she didn't want to. Maybe she wanted something better. She said the shakes were making her better. I had my doubts.

January turned out to be a gray and brown month. There was no snow, and every afternoon it rained just enough to keep my coat soggy and make the pages of my books curl. I caught a cold, and Molly kept me home for three whole days. I would stay in bed until Duck-Duck left for school, and then Molly would make me breakfast. Sometimes she made me soup for breakfast, which somehow felt like something you would do in a book. After breakfast, she read the newspaper and I read the funnies. She bought me lemon cough drops and let me watch television. I knew she was missing work, but she said it was okay, that staying home was what you did when you had sick kids. I wasn't really her kid, but it made me feel good anyways. I was sorry when I had to go back to school. I wanted to be sick for months.

January was still gray my first day back. I still felt a little weak too, like I had been eating soup for weeks instead of days. I made it through the day, but maybe I was still a little sick and that was why I couldn't keep up with Duck-Duck when we walked to school. Maybe being sick was why I wasn't as invisible as usual.

"Hey, you," called Frank as I walked toward my locker to leave after the final bell rang. He wasn't hanging out with Worm anymore. Now a skinny kid followed him around and tried to look as mean as him. I couldn't fight Frank and Worm, but on a non-sick day I probably could have taken Frank and Skinny Kid.

"Hey, ho," said Skinny Kid.

It made me smile a little. All I could think of was the dwarves: *Heigh-ho, heigh-ho, it's off to work we go. . . .*

"What you laughing at, slut? You can't even afford new shoes."

They weren't close enough for me to worry about having to get in a good defensive punch, so I kept walking. I didn't get why Frannie Synolds would make herself throw up because someone called her a name. An unimaginative name at that.

They were still trailing me, and now, from down the hall, I could see Darsa and her pack coming toward me. Duck-Duck was with her, second-in-command. I stopped at my locker, and they came closer and closer.

"Hey, Fishbreath, where'd you get those sneakers?" asked Darsa. "The trash?"

I kept my eyes glued to the stack of books in my locker. Math was on top of English, which was on top of social studies.

"Have you ever seen such disgusting shoes?" said Darsa. There was the whisper-growl of wolves. "Wouldn't she look perfect in one of those Save the Children ads?"

I pulled out the math book and put it in my backpack. I glanced up at Duck-Duck. If she spoke to me, maybe the others would back off.

"Hey," I said, catching her eye. "Are we walking home together?"

Duck-Duck stiffened and quickly looked away. Without a word, she just walked right past me. I buried my head in my locker. If I couldn't see, maybe it wouldn't be real.

They all kept walking, but I could still hear them.

"Oh, my God," Darsa said. "You're not friends with that skank, are you?"

I heard a little voice murmuring, "No, of course not. I just help her with her homework."

Darsa and the wolves snorted. "Can't she just text you questions? Oh, right, she doesn't know what a cell phone is." And then a faint Chrissy giggle.

I grabbed my coat, slammed my locker shut, and stumbled out of the building, unsure of where I would go but knowing I had to get out of there before I heard anything more.

But just then a miracle occurred.

"Carmel," said a familiar voice, "I was just coming to look for you."

I whirled around, looking for the face. It was my mother.

"Come on," Keely said. "We have to go."

I'd never been so happy to see her. Other kids always had

parents showing up to take them to doctor appointments or on special camping trips. I never did, until now. I was alone with my mother. It didn't matter where we were going.

"Come on," said Keely, walking toward the parking lot. "We have business today. Don't you remember?"

I didn't remember, but I was so happy to see her, I just got into the pickup.

"Thanks," I said. "That was perfect timing."

"Glad I could help," said Keely. "That's what mothers are for, right?" Her foot fumbled with the pickup's pedals before we started rolling out of the parking lot. "Do you have many friends at school?"

That was the first time she had ever asked about something real. Maybe therapy was doing her good.

"Not really," I said. "Girls can be mean." I got a sudden lump in my throat when I thought of Duck-Duck. "I thought one of them was my friend, but I was wrong."

Keely put her hand on my leg. It was something Molly would have done. "It's okay. You're better than they are." She took her hand away.

"Thanks," I said. I hadn't realized how cold I was until she touched me.

"No, really," said Keely. "You are. That's why you have a mother who cares." She turned left. "Now you can do something for me."

I should have worried when she said this—after all, it was totally bad logic—but it sounded like a TV-mother question:

"Do something for me," TV-Mom would say. "Don't ever think you're not good enough," or "Remember, you're the best kid in the world, okay?"

"Sure," I said. "What's up?"

"Have you had plenty of shakes today?" Keely asked. The pickup's speed increased. "I just need a little pee in a cup. Just an inch or so. They don't need a full cup."

She looked like she was asking me to buy her a can of Red Bull on my way home from school.

"You want me to fake a pee test for you?" I said. "You did drugs. I knew it."

"Not drugs, silly. I wouldn't do that. I just may have been in the same room where people were smoking a little pot. You wouldn't want me to fail the test for something bogus like that, would you? Then I would never get full custody. You don't want to live with that nasty blond girl for the rest of your life, do you?"

"It's like lying," I said, but I didn't say no.

"Mothers and daughters look out for each other," she said. "It's no big deal. I'd do the same for you."

We pulled up in front of the health clinic, and she opened her purse. Inside was a little cup wrapped in plastic. "All ready for a deposit," she said, trying to make a joke but not getting it quite right.

We walked up the stairs and took a quick left at the restrooms.

"Here you go." She put the cup in my hand and pushed me toward the bathroom. "Don't spill any."

The bathroom was a single. I stood with my fingers laced around the cup for a minute, thinking about peeing and lying. I had to admit that Keely had improved a lot since the Birge Hill days. She had actually shown up for every visitation appointment and seemed to really want to see me. She had never cared whether or not I had friends before. Maybe if I did this for her now, she would want to do things for me too. Maybe we could have a little apartment not too far away from school. Maybe she could get a job at Walmart or maybe even T.J. Maxx. She could buy me new clothes and we could make spaghetti and meatballs for dinner.

I unwrapped the cup and sat down on the toilet.

It was a lot harder to get pee into a cup than you would think. When I was done, I had to wash my hands with soap and also wash the outside of the cup because it was all wet with piss. A little soap sloshed into the cup, but I figured that would make it even cleaner and they would be even nicer to Keely.

"That's my good girl," said Keely, and she hid the cup under her sleeve and went into the pee office to give them the deposit.

17

School was getting worse and worse. Every day, I felt like I was walking the halls with a rock in my stomach. Every time I saw Duck-Duck, I walked the other way, but the rock kept getting bigger. I told Molly I needed a separate bag for lunch so that she wouldn't put mine in Duck-Duck's blue lunch box.

"Our schedules are different," I said. "It's hard to coordinate."

Molly looked like she wanted to say something, but then she didn't. The next day, Molly put my lunch in its own brown paper bag. If I told her the real reason, she would make me move away. After all, it was Duck-Duck's house first, and Duck-Duck was Molly's daughter. I started wondering if Birge Hill could be fixed up, and if the heat would still work if I bought oil.

Then one day when I got home, Molly was waiting for me.

"Fishy," she said, "when I was at work, I got a phone call from Candy Phillips."

This was a bad sign, since Molly almost never took messages from any of the Social Service ladies. She was always insisting that they speak directly to me or to the both of us.

"What?" I sat down on the couch. I crossed my arms and stuck my fists under my armpits.

Molly came over to the couch and sat down next to me. She looked sad, but didn't look like she was going to throw me out.

"Candy said Keely's visitation rights have been suspended until further notice. Something about one of the conditions not being met. She didn't tell me anything else." Molly patted my leg. "I'm sorry, honey."

I wasn't exactly sorry and I wasn't exactly surprised, but my stomach started to burn, and I started trying to figure out which condition Keely had screwed up.

"Did she stop going to therapy?"

"Candy didn't say. Maybe if you asked, she would tell you."

"Whatever," I said. "It doesn't matter."

Molly gave me a blue-squinty look.

"It's true," I said. "If she doesn't care enough to do what she's supposed to, why should I care?" I almost said, "Why should I give a rat's ass?" but that was what Grandpa would have said. Molly never even said *give a shit,* let alone talked about rats and horses and pigs and their asses.

"Okay," said Molly. "But next time we see Candy, we can still ask. Just for curiosity's sake." She looked so sad that I was certain that if I were Duck-Duck, she would have hugged and kissed me right then. I moved to the far side of the couch.

"Whatever," I said again.

"If you want to talk about it now, I have time," said Molly. "Or if you'd rather talk later, just let me know."

"Nope," I said. "I'm good."

Instead of talking or thinking about it, I had dinner. Instead of talking or thinking about it, I thought about gingerbread.

Molly's gingerbread was more like cake than cookies. It had a bite that didn't hit your tongue until after you swallowed. I counted the number of bites and the number of chews. It kept me from thinking about visitation rights and suspensions and giving a shit.

After school the next day, I took the long way to Molly's. I walked through the cemetery, up and down the rows of dead people. I decided I would call Candy and ask if we could just act like I was sixteen already. If the Department paid up the electricity and started me off with a tank of oil and a little propane, I could move back to Birge Hill and fend for myself. Now that I knew how to cook, I could make better food than we used to have. If I could get a SNAP card of my own, I would be okay. Maybe Candy would drive me back and forth from the grocery store once a week so I wouldn't have to walk.

I made my way to the street on the other side of the cemetery. I decided I would go home and tell Molly that she had been very nice to take me in but I needed to be on my own now. I was wondering about the paperwork I would need to become independent when I realized that I was being followed.

It wasn't hard to figure out. The green pickup spit black

smoke whenever she hit the gas, and it made an unmistakable *cough-gag* when she gunned it. At the end of the block, Keely caught up with me and stopped. She leaned over and pushed open the passenger door.

"Get in," she said. "Hurry up."

I got in.

"What are you doing here?" I asked. "I thought your visits were suspended. What happened?"

"You fucked it up — that's what happened," said Keely, banging her hand on the steering wheel. "They said the sample was contaminated, so they made me do a second test right there, with a lady watching me pull down my pants."

"And you failed."

"Damn right I failed, kiddo. I told you I might have been where people were smoking a little pot. Why couldn't you get one thing right?" She looked like she was going to spit, just like Grandpa.

Suddenly I was really mad. "Hey, maybe I spilled a little soap," I said, "but it was your pee that had drugs in it, not mine."

Keely started like she was going to yell or hit me. Then she stopped and half smiled. "You're right," she said, and took a deep breath. "Think of the Four Freedoms: Cleaner, Concentrated, Secure, and Free. An answer will come to you."

She reached behind the seat to grab her purse. She pulled out a plastic bag of shake mix and a cup.

"I already have a shake. Let me make one for you," she said, and she measured out white powder and water into the cup.

"Here you go." She handed me the cup. "You need a pick-me-up."

I took it and drank some as Keely started the car. Suddenly the day seemed longer and more tiring than any day yet, and I fell asleep as Keely drove off.

18

When I woke up it was dark, which confused me. I'd just been at school, and it had been light out. My eyes were throbbing like I had a cold or had been hit.

As my eyes started to adjust to the dark, I realized I was in a one-room shack lying on a lumpy pad on the floor. I saw Keely on another thin mattress nearby. I sat up to see better, and she suddenly spoke.

"Don't even try. The door is locked, and I've got the key. You're going to live with your mother now, like daughters are supposed to."

"Where the hell are we?" If I had been out for a long time, who knows where she had taken me.

"Every time you have a question, think of the Four Freedoms: Cleaner, Concentrated, Secure, and Free, and an answer will come to you," said Keely.

My head felt heavy and my throat was incredibly dry. "What was in that shake? What did you do to me?" I said to her.

Keely didn't answer. She just stretched and rolled over on her mattress.

"We can't live here. What about school?" I said. "You can't keep me here all day and night. I have an oral report due tomorrow."

"You're smart enough already. You don't need more school."

Lying there in the dark, I tried to think of an answer to that, but then I fell back to sleep.

When I woke up again it was day, and my mouth was so dry it hurt. I was still in the shack. In the daylight, it looked even worse. There was electricity but no sink and no toilet. Cartons of shake mix and bottled water were stacked up, lining the entire wall. Keely was obviously planning on being here for a while. I could hear a river nearby. Keely was standing by the window, screwing on the top to her shake-up cup.

"I know I wasn't a good mother," she said, not even looking at me. "I was too messed up. But things are different now. I'm going to make it up to you." She sounded a little shaky, but she banged the cup against her palm and took a swig.

"By taking me prisoner?" I said. "That is just plain stupid."

"A mother knows what is right," she said. "And it's right that my daughter be with me now." She glanced up at me, but then looked back at her cup.

It made me wonder what made someone a mother. Popping out a baby? If you popped one out and then got on a bus to California the minute after, were you still a mother? What if you popped out a baby and then lived with the baby, but all the time you were wishing you hadn't had it and wished the baby wasn't living with you? I thought of Molly, who had wanted a baby so much that she borrowed sperm from a bank and then homeschooled too.

"So, what I think doesn't count?" I asked, scanning the walls and windows of the shack. I wondered if there was a way to pry open the little windows. "How are you going to provide a 'good home' now?"

"They were going to take away my daughter," Keely said. "They might have never let me see you again if I didn't pass all their stupid tests. I couldn't take the risk."

"So, running away is less risky?" Nothing I said seemed to sink in. "Good luck with that."

"I used to think it was all about luck—good and bad, but mostly bad," said Keely. "But now I know it is within my power to change my own life. I don't have to just be a passive participant."

"Change away," I said. "Just don't go changing my life."

"Simple, Simple, Simple," she answered, and handed me my very own shake-up cup.

For the first week or two, I tried every way I could think of to escape.

Whenever Keely went outside, I tried pulling out the window nails, but I only got splinters in my fingers. We didn't have metal forks or spoons, but whenever Keely left for even ten minutes, I tried digging a hole in the wood wall with a screw I pulled from the electric heater. After a week, I had made only a tiny pile of shavings. At that rate, I'd be there till spring.

When I ran out of ideas, I would ask myself, *If Duck-Duck was still Duck-Duck and not a wolf-girl, what would Duck-Duck do now?* But I never got further than standing on a chair looking out the tiny window at the white rushing river. There was still very little snow; the trees were black and naked. In the mornings, the ground was white with frost. If Keely had fallen in the river now, she would have become ice. We were probably miles from the nearest house.

"Where the hell are we?" I asked again, despite knowing that Keely would never answer me.

"Home," said Keely.

"And where exactly is 'home'? Arizona? Timbuktu?" I knew I sounded snotty, but surely she would at least tell me what state we were in.

"Simple, Simple, Simple," she said.

"By 'simple,' are you saying we're still in New York?"

Keely didn't answer. On the frosty windows, I finger-wrote backward S.O.S. messages, figuring that even if Keely saw them, she wouldn't know what they meant.

"Molly and Duck-Duck are going to miss me, you know," I said. "They'll send the police out looking for me."

"No, they won't," said Keely. "You never belonged there. They didn't really want you. They were just being charitable. You don't want to live on charity."

"The Social Service ladies will send the cops to look for

me," I said. "They'll put me on TV. They'll put me on milk cartons." I tried to sound certain. Duck-Duck would have.

Keely was counting her cigarettes. "That's why I told everyone I was going to take you to my apartment in Arizona," she said. "All those ladies, as you call them, will be looking for you far, far away from here." She gave a weird smile. "You think I'm dumb—I know."

The shack had an electric heater but no running water. We went outside in the cold to piss and poop, and we washed with wet wipes and cold water brought in from the river after we broke through the ice. Pooping was painful, your bare ass out in the cold. At first I hoped someone would walk by while I was squatting there with my naked butt in the wind, but no one ever did. Keely was always standing ready to grab me when I was done. If I tried to run, where would I go? We were out in the woods, and I didn't even know what state we were in. I didn't want to think of the warm lion tub at Molly's house.

Every day, I tried to think how lawyer logic would solve this problem, but as the days passed and I was still a prisoner, thinking grew harder and harder. It was as if Duck-Duck and her warm lion tub were in the real world, and I had gotten stuck in a cold imitation world. Or maybe it was the opposite.

This cold fake world had no other people in it besides me and Keely. In the mornings, I saw animal tracks—squirrels, foxes, even bears—in the frost but never any human tracks. I wondered if we were in Alaska or Maine. Somewhere lonely with a lot of predators.

After several weeks of cold woods, I almost started to believe that Keely was right and that Molly hadn't noticed I was gone. Or maybe she had noticed but didn't care enough to tell anyone. Then I thought of the chicken in the oven, and I knew Molly would notice and would care. Duck-Duck might be too busy with Darsa, but Molly would care.

Keely didn't read newspapers, but she had stuffed them in the window cracks for insulation and used them to cover holes in the floor of the pickup. I excavated weeks' old *Country Journal* pages; they were all too old to mention a search for a kidnapped thirteen-year-old girl.

My backpack and books had never made it to the shack, so the only other reading materials apart from the old newspapers were the black-and-yellow Auga-L shake containers. Every morning at breakfast and again at lunch and dinner, I read the Auga-L ingredients, the nutritional requirements, and the claims to serenity. I missed Harry Potter and Nancy Drew like they were my long-lost brother and sister.

The shack's little windows were rigged to slide open only six inches. They were high up off the ground too, so even if I did break one and managed to fit through it without slicing myself to pieces, I would still have to jump ten feet down. The door had a wooden bolt on the outside, which Keely conscientiously slid into place every time she left. I kept thinking she would forget about the bolt, just once, but she never did. The door locked on the inside with a key, which Keely never put down, even to pee. There was no phone, no computer, no TV. All I could see outside were trees and river.

We would wake in the late morning and have a shake. Then

Keely would leave—for a walk? to go to the stream? to the pickup?—always bolting the door behind her.

For lunch we would have another shake, and then Keely would nap.

In the afternoons, Keely would let me out for half an hour, tying a rope to my leg and watching me the whole time. At one point she decided mothers and daughters should play games, so we played tic-tac-toe and Go Fish.

"Games give us a chance to bond," she said in a voice I knew was not hers but the therapist's.

For dinner, yet another shake. Sometimes Keely would go out again for a smoke, and then, at night, she would lock the door with the key, which she put in the pocket of the sweatpants she wore as pajamas, and we would go to sleep for the night.

It was boring, but it was also almost relaxing in a way. No homework. No shopping for food. No math class. I knew Duck-Duck would think I had gone soft by not trying to get away anymore, by relaxing into the repetitive life of a prisoner.

I started to think the shakes were slowly erasing my memories of real food.

"Cleaner, Concentrated, Secure, and Free," Keely would say.

I decided she was convinced that if we both drank enough shakes, we would become a normal mother and daughter.

I tried asking her questions from time to time.

"How long are you going to keep me here? Till I'm eighteen? Are you out of your mind or something?"

"No, I'm not. You're my daughter, and I am doing what's

best for you. They can't take you away from me," said Keely, click-clacking her teeth and starting to head for the door.

"Give me a break," I said. "You're only doing this because you couldn't hack having a job and going to therapy."

"Carmel, you just got to face facts. I'm your mother," said Keely.

"My name isn't Carmel anymore, Mom, it's Fishkill."

"I named you Carmel. Carmel Fishkill."

"And I named myself Fishkill. Fishkill Carmel."

"Cleaner, Concentrated, Secure, and Free," she said, and banged the door shut.

Having conversations with Keely was a bit like talking to a cat. Sometimes she seemed to understand English. Sometimes she didn't.

Gradually, Keely started talking more. At first it was in little spurts. Then the chats got longer. None of the conversations ever felt finished, though.

"I was going to kill him, you know," Keely said one morning, mixing up my first shake of the day.

"Kill who?"

"Pop. I was going to kill him if it got bad enough."

I thought about this. Wasn't the hitting stick bad enough? Wasn't the rationed toilet paper bad enough?

"It was already pretty bad," I said.

"I was going to give it until you were fourteen. If he hadn't kicked off by then, I was going to kill him."

Fourteen would have been a long time to wait. "Why fourteen?"

"He didn't come into my bedroom until I was fourteen," she said, and then she went outside to pee.

She stayed outside for a long time.

Keely was still outside when I had a memory. It was a weird memory, as if I were seeing it through a rusty screen. I wasn't sure if it was really a memory at all.

In the memory, I was really little. I walked smack into the corner of the kitchen table and hit my head. There was blood, and it hurt and I cried. I must have been really, really young, because I hadn't yet learned you shouldn't cry, you shouldn't make noise. From far above me, Grandpa's foot came down on my hand and almost crushed my fingers flat. Suddenly Keely was there. She pushed him hard and he stumbled back, off my hand, into the refrigerator door.

And then Grandpa hit her, and hit her again, forgetting about me. My hand throbbed, my head bled, but I stopped crying. I never cried again.

Maybe Keely had tried to protect me after all, and I never noticed. Maybe I noticed but then forgot. Maybe I remembered but it wasn't a real memory. It made my head hurt just thinking about it.

When Keely finally came back in, she changed the subject.

"When I was young, I wanted to go to the Mildred Elley School and become a cosmetologist," she said. She poured some shake mix into a cup. "That's someone who knows how to cut hair for fashion models and do their nails and stuff."

"I know what a cosmetologist is," I said. "Why don't you do it now?"

Keely shook her shake for much longer than it really needed. "It's too late. I lost my chance," she said, and she took a swallow of vanilla shake.

"It's not too late," I said. "Molly says you're still young. You could re-carnate. That's what I did." I told her a little, just a little, of becoming Fishkill. I didn't tell her the whole story, the way I told Duck-Duck and Molly, but just a little so she would know I knew what I was talking about. "Like, do you really want the name Keely? Or Jamison? That was Grandpa's name, but that doesn't mean you have to keep it."

Keely looked at me as if I had appeared out of a green bottle, like a genie. "But that's my name."

"Wouldn't you rather have a name with a story to it?" I asked.

"What good is a story?" said Keely. "Keely's my name."

"If you want it to be," I said. "And if you wanted to, you could go to hairdressing school."

"Cosmetology school," she said.

"Whatever."

I thought about hairdressing. Keely never had her hair or nails done until after she fell in the river and ran away with the Reno Man.

"Did you start wearing lipstick because you wanted to go to cosmetology school?" I asked, but Keely was already leaving, sliding the big bolt over the door so I couldn't escape.

I thought of Molly. I was sure she had never had a father like Grandpa. She had a real job, a real car, a real life. If Keely had ever had one person who wanted her the way Molly wanted Duck-Duck, would we be here in this shack right now? It made me sad, thinking of Keely wanting things to be different and never succeeding. Even though I was still mad that she had kidnapped me, I had to give it to her that at least she was actually trying to make her life different.

When Keely came back, I said it fast so she couldn't run away before I said it.

"Thanks for wanting to kill him."

She glanced at me. For a second, she looked almost like, if she were Molly, she would have hugged me. "Sure," she said, "no problem," and then she went back outside again, even though she had just come in.

The next morning, when I looked out the frosty windows, there was only white, like a coloring-book dream with no color. It had snowed a heavy foot overnight. If I'd been at Duck-Duck's, Molly would've made us hot chocolate and we would've gone sledding. That is, we would've gone sledding if Duck-Duck were talking to me. Maybe the hot chocolate would have had little marshmallows on top.

Instead of taking me sledding, Keely shoveled a small path to the stream. I left the shack only once that morning, to pee. Inside, I lay under the blankets, staring at the ceiling while Keely shook up shakes. I wished again for a Harry Potter book. Keely never read Nancy Drew or Harry Potter or *Harriet the Spy*. She wouldn't have read *Charlotte's Web* or *Little Women* or *The Secret*

Garden. I wondered if I could convince Keely to visit the local library if I promised to read Harry to her. I could start with the first book, and we could read our way through the winter.

A sudden thought shook me.

"If you couldn't read, how did you read the Fishkill/Carmel sign?" I asked.

Keely shrugged. "When you were coming, I kept asking Pop, 'Where are we?' I thought if we were close enough to a hospital, he might take me."

"What did he say?"

"He said we were in 'Carmel or Fishkill, or some crap place like that.'" She shook the cup slowly while she stared into space. "Carmel is such a pretty girl's name, don't you think?"

"Yeah, sure," I said, but my mind was spinning. All my life I had imagined how I was born: my mother lying on the backseat, pushing and screaming. Then, just as I popped out, my mother raising her head high enough to look out the window, seeing the green sign, glowing with reflective white letters like a cosmic message, and then falling back on the seat, exhausted but satisfied. It never occurred to me that the story I told myself wasn't actually how it happened.

Maybe there were other things I made up too. Maybe I should find out.

"Who was my father?" I asked.

"Shakes are ready," said Keely. "Drink up."

"Who was my damn father?" I asked again, but Keely just drank from her cup and cut her fingernails.

That night it rained a cold winter rain, and all the snow disappeared, as if it had never been.

I began to dream about peanut-butter-and-jelly sandwiches. Every morning I would dream I was biting into a PB&J on whole wheat, but every morning I woke just before the peanut butter touched my tongue. Sometimes I dreamed of a glass of milk. In the dream, the glass always slid farther away when I reached for it, and I could never get even a swallow.

If I was stuck with Keely, maybe I could at least convince her we didn't have to live in the shack. Maybe we could live in one of those double-wide trailers with two bedrooms and a pretty backyard.

"If we had a real kitchen," I said to Keely, "I could make you spaghetti and meatballs."

For a second it looked like she wanted to hug me. If she were Molly, she would have.

"Simple, Simple, Simple," she said instead.

I decided I wasn't going to get discouraged. Maybe she just needed a little time to get used to the idea. I wanted to say, "We could have a real home like they do in *Little Women*," but Keely had never read *Little Women*, and we would never be close like that anyway.

I wondered why Keely had never learned to read. She had gone to school; I knew that. What exactly was wrong with her?

"Did you have bad reading teachers?" I asked.

"I guess not," she said. "It just never made any sense to me."

How could reading not make any sense? "Do you know the alphabet?" Maybe those S.O.S. signs were a mistake.

"Sure," she said. "What do you think I am, a baby?"

"Then why can't you read words?"

She shrugged. "I don't know. I just can't. Too many letters or something."

This made even less sense.

"Didn't they teach you?" I said. "And you can't write?"

"I can draw fine," she said.

I had never seen her draw, same as I had never seen her even try to write. If forced to, she would sign her name with a big scrawl that looked like a *K* with a *Y* if you held it sideways and squinted.

"Why don't you draw me something?"

"No pencils," she said and left the shack, carefully pulling the bolt across behind her. She didn't come back for hours.

It grew dark. Wet snow began to fall again.

The days started to run into one another. Sometimes it felt like we had always lived in the shack. I had more questions than I could count. Sometimes Keely would actually answer, but I had to catch her by surprise. What I really wanted to know was, why hadn't she tried a little harder?

"Why didn't you just follow the Social Service rules?" I asked. "You already had some visitation. You could have worked up to reunification."

Keely shook her head. "How can one person remember all those rules?" she said. "One lady would tell me I had to go to therapy or I'd lose visitation. The other would say if I didn't go to the parent meeting, I'd lose visitation. But the meetings were at the same time. I was screwed no matter what. And if I didn't follow all their rules just right, you would have ended up with that fag lady and her daughter for good. If you stayed there, you would have ended up perverted."

"Fag lady?" I said. At first I couldn't even figure out who she was talking about.

"Your little friend's mother, Molly Farina. Why isn't she married? Where'd she get that kid? She's just not normal—you can tell from her hair."

I sat down on the edge of the mattress in amazement. If Keely had told me she had learned to make French wedding cakes, I couldn't have been more stunned. Not married? Where's the kid from? Not normal? I almost laughed.

"Don't you know those are the same things everyone asks about you?" I said.

"There's nothing wrong with my hair," she said, "and I'm not a fag." Then she vanished out the door into the woods.

When she came back, I said, "You know, those are exactly the kinds of things Grandpa would say. Don't you know that if you talk like him, you're going to be like him?"

Keely acted as if she didn't hear me and started making yet another shake.

That night I had a dream that the moon had turned into a woman with spiky hair.

"Is there really cheese up there?" I asked her. "Or is it cake? Can I come up and see for myself?"

The moon lady just smiled, and then a cloud passed in front of her face and she disappeared. I kept watching for her, but all I saw were gray hailstorms moving in from the west.

We entered a dark season of shack winter, when each breath had a frozen, pained edge and it felt like winter would last forever. It was probably almost March, although I had lost count of the days. I was always cold. We had to leave the bottled water right next to the electric heater to keep it from freezing.

"We're going to move on soon," said Keely.

She didn't look like she was moving on anywhere. She sat on the floor, leaning against the cabin wall with a vanilla shake in her hand. It almost looked like a beer, the way she nursed it. I could see her breath.

"Oh?" I said. "Sounds fun. Where to?" It would be bad if we moved on. It would make it less likely that anyone who cared would find me. The farther we moved from home, the fewer people would know us. Even if I ran away to the police, in another state they wouldn't believe a kid's story over a grown-up's.

"We're going to California," she said. "Where the movie stars are."

"I thought you wanted to go to Arizona."

"They're pretty close. We'll visit Arizona on the ride out. They will have stopped looking for us by now."

I couldn't believe she thought her truck would make it all the way to California. Maybe she had another plan.

"Plane tickets are expensive," I said. I watched her smack the bottom of her shake cup, trying to dislodge some leftover drop.

"Don't be silly," Keely said, but she didn't add "We're driving" or even "We're taking the train."

"Are we going to walk?" The truck was almost dead. Wherever she had it stashed.

"Simple, Simple, Simple," she said, and then she went out for a smoke.

When I got free, I was going to take every dictionary I saw and tear out the page with the word *simple* on it. Meanwhile, I just hoped we wouldn't *simply* disappear before some lost hunter *simply* stumbled on the shack and *simply* wondered why there were so many *simple* cigarette butts on the *simple* ground.

When she came back, Keely repeated, "We're going to California."

"How about you go to California and I stay here?" I said.

"We're a team," said Keely. "A mother-daughter team."

The only time we had been a team was the time Grandpa had shot a garbage raccoon. Instead of throwing it into the woods, he left it in the driveway for days. When it was gushy and full of flies and worms and had birds pecking its eyes, he told Keely and me to clean it up.

"You think we have a maid or something?" he said, and then he stood there until we got shovels and moved it out of the driveway. The body was hard to pick up all at one time because the shovel was too small. We didn't want to pick it up with our hands, so we had to cut it up, dripping rot, and cart it away piece by piece. We had to work together to get rid of the raccoon before one of us puked on the driveway and got in worse trouble.

"Got a weak stomach?" he said to Keely, who wobbled as a piece of intestine fell off the shovel. "Should we cook it for dinner?"

"We're not a team," I said to Keely now. "We never were. We were a chain gang."

Since Grandpa was gone, there was nothing at all chaining us together anymore. Not even a rotting raccoon.

"C.C.F.S.," Keely said, and she drank another shake.

19

Early one cold morning Keely went out and didn't come back until almost noon.

"Where were you?" I asked.

Keely didn't answer. She mixed herself a shake and paced. It made me nervous. Maybe she had decided we'd leave for California that day. I sat down on the mattress and tried to pretend I wasn't anxious. Sitting there, low to the floor, I spotted a small scrap of paper that I was sure hadn't been there before. It was right near the door, like it had been slid underneath. I didn't run to look but got up and wandered around the room as if I were just stretching my legs. I worked my way to the front door and bumped Keely's coat, which fell off its hook. Leaning down to pick up the coat, I scooped the paper into my palm and went back to the mattress. I pulled the covers over me and read the note — "Free the M&Ms!" — written in red, blotchy letters that had to be blood.

Duck-Duck! How had she figured out where I was? Where was she? Yesterday, when Keely took me out for a walk around the shack, I hadn't seen anything vaguely ganglike. Just the idea that someone was looking for me made me yearn even more for the outside world without vanilla shakes.

I waited until Keely went out again. I heard her pull the heavy wooden bolt across the door, and I waited until I thought she would be out of sight. Then I started looking out every window, trying to see if I could spot signs of anyone outside. I stood on a chair and breathed on the windows to finger-write backward S.O.S. signs. If helicopters were searching, though, my S.O.S. signs wouldn't do any good. I would need a sign on the roof.

But no helicopters buzzed overhead. No police cruisers came speeding up to the shack either. A few minutes later, I did hear a *tap-tap-tap* on the back wall, and I saw a red mitten flying up past the back window. I raced over, stood on a chair, and jerked the window up the six inches it would go.

"Hello?" I cried. "Who's there?"

"Shhh," whispered Duck-Duck. "She might have the cabin tapped."

Peering out the window, I could see the top of Duck-Duck's head and the tip of her nose. It was a beautiful nose.

"Oh, my God, I'm so glad to see you," I said. "Did you get help? Is someone going to get me out of here?"

"Shhh, she could be recording us. I'll open the front door," whispered Duck-Duck, "but we have to make a plan."

The idea of Keely rigging the shack with a recorder was laughable. I heard Duck-Duck struggling with the front bolt and then the door opened. The cold had made her cheeks as red as her mittens, and her blue-and-white coat stood out against the gray wooden walls. It was as if the weeks of shack life had been a black-and-white movie, and then suddenly, a full-color Duck-Duck appeared.

"A plan? Run like hell. Keely can't be far away. Let's get out of here."

"No, no. We have to think ahead." She paused for a second. "I've got it—Keely's got to think you're dead."

"Huh?" I said. "Why do I have to be dead? Won't Keely just go to the police?" I looked out the open door. Sometimes Keely left for a couple hours. Sometimes it was only fifteen minutes.

"Think about it. Keely won't go to the police. She kidnapped a minor, even though it was her own daughter. And she's not going to tell the cops her daughter is dead. She'd be the primary suspect in a snap." Duck-Duck snapped her fingers to show how quick. "She'll leave town to escape arrest, and we'll be free and clear."

"That plan sounds overly complicated," I said. "How about we just run? Now?"

"Complicated is good," said Duck-Duck. "If she thinks you're still alive, she'll follow us, and she could try to kidnap you again. So how would you like to die? Stabbing?"

Duck-Duck's golden hair made me think of Yodels. Her red mittens reminded me of Molly's baked chicken. Her blue, blue eyes spoke of lemon cupcakes.

"How'd you find me?" I asked as Duck-Duck started unzipping her backpack.

"It was easy. The police were supposedly doing their Amber Alert thing, and Mom was making phone calls to everyone under the sun. I think she even called our senator. But after two weeks, it was obvious no one was logical enough to find you. The cops thought she was far away. I tried to tell them that they should try thinking like Olivia Benson from *Law and Order SVU;* there's no way that truck would make it to Arizona, but no one listened to me. So I Googled the closest Auga-L supply location and staked it out. It was just some lady's house. You can mail-order the shakes, but that would take having a mailbox or an address, and Keely wouldn't want to be found. Besides, she wouldn't be able to read the order form. I figured if I checked out the lady's house enough, Keely would have to stock up at some point. I got lucky. When she showed up this morning, I hopped in the back of the pickup while she was inside the house. I covered up me and my bike with her tarp, and she drove almost straight here. She left footprints from the truck to the shack. I skipped school to track you down," she added.

"But how will we get back? How far are we from Salt Run?" I could see Keely being so out of it that she didn't notice a girl and a bike in the back of her truck, but I never would have been brave enough to test it. Only Duck-Duck would have done that.

"We're downriver from Birge Hill," said Duck-Duck, rummaging in her backpack. "About five miles into the woods. We can go home on my bike."

The death scene, Duck-Duck said, had to be highly visual, since Keely couldn't read a suicide note. "It's too bad. You could have written a real good one saying you were dying of loneliness and life wasn't worth living anymore. Lots of blood is key to a good murder scene," she explained. "If I had had more prior notice, I could have made totally realistic fake blood. But this will have to do," she said, and she fished a can of tomato juice from her backpack. "If they test for DNA, it wouldn't pass, but Keely won't tell the cops, so she'll never know. We want Keely to feel real guilty and, tortured by her role in your death, cross state lines as fast as she can."

First we broke a window from the inside. We poured fake blood on the ragged glass edges and tore one of my T-shirts into shreds and draped it along the sill as if I had cut myself, dragging my body across the shattered glass.

"You sever an artery on the window glass," explained Duck-Duck. "Blood gushing from your neck, you stagger to the river to end your life."

I made deep, staggering footprints to the river, as if I were having trouble walking. Duck-Duck walked behind me in my footprints so there would be only one set of prints leaving the shack. She dripped the last drops of tomato juice along the frosty footprint path and the edge of the river. "Here, put your handprint down near the edge of the water and drag it in like you changed your mind at the last minute but it was too late."

She picked hairs off my sweater and rounded off the number with a few pulled from my head. "We'll stick a few here and there so it's more realistic." Duck-Duck stepped back to cast an artistic eye on the death scene.

To avoid footprints leaving the river, we waded upstream, breaking through thin ice, to find where Duck-Duck had stashed her bicycle. The water was bitterly cold, but somehow didn't feel as bad as spending a whole winter in a lonely shack.

"Nice work," she said as we sloshed along, clinging to bushes to keep from slipping on icy rocks. "Keely will feel totally guilty and never tell a soul. She could be up for involuntary manslaughter if she told anyone. Oh, and I found your backpack in the pickup. I stole it back for you. It's with my bike."

Suddenly I felt awkward. We hadn't seen each other for weeks. I knew where I had been. What had Duck-Duck been doing all this time?

"How's soccer?" I asked, shivering. I wondered if sports discipline included breaks for missing-person searches and what Darsa thought of that.

"Oh," said Duck-Duck without looking at me. She kept trudging through the ice and water. "I quit."

"Why? Weren't you going to be a division something?"

"I wasn't any good anyway." Suddenly Duck-Duck sounded like someone I didn't know. Like she was unsure or scared or just plain ashamed. It reminded me of something, but I couldn't quite put my finger on what.

"Darsa made you quit, didn't she?" I said.

"No," said Duck-Duck, "I just quit."

Now I knew what her shame reminded me of. Keely.

"Was she mean to you?" I had just been a prisoner for weeks. I felt like I hadn't really talked in months. I definitely didn't have the patience to talk around stuff.

"Yeah, kinda," said Duck-Duck. "But I wasn't really dedicated enough."

"That's bullshit," I said. I knew I was being snotty, probably from weeks of eating nothing but serene shakes. "Whatever she did to you, it's because she's a bitch. I'm an expert on mean people, and I can tell you for sure, it had nothing to do with practicing or soccer, or anything you did or didn't do, or anything else logical."

Duck-Duck trudged along. "At first it was little stuff. She told the soccer club coach I lied about how many practice runs I made. He believed her. Then she and Sheila took my training time slot at the gym and left chewed-up gum in my lock."

"I'm sorry," I said. I wasn't exactly sorry, because if you took up with someone like Darsa, what could you expect? But I couldn't say that, even as grumpy as I was after being a shake prisoner for weeks.

"It's okay," said Duck-Duck. "It doesn't matter."

"Did you tell your mother?"

Duck-Duck climbed up the bank, out of the river, and I followed her. We were both shivering now. My toes felt like they belonged to someone else.

"No," she said really quietly.

I knew why. "You thought it would have made everything worse," I said. "But then it got worse anyway, right?"

Duck-Duck clutched her arms around herself. She was almost whispering. I had to catch up to her to hear.

"You were right, you know. About Darsa," she said. "Darsa texted the whole team that my mother was a fag and I was one too. I didn't find out until a week later. Everyone was laughing behind my back and acting like they shouldn't get too close to me in the locker room because they'd get contaminated. They burned my socks in the sink because they said I was contagious. I couldn't tell my mother that."

She was crying, or I thought she was crying. We were totally soaked, so maybe it was just loose river on her face.

I thought about Molly with her spiky hair and her big shoulders. She probably wouldn't be bothered by little girls calling her a fag, but still I knew why Duck-Duck didn't tell. Molly would have been upset that who she was had caused Duck-Duck pain.

"You're right. I wouldn't have told her either," I said. "But next time, punch Darsa in those big boobs and don't quit soccer unless you want to."

Duck-Duck sniffed, but she gave a little giggle too.

"Can we get out of here now?" I asked.

"My bike is just on the other side of that rock," she said, pointing ahead. Then she said, "I'm sorry I was mean. You know, at school that last day. I was going to apologize when we got home, but you were gone. I was afraid I'd never see you again."

"It's okay," I said. "We're good. After all, you rescued me, right?"

My feet were wet, shaky icicles, but I held on tight while Duck-Duck pumped us back home.

"Mom!" she called when we got to Cherry Road. "Look who I found!"

When we opened the front door, Molly looked like she was going to cry. Then she hugged me until my face felt flat, and then she started making phone calls to everyone under the sun. I went upstairs to the lion tub and lay in the hot water until my fingers shriveled into warm raisins.

Molly still looked on the verge of tears, but she pulled it together and made us Black Moon Chili for dinner. It was called Black Moon because it had black beans and black olives, but all I cared about was that it wasn't a vanilla shake. Molly and Duck-Duck and I had dinner, the first nonshake food I'd eaten in weeks. How many weeks? I had to ask because I'd lost count. It was only three and a half weeks, but it felt like months, or maybe even a small year.

And then I went to bed in the pink pop-up bed with pillows and blankets and clean sheets underneath. I thought I would fall asleep quick, I was so tired from the icy river and the bike ride, but I didn't. I lay there and thought about Duck-Duck. She had said sorry. *Sorry I was mean.*

Teachers would tell us, "Say you're sorry," and then they'd want the other kid to act like he wasn't still pissed off that Pepsi had been poured into his chicken-noodle soup. This was called *accepting an apology.* Sometimes the apologizer would say, "I'm sorry . . . but you were asking for it," or "I'm sorry you're a cry-baby." Then the teacher would get mad, and they'd all be back where they started.

Real apologies left you open to attack, because then you couldn't do it again without everyone knowing you knew it was wrong and you were still doing it anyway.

Real apologies were like what Duck-Duck meant: she knew she messed up and she wasn't going to do it again.

And then I started getting confused, thinking about real apologies, and how once you pour Pepsi into soup, it can't be un-poured, but really I was already asleep.

20

The next day, I gave my statement to Officer Sam and Officer Greg. The Social Service ladies descended on us too, but after we convinced them that Keely hadn't maimed or starved me to death, they retreated. Molly came with me special to the school, to make sure there weren't any problems.

"Including the times she was out sick, she's missed more than a month of classes," said the counselor, as if it had been my fault, "and she was struggling as it was. We'll probably have to hold her back a year."

I could see Molly's back get stiff.

"It's only March, and you're deciding already she's a grade behind without any proof?" she asked. "I'd like to have some testing done before you decide she's behind."

Keely would never have said that. Keely wouldn't have shown up for the meeting in the first place.

"I don't think we have any testing accommodations available just now," said the counselor, but then she looked at Molly, who was giving her the same blue-lightning stare she gave Duck-Duck, and the lady changed her mind. "But I'm sure we can work something out."

"I'm sure you can," said Molly.

At the time, I was happy, but then the next week, I had to take tests for hours. I did reading and math, and science too. I kept looking out the classroom window, where it was sunny and bright, and I kept thinking this was almost as bad as being stuck in a dark shack all day.

They didn't tell me the next day, or even the next week, how I did. The counselor said I had to come back with Molly, and they would talk to both of us.

"That's not good news," I said to Molly. "I mean, if the tests were fine, they would just say everything's fine and not need to talk. They must want to hold me back."

"Don't borrow trouble," said Molly. "We'll just go in and talk to them. If need be, we'll make them pay for a tutor. It wasn't your fault you missed school."

And then I realized there was a little part of me that thought it *was* my fault, that if I had good enough genes, I never would have been caught by Keely in the first place. If I had been good enough in math, I would have figured out a way to escape. But when Molly said that, out loud, I realized she was right. It wasn't my fault. Why punish me for Keely's crime?

When we went to school to find out how I did on the tests, I got nervous and had to hold Molly's hand. But the funny thing was, the counselor, Miss Treadway, and the testing teacher were all sitting there looking nervous too. One of the Social Service ladies was there, I guess to make sure I was doing school like I was supposed to. I must have been gripping Molly too hard, because she stretched her fingers a little, like they were losing blood.

"Sorry," I mumbled.

"Do you have the results?" said Molly. "I'd like to take a look."

Miss Treadway didn't look too happy. She looked twitchy, like Molly was making her itch. "Well, we have the results," she said, handing the paper to Molly. "Here, you can see the breakdown."

I looked over her shoulder and saw a bunch of graphs and numbers and percentiles. I nodded like I understood.

"She's in the ninety-ninth percentile for math and reading," said Molly. "And eighty-fifth percentile in science." She squeezed my hand quick, like she knew it all along. Maybe she did; I sure didn't. "You still think she should be held back?"

"We think perhaps we underestimated her abilities," said the testing teacher. She wasn't looking up at Molly. She was looking at the paper, as if what she had to say were there, written in code. "Fishkill really should be in the upper-level English class and at least grade-level math." She was mumbling now.

"I thought so," said Molly. "Could you write up that evaluation for me and make sure it goes in her file? And can we switch her classes now instead of waiting until next year?"

They argued a little about that, but since I had been gone

for three and a half weeks and going back to the old classes was almost like going back to a new class, I got bumped up to Duck-Duck's math class. For English, I would get special extra assignments. Next year I would be in top classes for both.

After the meeting, I went to gym, and Molly went back to work. When I got home, Molly gave me a little card with a picture of a tiger with green eyes and a swimming pool. Inside she had written, "To my green-eyed girl. Keep up the great work. Love, Molly."

I didn't know how to say thank you. Duck-Duck would have hugged and kissed her, but I didn't know how to do that really. I put the swimming tiger card in my backpack and carried it with me every day, next to my emergency Yodel.

Something else that was different when I came back was that Duck-Duck had breasts. Not big boobs like Darsa, but little ones, like shells. They were pink. I kind of saw them through her shirt, but then at night, we took off our clothes to go to bed. I saw her looking at my chest. I didn't have any boobs, not even little ones. Maybe I wasn't going to get any. That would be okay with me.

"Mom promised she'd buy me a real bra," said Duck-Duck, "but we haven't gone to the mall yet."

I giggled. "Your mom hates the mall."

"Yup." Duck-Duck put her hands on the sides of her little breasts. "Maybe if I get a bra, it will look like this." She squeezed her tits together, making them stand out, almost like Darsa's.

"No, more like this," I said, putting my hands beneath her

boobs, pushing them up so they were standing out and up, both at the same time. Now they really looked like Darsa's.

Duck-Duck suddenly turned pink, the same pink as her nipples, which got a little pointy. I didn't take my push-up hands away, but I touched the nipples with my thumbs to see if they were soft or hard.

"Do they hurt?" I asked.

"No," she said. "Can we kiss like in the movies again?" She looked a little sad, like she had lost something but didn't know what.

I liked that she wanted to kiss again. So before bed, we French-kissed, Duck-Duck with her little boobs, and me with none.

I was back at Cherry Road and I was back in school, but somehow everything felt off, as if while I was away, somehow the school building had shrunk and the library had gotten smaller. The pictures on the wall near the gym entrance, of jumping jacks and toe touches, now looked yellowed and old, like they had been put up a century ago. I could have sworn the milk cartons in the cafeteria had less milk. When I told Molly these things, she said sometimes we grow up in spurts. She said that because we are different, everything around us looks different.

I wasn't so sure how this applied to Duck-Duck, though. Duck-Duck wasn't the same either, and she hadn't gotten locked in a shack. At school she had become timid, like she was afraid someone would jump her or call her a bad name. At home she acted pretty normal, but then we would go to school, and she would get un-Duck-Ducked again. I watched carefully to see if she was puking in the bathroom or banging her head against lockers.

"When they're not pretending I'm invisible, they still call me names," she said one afternoon. "Stupid things like slut and dyke-wad. I try to pretend I only speak sign language and can't understand what they're saying, but it doesn't really work." She looked a little like she did in the river.

"Names aren't so bad," I tried to tell her. "At least they're not hitting you or filling your notebook with glue or stealing your lunch. If they're just calling you a freak or a fag and not stealing your underwear during gym, then just stay away from stairways and walk quick in the halls. Just keep your eyes open."

"At lunch, if I put down my sandwich for a second, they drop gross used napkins on it. My mother would say I should just ignore Darsa and go about my business. She would say, what goes around comes around, but meanwhile I'm only eating granola bars for lunch." Duck-Duck started slicing her cinnamon toast into quarters instead of just in half. I watched the buttered quarters become buttered eighths become buttered slivers and then buttered crumbs. Maybe she needed more than just advice. Maybe action was required.

"If you just let it go around, Darsa gets away with it," I said. "That's not right. Sometimes a little revenge makes you feel better."

Duck-Duck seemed to be considering this. "Revenge isn't exactly wrong," she said. Her buttered crumbs were looking more and more like birdseed. "It's not very Zen, though."

"We could push her down the stairs," I said. It seemed the obvious thing to do, Zen or not.

"No, there would be witnesses and forensic evidence," said Duck-Duck, "and we could get suspended. Anyways, physical violence against girl evil doesn't work." She stirred her birdseed. "No, it has to be like that old movie with the train and the piano music. Subtle revenge."

"Huh?"

"I forget the name of the movie. We borrowed it from the library. The good guys have to get back at the bad guy because he killed their friend, but they have to do it so that he never knows and can't get back at them later. They con him out of hundreds of thousands of dollars but he never knows it was them."

I doubted I could do subtle revenge, but if that would make Duck-Duck feel better, I was willing to try.

"So, what's as bad as being pushed down the stairs but won't be tracked back to us?" I asked. "Could we get her so confused she falls down the stairs without even being pushed?"

"That's a thought," said Duck-Duck. She sounded impressed, as if I had come up with a scientific truth or proof. She stopped murdering her toast. "I've heard of apps you can put on someone's phone that make it ring when there are no calls and not ring when there are. Darsa is so hooked on texting, it would screw her up for days. I bet there's an app that makes any outgoing texts go to the wrong number. It would cause havoc, pure social havoc." Duck-Duck's eyes lit up like the night-lights Molly had plugged in so I wouldn't get lost on the way to the bathroom.

"But wouldn't we have to steal her phone and know her password to be able to download the apps?" I asked.

"Uh," said Duck-Duck. "Right." And her lights went out again.

I felt bad, as if I should have protected Duck-Duck from all this and didn't. I should have warned her earlier about the wolves.

"What's really, really important to Darsa?" I asked.

"Soccer," said Duck-Duck.

"Besides soccer."

She looked at me blankly, and then she smiled. "Her reputation."

"Her good name?"

Duck-Duck laughed. "No, her bad name. Teachers think she's nice and sweet and athletic. Girls think she's popular, all-powerful, and mean. In order to be all-powerful, everyone has to think you don't care about anyone else."

"I don't get it," I said.

Duck-Duck ran and got her computer. She opened it and clicked a quick click. "I," she said, "single-handedly, am going to give Darsa a new reputation." She opened a document and started typing. "When I'm done, Darsa will be the goody-goody of the year. She'll *hate* it."

"What, are you going to sign her up for the glee club, the chess club, sewing circle, and gamers international all in one day? She'll just say it wasn't her that signed up and make fun of anyone who thought she did."

Duck-Duck typed faster.

"Are you going to sign her up for that bake-sale charity group that gives money to underprivileged children in Africa?"

"Nope," she said modestly, "it's more genius than that. She has to think she wants it, but then when she realizes she doesn't, it will be too late."

Twenty minutes later, Duck-Duck stopped clicking and let me look. The top of the page read, "SCHOOL ESSAY CONTEST: *My Greatest Accomplishment*. By Darsa Peterman." The title was in fancy writing that wound the *G* around the *r* in *Greatest*.

"You wrote an essay for her?"

"Not just any essay. A winning essay-contest essay."

"If *you* won, then everyone would know you were the smart one," I said.

"No," said Duck-Duck, "Darsa is going to win this contest. Even with the few typos and dumb things I put in to make sure they don't track it to me."

I started reading.

School Essay Contest: My Greatest Accomplishment
by Darsa Peterman

Some people say that an accomplishment means something concrete that you do, like build a school or get a college degree. I think that an accomplishment can be something more simple,

like a emotion or a feeling. I think an accomplishment is also doing some thing with that feeling.

When I was nine my father left my family.
We didn't know he was leaving for good at the
time but now we know he isn't coming back.
At first I was sad. Then I was mad. Now I am
resigned ??? that we have to be a family without
him.

After a year I realized that although my
father leaving us was a bad thing it was also a
good thing. Because I had to be sad and then
mad, I started to empathize with people who
have hard things happen in their lives. Empathize
means to feel bad for someone. I feel that now I
empathize with people who have problems like
the poor and the handicapped. I think because I
had troubles in my life, I care more about other
people who have troubles too.

I have a clear vision in my brain of what
the world should be like. I think we all should
work to advertisse for charity work. We should
all support kids who aren't good in sports and
maybe have trouble with subject like math and
english. Sometimes a person is kind and innocent
but then they have trouble learning and are hor-
ribly misfortunate.

We should all empathize with each other and

there would be no more bullying. I myself am certainly willing to make this true. I am going to volunteer two hours every day to help kids not be picked on. We should make our school a place other people are jealous of and make an extraordinary change in this world forever. This would certainly be a great accomplishment.

It was quite an essay. It even sounded like Darsa, if Darsa were someone who said nice things and cared about people. "What are the question marks after *resigned*?" I asked.

"It means I'm still thinking about it. *Resigned* might not be in Darsa's vocabulary, and if this is going to work, people need to believe it came from her," Duck-Duck said. "I haven't finished the editing phase. Maybe I'll spell it wrong."

"Did her father really leave?" I said.

"Well, her parents got divorced. It has to have enough truth in it to make people believe she wrote it. I couldn't write that she grew up in an orphanage from the age of two, because it's too far from the truth, but desertion sounds close enough." Duck-Duck hit spell-check and counted how many mistakes she had put in.

It turned out that writing the essay was the easy part. The next phase was more difficult.

"We have to steal Darsa's real essay and replace it with mine," said Duck-Duck, "before the April fourteenth deadline. We have to figure out how to find it with all the office ladies sitting there."

"I could start a fight in the hall as a distraction, and you could go for the box," I said.

"Start a fight? How are you going to start a fight in that time frame? Don't you need some buildup?"

Duck-Duck obviously didn't have a lot of fight experience.

"Don't worry," I said. "I'm an expert. Worm is good for a fight anytime. Just leave it to me."

On the last day the essays were due, we prepared for our super-undercover op. *Op*, Duck-Duck told me, meant *operation*, which wasn't surgery but something the Army said when they had secret missions.

"It's like gang activity," she said. "But with more helicopters."

First, we walked past the office as if we had no intention of going in but were on our way to the gym. When I got just past the office, Duck-Duck dropped back. I took the milk from my lunch bag, opened it, and waited.

I could see Worm coming from all the way down the hall. Just as he trudged past me, I spilled the milk all over his huge feet.

"Whoops," I said real loud, so Worm would know I'd meant to do it and was only pretending like I hadn't. "Sorry." Milk splashed on his new red sneakers and wet the bottom of his pants. Any second it would be leaking down into his socks.

Just like I knew he would, Worm went for me, and I bent low so he wouldn't knock me over when he hit me. But the fist never came. I looked up, and he had stopped just in front of me, his eyes squeezed shut and his fists clenched. He was holding his breath.

"What's the matter with you?" I said. "You look like a blow-fish."

"I'm trying not to hit you, freak," he said, and jammed his fists into his pockets.

"Huh?"

"Mrs. Clavel said I can't hit anyone else or I'll be expelled. I'm trying not to hit you." He sucked in a big breath and held it.

Mrs. Clavel was the psychologist who worked in all the schools. I had been to see her once, years ago, and she told me she was sure Grandpa had my best interests at heart.

"Fine, Worm," I said, "don't hit me. But can you at least yell a little?" Worm looked confused. "If Mrs. Clavel asks, you can tell her you were using your words."

"Yell?" he said. "Sure," and he started hollering. I hollered back and lunged at him as if I were going to sock him in the chest, and he fell back and hollered again. The office ladies ran out of the office and pulled us apart, and in the shuffle I saw Duck-Duck slip in toward the box of essays.

I kept it up until I could see that she was out of the office and down the hall, and then I said, "It's okay. He didn't hit me or anything, so I guess it's all right. Forgive and forget."

"Yeah, me too, shithead," said Worm.

After telling us twice about noise rules and cursing rules and disruption rules, the office staff gave up and went back inside.

"Thanks," I said to Worm. "I owe you."

"Whatever," he said, but he was still looking at me. "What did you call me before?"

Then I realized I had slipped up and called him Worm to his face.

"Norm," I said. "I called you Norm."

"No, you didn't. You called me Worm."

"Sorry," I said. "I'll call you Norm from now on." I couldn't think of how to get out of this one. He would probably break his promise to Mrs. Clavel and break my nose.

"Worm," said Worm. "What a gross name. Cool."

Boys were really weird.

"Glad I could help," I told him, and ran down the hall after Duck-Duck.

"Did you find it?" I said when I caught up to her.

"Sure did. It was right on the top. Now we have to run to the library and print out her new essay in the same font. We don't want her saying it can't be hers because her computer doesn't have Apple Casual."

So we ran to the library, and I started talking to the librarian about how to look up the word *photosynthesis*.

Duck-Duck printed it out and grabbed her paper, and we slunk back down the hall.

"I'll just drop it in the contest box," she said, "like it's mine."

We went to next period, feeling like we had made "a great accomplishment."

Now that we were planning subtle revenge, it was easier for Duck-Duck to be Zen.

Because I had poured my milk on Worm's feet, I didn't have any milk left for lunch, but Duck-Duck was letting me share hers.

"I look at Darsa now," said Duck-Duck, "and I think of our winning essay."

It was almost as if Darsa knew we were talking about her, because just then she passed our table. She stopped and stared at Duck-Duck's avocado-tomato sandwich on sesame-rye bread.

"*That* totally looks like dog shit," she said. She smirked at her new second-wolf-in-command.

Tina was almost fat, but she wore really tight new clothes, and her father had a lot of money. On cue, she giggled hysterically, as if Darsa were going to win the annual comedy award. "Ohgod," she agreed. "Isn't it terrible? Like something out of a horror movie. Look, it has lice," she said, gesturing toward a sesame seed.

"But Miss Fish-gills has something even worse," Darsa said, smiling. "What on earth are you eating?"

I had finished my sandwich and was on to the granola pudding that Molly and Duck-Duck had invented the night before. I liked it, but Duck-Duck said she didn't think they would serve it at the royal wedding.

I kept chewing. Then I thought of the essay and smiled. The smiling was a mistake.

"Hey, food-stamp kid, who you laughing at? Your mother left you because you're such a loser, and you're laughing at *me*?"

Duck-Duck had said Zen meant you were really, really mellow and things didn't bother you or give you a stomachache. I was trying for that, especially since we already had a subtle revenge plan, but somehow the granola pudding ended up on Darsa's chin and down the front of her dress. The milk that came next probably even got her bra wet.

You'd think I'd thrown gasoline on her.

"AAAAHHHH!" Darsa screamed. "I'm allergic to dairy! I'm going into anaphylactic shock. You bitch! I'm going to kill you!" She dug her hand into her purse and whipped out an EpiPen. "You piece of trash!" She lunged at me with the EpiPen.

At any other time, the lunch ladies would have heard her, and I would have been in big trouble, but just at that moment, the bell rang and an eighth-grade boy hit a girl who had the lungs of an elephant. Even Darsa's shock waves couldn't reach the adults. I grabbed Duck-Duck and we ran, blending in with the moving crowd.

We hid in the bathroom for five minutes before we went to our next class.

"Remind me to tell my mother I need an EpiPen," whispered Duck-Duck. "Doesn't it look like it would come in handy?"

"We don't need it," I said. "We have our essay to look forward to."

"Right," said Duck-Duck, and she took a deep breath. "Zen."

"Calm Mind," I said, and I took a peek out the door to see if the coast was clear.

On April fifteenth the contest winner was announced during all-school assembly. I was as excited as if I had an essay in that box.

First we had to sing the National Anthem and the school

song. Then the principal talked about the new floors in the boys' locker room. Then the school nurse talked about germs and hand-washing.

"Hello," I said to Duck-Duck, "I think we know how to wash our hands by now."

Finally, it was contest time.

"What do we do if she doesn't win?" I whispered to Duck-Duck.

"Don't worry," she said. "She will." The principal walked onstage.

"We are pleased to announce the winner of this year's essay contest," said the principal. "The topic was *My Greatest Accomplishment*. We had so many wonderful writers, it was hard to pick."

"I bet," whispered Duck-Duck.

"The winner is a wonderful young woman . . ." he continued.

"Young woman," echoed Duck-Duck. "Halfway there!"

". . . who has used personal hardship to make herself a better person. She did not become bitter or vindictive but became an asset to our community. I am pleased to announce that the winner is . . ."

"Announce, already," Duck-Duck whispered.

"Miss Darsa Peterman!"

We clutched each other's hands and laughed. It was like winning money from a scratch ticket. We looked around for Darsa.

She was sitting right up front, smack in the middle. Head wolf sitting at the front of her pack.

"Come on up, Miss Peterman," said the principal.

Darsa stood and walked slowly up to the front, smiling, letting everyone see her boobs.

"Darsa," said the principal, "your essay was a wonderfully inspirational piece of writing."

Darsa smoothed her hair and smiled her cheerleader smile.

"Of course," she said. "Anything to inspire others."

"Gag me with a spoon," murmured Duck-Duck. "That's such garbage. Her real essay was a mediocre piece on soccer and nutrition. She thinks protein bars are the gateway to heaven. How is that inspirational?"

"We are going to post your essay on the school website," continued the principal, "so everyone can learn from your wonderful attitude."

"Thanks so much," purred Darsa.

That afternoon, the essay was posted on the school website, along with a picture of Darsa.

Parents immediately began posting comments. I wondered why they weren't at work and why they cared so much about a kids' contest.

"Great work!" said one mother.

"Everyone should follow your shining example!" said another.

"They use too many exclamation points," said Duck-Duck.

Kids weren't posting comments about the essay, just parents.

"Maybe the kids are all too stunned to post," was Duck-Duck's guess.

But then the whispering started. I noticed after fifth period. Every time Darsa walked down the hall, kids stared at her.

"What's your problem, slut?" said Darsa to one girl. The girl giggled.

Giggled. At Darsa. Darsa's face grew dark and she sprinted toward the library to go online, since the principal had outlawed using smartphones during school.

"I have to go to English. I'll get in trouble if I'm late," I said to Duck-Duck. "They won't care about you, though. Run after Darsa and see what happens."

"Not run," said Duck-Duck. "Trail."

"She went ballistic," whispered Duck-Duck when we met after my English class. "She ran to the principal's office, and I watched her through the office window. I think she was going to tell him that she didn't write the essay, but before she could, he said he wanted her to know he had called her mother and told her what an extraordinary daughter she had. He said he was going to make Darsa head of the anti-bullying task force."

"What did she do?"

"It was hysterical. She couldn't figure out what to say. She looked like she'd been beaten bloody but there was no blood."

"Cool," I said. Subtle revenge was kind of fun. "You feel any better?"

Duck-Duck didn't say anything, but she smiled a big smile and flicked her blond hair. "Let's go to the cemetery this afternoon," she said. "We haven't had a gang meeting in a long time."

21

Under the cemetery quince tree, we came up with our next gang goal. We didn't know it was a goal at first. We thought we were just drinking juice and talking about Keely.

"You think your mom will try to steal you again if she finds out you aren't dead?"

I had almost forgotten about the bloody death scene. Where had Keely gone after I escaped the shack? Did she really think I was dead? Would she come looking for me? Maybe almost losing me like that, thinking I had bled to death in the cold, would change her, make her try to be a real mother like Molly?

"Naw," I said. "Even if she tried it again, everyone would know it was her right away. It couldn't work a second time."

"That's true," said Duck-Duck. "They probably have a permanent BOLO out on her already."

"What's a 'bolo'?" I reached inside Duck-Duck's backpack and pulled out a granola bar. I tore off the top of the wrapper and started making a careful slit down the side. I hated it when the bottom was all crumbs. You couldn't split it evenly.

"'Be On the Lookout.' It means the cops tell all the other cops that someone is bad news, and they tell everyone the license plate number, and every cop all over the country will memorize it and be on the lookout."

I broke the granola bar and gave a perfect half to Duck-Duck.

"Maybe," said Duck-Duck, biting off a piece, "she's gone for good."

Despite the fact that she had kidnapped me, despite the fact that she had made me drink shakes three times a day for weeks, this made me a little sad.

"Do you have any other family?" Duck-Duck asked.

"Nope," I said.

"Other grandparents?"

"I guess they're dead now, but who knows?"

"Didn't you ever ask?"

In fourth grade, we had a unit on family trees. We were supposed to draw a tree and write out the list of names of everyone in our family, all the way back to olden times. I had no clue what to put on mine. I hardly ever asked Grandpa direct questions. It was better to try and blend into the wall, but suddenly I had really wanted to know. I decided it was worth the risk of being hit with the stick.

"What was Grandma like?" I had asked Grandpa.

"She was a bitch," he had said. "What did you expect? The queen of England?"

"I tried to ask about my grandmother once," I said to Duck-Duck, "but Grandpa wouldn't tell me. I told him I was sad I had never met her, and he said, 'My heart pumps piss for you.'"

"He said that?" said Duck-Duck.

"Yup. He wouldn't even tell me her name."

"People deal with death in different ways. Maybe he was just grieving. My mother said that when Ellen's sister died and Ellen poured all the salad dressing down the garbage disposal."

"No," I said, "it wasn't like that. He was just an asshole."

It made me wonder how a person became an asshole. Was it genes, or food, or mold in the walls? Grandpa must have begun very young to get so good at it. *There's something good in everyone,* one of the first Social Service ladies said. *You just have to find it.* Maybe when Grandpa was five years old, he would pet kittens and not drown them. Maybe he wasn't an asshole then. I doubted it, though.

"I can't imagine who would want to be with Grandpa," I said. "Let alone marry him."

"Maybe Keely came from a surrogate," said Duck-Duck, "or she was an incubator baby. Maybe your grandfather put sperm in a box and he bought eggs from a donor and they incubated Keely."

I tried to imagine Grandpa going to the hospital with a lunch box full of sperm because he wanted a baby.

"No way," I said. "He hated kids. He would never make one on purpose. Also, it probably costs a lot of money to incubate, and he was really cheap."

"It's true," she said. "You can goof up and make a baby the regular way, but surrogates and incubators take premeditated intent plus cash."

I wondered how much money it cost Molly to buy sperm from the bank to make Duck-Duck, but it seemed rude to ask.

"We could do research and find out if your grandmother existed," said Duck-Duck. "We could at least find out her name. It could be our next goal. She's a missing person, and no one is looking for her except us." She ate the last of her granola bar and licked her fingers. "I bet we could find her on the Internet." She pulled paper and pencil out of her backpack and started drawing family trees. She added leaves and roots as if they were real trees.

"My family isn't on the Internet," I said. "You'd have to be married on paper and born in a hospital. I bet no one was."

"We're all on the Internet now," said Duck-Duck, adding some vines that looked like poison ivy. "But we should think of a more interesting way. Gangs like things complicated and risky. Nothing risky about the Internet. Unless you're looking at dirty pictures, of course."

I wondered what her idea of risk was. Keely's idea of risk was buying a scratch ticket. I waited.

"We can steal your file from the social worker's office," said Duck-Duck.

"Oh, God," I said. "Why don't we just print a label that says BEHAVIOR PROBLEM and glue it on my forehead?"

"No, really. We won't get caught. I have a super plan."

Duck-Duck told me her super plan. It didn't seem so super to me.

"No way," I said. "I can't act like that. Candy will think I'm on drugs and send me to the ER."

"Sure you can," said Duck-Duck. "Distract the target. Just give her a lot of eye contact and say sappy things. Get her to *em-path-ize.*" She drew out the last word and made her blue eyes get really big so I would know just how sappy. "Let's give it a try. What's the worst that can happen?"

I didn't want to think about that.

Even though I still thought buying a scratch ticket was a better idea and had a better chance of winning, the next day we went down to the Social Service lady's office. Duck-Duck hid around the corner while I went in.

"Hi," I said. Candy was sitting at her desk, writing. I wondered why they had computers if they were going to waste all that paper anyway.

"Hello, Fishkill. So nice to see you. What's up?"

"Well," I said, gathering my lie-making abilities, "I just wanted to talk."

This was a magic phrase.

"Talk?" Candy smiled. "Why, certainly. What's on your mind?" She pulled out my file and moved a second chair closer to her. "You've been through so much."

I sat down on the chair but then pulled a tissue out of my pocket. "Well," I said, and coughed a little. "I was just thinking"—

I coughed a bit more—"I wanted to ask you . . ." And then I had a humongo coughing attack, like I might have scarlet fever or something contagious.

"Goodness!" said Candy. "Would you like some water?"

I nodded and stood up, coughing some more. I almost convinced myself there was actually something clogging my lung tubes. I stumbled out toward the water fountain.

Sure enough, Candy followed me out of the office with a hand on my back. I coughed myself down the hall slowly so Duck-Duck would have time to look around the room. Then I leaned over the water fountain and drank, slowly. Candy started to move away, and I gripped her arm as if I needed her in order to drink, and she waited.

"You okay?"

I nodded and took a few breaths. It was probably possible to kill yourself by fake coughing.

"You need some more?"

"Maybe a soda?" I said. My voice was kind of hoarse, like it would be if I were dying of scarlet fever. I read a book once about Helen Keller. She had something like scarlet fever and then she was deaf and blind. They didn't say anything about her being hoarse, but I bet she was.

"Sure, no problem," said Candy. She walked to the soda machine down the hall and pulled out some change. "What kind do you want?"

"Orange?" I said.

"Here you go," said Candy. "You okay now?"

"Yes," I said. "Maybe it's allergies." I stood near the water fountain and popped the can open. I took a sip. Then I took another sip. I coughed a little cough.

Before I could stop her, Candy started walking back to her office. She reached her door and jumped a little jump.

"And what are you doing, missy?" Candy actually sounded mean. "Give me that." She was probably mad that she forgot to lock her office door. She grabbed a file out of Duck-Duck's hand.

I could tell Duck-Duck was about to give a legal speech, but I interrupted.

"It's not her fault," I said. "It was my idea. I just wanted to find out some things."

Candy looked at me. She was still pissed off, but she didn't seem quite as nasty. "What do you need to find out? Why on earth didn't you just ask me?"

I couldn't think of an answer to that.

"Ask your question," said Duck-Duck. She made her eyes wide and gave me a little poke. "You just want to know things, *right*?" She shoved her foot into my foot.

"Yeah," I said. "Ummm."

Candy crossed her arms and made a face. It was almost a snarky playground face, not a Social Service–lady face. "Umm, what?"

"What she means," said Duck-Duck, "is she wants to know whatever information you have in the files about her maternal grandmother."

Candy looked at me. "Is that all you want?"

"Yeah," I said. It sounded stupid when she said it that way.

"You could have just asked." She picked up the file and started flipping the pages backward. Then she put it down on the table and kept turning pages. Back, back, back, still no grandmother.

"Huh," Candy said. She probably was a little embarrassed. I would have been if I had just made such a big fuss and then wasn't able to come up with the answer. "It's not here."

"Was it censored?" said Duck-Duck. "Was the information redacted?"

Candy stared at her like she didn't know what *redacted* meant and didn't want to admit it, but then she said, "I guess the original records were incomplete."

"You knew my mom when you were little," I said. "Do you remember if her mother was around then?"

"No," she said. "She wasn't. It was always just your grandpa and Keely."

"What about your files on Keely?" pushed Duck-Duck. "Maybe it's in *her* files."

"That's confidential," said Candy. She stopped looking embarrassed and started looking definitely unfriendly. She probably wanted Duck-Duck to stop hassling her.

Duck-Duck heaved a big sigh. "Well," she said, "that would be true if the information that was *supposed* to be in Fishy's file were actually there. But because you folks screwed up, it's necessary to access Keely's file. Get it?" she added when Candy looked confused.

"Hold on," said Candy. She started to leave the office. "Do not touch *anything*." She locked her drawers and her file cabinets, looked at us threateningly, and went down the hall.

We waited, every once in a while checking to see if she was coming back yet. Just as I was giving up, Candy appeared. "Okay, here we go," she said. She handed me a piece of paper. "Is that good enough?"

This paper was definitely redacted. Candy had blacked out all the information on a page of Keely's file except one thing. Under *Mother* it said Mary Esther Jamison. Under *Father* it said Leroy Jamison. Grandpa.

"Her name was Mary Esther," said Duck-Duck. "Cool."

Not so cool was that after Mary Esther's name it said *Deceased*.

"She's dead," I said. "I would be too if I had married Grandpa. I wonder why she married him in the first place." Mary Esther sounded like the name of someone who would marry a William or a Frank, not a Leroy. Especially not a Leroy.

"That," Candy said, "is beyond my purview."

"Well, it's a small lead," said Duck-Duck. She flicked her blond ponytail. "Come on, Fishy. I think that's all this informant has to offer."

"Sorry," I whispered to Candy as we went out. "Thanks for the soda."

The next day we were going to follow up on Candy's lead and figure out why Mary Esther married Leroy in the first place, but Duck-Duck decided to start learning tap. I thought tap dancing sounded even more dangerous than soccer, but I kept my mouth shut. I did say I wouldn't be caught dead in one of those leotards.

"No, you should get one!" Duck-Duck laughed. "A pink

one! I don't think you can wear sneakers, though." She fluttered her blond eyelashes at me. "I think you'd look cute."

"No way," I said. "I'm going food shopping with Molly."

"That's what I like about you," said Duck-Duck. "You're so flexible and open-minded." She poked me in the side and did a little tap dance. The light shone off her blond hair. I almost told her she looked like a movie star, but then I didn't.

"Maybe next time," I said.

After we dropped Duck-Duck off at tapping school, Molly and I drove to the fancy food store. It was the beginning of May, and there were hanging flower baskets outside. Flowers spilled over the edges of the pots: pinks, yellows, sky blues. We stopped for a second to look. I picked a cart, and we went in and turned down the fruit aisle. There was a little tray with pieces of free mango. Each slice was speared with a blue toothpick. I picked up a toothpick and ate the mango. It was smooth as it went down, but furry too, like a sweet sun that used to live near blue water. I held on to the toothpick when I was done. I poked it between my teeth and chewed on the end.

We had reached the end of the fruit aisle when I heard her.

"What the hell is this? It tastes like orange shit."

I gripped Molly's hand.

"This store always did have weird food. God, I can't get this stuff off my tongue."

It was Keely, and she was so loud that people were looking at her. I pushed Molly, but she didn't move. If she had been Duck-Duck, she would have known what I meant right away.

"What's the matter?" said Molly.

Keely turned, and I knew we had been seen.

"Hello, *girls,*" said Keely. "You should taste this crap. It's like slime on a stick." She started moving toward us. I knew she was drunk.

I was still pushing Molly, and finally she took a few steps.

"Running away?" Keely yelled. "Afraid the court will find out you're a fag?"

Molly pushed the cart between us and Keely. "Hon, *fag* is for men. The word is *dyke.* Get your terminology straight." She smiled just a little, like there was a joke only she was in on, but she kept a firm, almost crushing grip on my hand. "If you want to talk to either of us, you can contact Social Services. Or, better yet, my lawyer. If you follow us, I'll call the police."

"Bitch!" growled Keely. "Pervert! You ruined my life! You'll be sorry!"

We left our cart in the aisle and walked out. There wasn't all that much in the cart yet—we had only gotten through the fruit aisle—but I felt bad for the apples sitting there all alone in the plastic bag.

We quickly got back into the car and Molly drove out of the lot. She called the cops to let them know Keely was in town.

"We can do our shopping tomorrow," said Molly. "Are you okay?"

I didn't say anything. I didn't know if I was okay or not. I realized I was still gripping the toothpick.

"Why can't she just be . . . ?" I couldn't finish my sentence. Why couldn't she just be a regular mom? Why couldn't she just be someone who didn't drink beer? Why couldn't she just act normal? I almost started crying, which was dumb. Crying wouldn't make Keely love me enough to follow rules and not act wacko.

"Yeah," said Molly. "I know." I believed her too. She seemed to know exactly what I was going to say, even though I couldn't finish my sentence.

We stopped for milk, since we hadn't really shopped. We bought three Hershey's Kisses, too. Then Molly started the car again, and we went to pick up Duck-Duck from tap dance class.

The dance school was up on the second floor, above the hair salon. Molly and I got out of the car and watched women get their hair washed and cut while we waited for the *tappity-tap-tap* to stop from overhead. I tried not to think about our encounter with Keely.

"Would you like to get your hair cut?" asked Molly. "Think about a style you might like, and the next time we bring Chrissy to tap, you could get your hair done."

We watched one woman's hair turn from gray to black.

"Did you see the goo she put on that woman's head?" I said. "Gross."

The woman's now-black head turned curly. She looked like a poodle.

"I'm done!" said Duck-Duck. She had run down the stairs, and we hadn't even noticed. "So, are you going to get a perm?" she asked, smiling, as we turned away from the poodle-headed lady.

"Yeah, right," I said. "Let's go, tap-girl."

I got into the backseat of the car. Instead of going around to the door on the other side of the car, Duck-Duck climbed in on my side and pushed her dance bag against me.

"Slide over, Fishy," she said. "It's muddy over there. You want me to get my dance shoes dirty?" She pointed her sneakered feet like a prima ballerina and then picked up a foot to examine the bottom, miming horror and dismay.

I moved in but pinched her thigh to make her jump. "Dirty Ballerina. That's a good title for a porn movie." We giggled and pinched each other until Molly shushed us.

"I can't hear myself think," she said as we started to drive home. "When are you girls going off to college? Soon, right?"

And then there was a flash of green. A white scream.

22

Breathing under air is like breathing underwater. I was blind.

I heard someone say, "The passenger on the right . . ."

Am I the right passenger? I thought.

Air is heavy like water is thick.

A man as huge as a tractor pulled open a car door that didn't open the way a car door should.

Air steals sound like water steals breath. I was deaf.

I was leaving the world the same way I came into it—in the backseat of a car. It was how a story should end, all tied up neat. All tied up tight.

Under-air is heavy and slow. I was still.

I was the right passenger.

I was dead.

23

I woke up in a hospital bed. I saw tubes and machines. I heard beeping and crying. I was breathing air. I was the wrong passenger.

I remembered Keely's green pickup coming toward Molly's car at an impossible angle, like she wanted to ride up and over the middle of our car. I remembered the crash, although the doctors told someone I might not. I didn't remember sound, just light and color and dark.

Even though I was lying in the hospital bed, I wanted to ask if I was dead, but I couldn't make words.

I could hear Molly on the other side of the curtain, screaming and crying. I had never heard a grown-up cry like that before. If Molly had been stabbed, she couldn't have screamed or cried louder. Then they must have given her drugs, because soon she was quiet.

I didn't hear Duck-Duck.

I wanted to ask the nurses, what happened? Who was the right passenger? But every time they came near, it was like I was dead. I couldn't speak or open my eyes.

I didn't cry.

"How are we doing?" someone asked.

I blinked and opened my eyes a crack. A young nurse with braids all over her head was pulling a cart up to the bed

"You got pretty banged up, but nothing was broken," she said cheerfully.

I tried to focus my eyes on her face. Everything seemed a little blurry.

"You were asleep the last time I came by. I took your vitals and you barely woke up." She put the blood-pressure cuff on my arm. "I'm so sorry about your friend," she said.

I must have gotten a weird look on my face, because then she said, "Oh, no," and she ran away.

I thought she ran away, but maybe I fell asleep again because then suddenly there was a hospital social worker standing next to me. I hit her in the chest, hard, but she just grabbed me and held on.

"Go away," I hissed into her cold ear. "Go fuck yourself."

All I could hear was Molly screaming.

24

When Grandpa fell dead on the Birge Hill kitchen floor, it took us several minutes to get up the courage to go in close enough to check on him. I was sure if I got too close, he would grab me by the neck and squeeze. Keely must have thought so too, because she hung back by the door, clenching and unclenching her fists.

It was the clock that convinced me he was probably dead. It was suddenly ticking so slowly, so loudly, that I knew if he were still alive, he would have heard it and broken its hands.

"Grandpa?" I tested, but he didn't answer. "Grandpa?"

"Pop?" said Keely. She still didn't move.

I took a step toward him and then changed my mind. I grabbed the hitting stick from behind the door instead. I gave him a little poke and Keely jumped. I gave another poke, but still Grandpa didn't move. I dug the stick into his side and he didn't even twitch.

"I think he's dead," I said. "We should call nine-one-one."

"Why?" said Keely. "What can they do if he's already dead?"

"That's what you're supposed to do," I said. "Besides, there's no way the two of us can pick him up from the kitchen floor."

It took us a little while to make the call. Keely kept picking the phone up and putting it down. Finally, I grabbed and dialed.

"Nine-one-one," said the lady on the other end. "What is the nature of your emergency?"

"I think my grandpa is dead," I said.

The lady made me stay on the phone until the ambulance arrived. It wasn't just the ambulance. The fire truck and the police and the Highway Department man came too. I guess they all wanted to see for themselves if it was true. Grandpa always said people were nosy shits, and I guess he was right.

Because of the trailer and the ugly fence, the ambulance couldn't back up to the door, and the emergency people had to walk the stretcher around and across the muddy lawn. One guy stepped into a rut and sprained his ankle.

They put the stretcher down on the floor and lifted Grandpa onto it. *One, two, three,* they said, and then they all stood up. I knew he must really be dead, because one of the emergency men was also the guy who worked for the oil company, and Grandpa always fought with him about the bill. Grandpa called him the crap pit in a horse's ass. He would never have let the oil man touch him if he were still alive.

The policeman said he would drive us to the hospital, and we went because they seemed to expect us to go. We sat in the waiting room until the doctor came out and said he was

Very sorry, but Mr. Jamison was dead on arrival. He signed papers and made Keely sign them too. That was probably when they called the Department of Social Services, because Keely couldn't answer even simple questions about what to do with the body. Also, all the 911 people had been inside our house, and I could tell they weren't impressed. I saw the Highway Department man, who hadn't put even one finger on Grandpa, pull a bottle out of his glove compartment and squirt hand sanitizer on his hands, just like the school nurse did. He rubbed each finger like he had touched a pile of poop.

The policeman drove us home and asked if we were sure we were okay, and we said *Fine, sure, thanks, Officer.* Then he left, and we weren't sure what to do. Keely took a beer out to the porch, and I washed the kitchen floor with bleach. The smell hurt my nose, but somehow it seemed the right thing to do. Dead animals were supposed to be dirty, so dead people probably were too.

I thought bleach would get rid of the dead feeling that had descended on the house too, but it didn't.

Sleep is escape, except when it's not. Lying on the hospital bed, every time I shut my eyes, I had dreams of green trucks and black rivers. Hands reaching through windows and up out of lakes. Blood flowing from blue rocks. I wondered if Molly had the same dreams, but I couldn't ask. I heard the nurses whispering about us. Keely had flown straight through the windshield, they said; she hadn't been wearing a seat belt. Duck-Duck was wearing a seat belt, but in her case, it was more a trap than a help.

When no one was looking, I left the room and walked

around. All I had on was a blue-gray gown and weird little slippers that were really only socks. I touched my finger to the yellow line on the wall, following, following, following, and then I turned around and followed, followed back. Molly was lying still in the other bed. She hadn't even noticed that I had left.

After two days, we got a ride home from a lady I didn't know. Outside the hospital, May flowers had suddenly bloomed as if they had no idea the world was totally different now. The lady did all the hard things: she opened the door, turned on the lights, cleaned up the dishes. But that night, we were alone.

The first night home was the worst. The thought of sleeping in Duck-Duck's bedroom made my throat close up like hardened glue. I ended up on the living-room couch. I used my backpack as a pillow, the rough canvas against my cheek. Molly paced the house all night. Mostly she cried. Sometimes she talked to herself. She sounded as out of it as Keely ever did. I started to worry that she was.

The second night, I saw Molly open the liquor cabinet, and I heard the *clink-clink* of ice. I got up off the couch. Molly was standing at the counter swirling the glass with her finger, watching the ice go around and around in the clear liquid. She didn't look up when I walked across the room.

I picked up her glass and poured the alcohol down the drain. Ice hit the metal sink, and Molly's head sank onto the counter. I opened the refrigerator and looked for a replacement. There was milk, orange juice, seltzer, and a small bottle of lemonade. I gave her the lemonade since it had sugar, and sugar was good for shock. I read that once. Milk was healthy, but it wasn't very good for forgetting things, and Molly wanted to forget things.

"Drink," I said, and she did, but then she started crying again as if I'd never given her the lemonade.

Cry, people always said. *You'll feel better. Don't bottle it up,* they said. *Express your feelings,* the therapists told us. *It helps.* Crying didn't seem to be helping Molly much.

Nobody cried on Birge Hill. Not me, not Keely, definitely not Grandpa. The Social Service ladies asked if we cried a lot when he died. We didn't tell them it hadn't even crossed our minds. Kids at school cried a lot. Girls cried for little reasons. A spilled soda, a sad movie. Boys cried only for big reasons, like being hit in the balls with a bat or getting their foot run over by a lawn mower.

Maybe there was something on Birge Hill that dried up tears. Keely didn't cry when Grandpa hit her. She screamed and yelled. She clawed at the floor. I didn't cry either. Maybe we didn't know how anymore. Maybe only normal people cried.

Time was moving in a funny way. Every moment ticked by slowly, like slogging-through-the-cold-river slow. Then later in the afternoon, I had to try hard to remember what had happened in the morning.

I had forgotten Molly had a sister. Our third day home from the hospital, Patricia arrived from California. Patricia didn't have big shoulders or spiky hair. She had long reddish-brown hair that curled up at the ends. She had a green purse and shoes that matched. She had red lipstick and she had a pad for lists. Somehow I ended up on the list.

"We have to go shopping," she said to me, and then we were in her red rental car, driving to the supermarket and the bakery, and then we were in the department store, "because, even under the best of circumstances, Molly is so shopping impaired."

Patricia cried too, but when we went shopping, she stopped. She reminded me of Duck-Duck's description of how to learn math: she was focused.

"How about this?" Patricia held up a gray itchy dress against me. "I guess we're not going to the royal wedding in *that* one," she said, though all I had done was shudder.

Then she picked out black pants that felt like velvet and a blue jacket that was really just a shirt with a round turn-down collar and a little frill at the waist. She made me go try it on, and then she bought a bunch of underwear and socks and threw in two pairs of jeans, "as long as we're here."

She bought me a new pair of shoes to go with the velvet pants: black, with laces.

"You want sneakers too?" she asked, and then she just started going through racks because I couldn't answer.

If I had been with Duck-Duck, I would have picked out a pair with flashing lights, but now I couldn't even look at them. I picked a white pair with red Velcro.

It was a good thing Patricia kept grabbing my hand as we walked down aisles. I felt like I couldn't see so well, and I seemed unable to walk quickly anymore. When we got home, she made me take a shower, and then she cut my hair, right there in the kitchen. It was the first time since the accident that I had seen Molly almost smile.

"Don't fight it, Fishy," she said. "Patty is a force of nature."

Molly didn't eat for days. In the hospital, I could hear the nurses telling her, *Just eat a little piece of toast,* or *Just a little Jell-O, honey.* She only drank tea.

In the hospital, I ate whatever they brought me, but I couldn't taste it. It was as if I were there lying in bed but the food was on television. I would look at the tray and see the empty plate and the opened pudding container and know I had chewed and swallowed, but I couldn't remember tasting any of it.

A day later, people started coming over. Almost all of them were women. Big women with broad shoulders and spiky hair. Small women with strong arms. Fat women with large breasts and pocketbooks. They brought casseroles and sandwiches. They brought tan-colored cookies and something called Soybean Surprise. They brought salads and peanuts. The food piled up in the refrigerator and the freezer. The women would label everything carefully and rotate the dishes, but Molly still didn't eat. She lay in bed or she sat on the couch, staring at the wall. Sometimes she would cry, and one of the women would pat her and cry too. I met Ellen that week. I was surprised because she and Molly hugged and kissed and cried as if they hadn't been divorced at all.

"Has Molly eaten anything today?" Ellen asked me. She had ducked into the kitchen to get me alone.

"I don't think so," I said. I didn't say she hadn't eaten anything that I knew of since the accident.

Ellen came over and put her hand on my shoulder. She had short brown hair and muscles like a baseball player. "See if you can get her to have some dinner," she said. "I bet you can do that." Then she smiled at me, and I knew why Molly had liked her.

"You're tough like Molly," she said, and then she left.

But Molly wouldn't eat dinner. All the women left for the evening and Patricia went to bed, complaining of jet lag. Molly drank a cup of tea and fell asleep on her bed. She didn't even get under the sheets. I slept a little in the living-room chair, but then I woke up. The house was so quiet, you could tell there weren't enough people breathing in it. The clock said midnight.

Duck-Duck had said if you could read, you could cook. I pulled out the cookbooks with the prettiest pictures and read. I read about French meat; I read about Italian birds. I read about Cornish hens and Spanish oxtails. I read about chickens with little potatoes inside. I read about fishes laid out whole on platters with their eyes still in their heads. I read about blancmange, just like in *Little Women*. I read about mousse and puddings and flan.

Some of the ingredients I didn't have. Some ingredients I'd never heard of and didn't even know where a person would buy them.

I picked the recipe that sounded like what you should eat when your best daughter died and you hadn't had a real meal in days.

It was the most delicious mac and cheese I had ever had in my whole life. I tasted it before I made Molly sit down and eat a bowl. The macaroni had pushback, not like the mushy canned stuff the church ladies always gave us. I grated the cheese myself, two different kinds, plus a garlic that I banged with the metal crusher the way Molly did when she made spaghetti sauce. I even put in some mustard with the cream, which the recipe said was the right thing to do. I had my doubts, but in the end I was glad. I kept testing the elbows to see if they were done. I burned my tongue, but when I pulled the mac and cheese out of the oven, it was perfect.

"Dinnertime," I said, even though it was two o'clock in the morning. The funny thing was, Molly got up and sat down at the table like I was the mom and she was the kid. "Time to eat," I said, and she ate. I think it was probably the best mac and cheese she had ever had too, because she ate the whole bowl and then ate a little more.

The next night I made spaghetti, like Molly had made, but I made white spaghetti and meatballs. I overcooked the sauce a little and it stuck to the bottom of the pan, but it still tasted like a garden. The three of us ate that instead of the chunky yellow refrigerator casseroles.

Then I baked chocolate-chip cookies, like the ones Duck-Duck and I had made but with walnuts. It was hard not to burn them, because while I waited for them to bake, my brain kept running on about green trucks and blue cars. Then I remembered to set the little egg-shaped timer to remind me about each batch, and they all came out perfect. It was funny how a cookie could be perfect when everything else was not. It was funny how my brain could think about cooking and also not think about cooking, both at the same time.

The brain was weird. I was waking up in the day—as if I

had been asleep, but I hadn't—realizing that I had been thinking about Grandpa. And it wasn't really thinking; it was like I
was there, like he was here, again. Duck-Duck was gone, Keely
was gone, and all my brain could do was live at Birge Hill with
Grandpa. It made me mad.

One afternoon, a visitor named Nancy was in the living
room. She worked with Molly as a nurse at the hospital. I could
tell from her ID, which was attached to her coat.

"How are you girls doing?" she asked when she came in the
front door.

I didn't really answer her. I just hmmed and let her walk into
the living room without me. Molly mostly lay on the living-
room couch—when she wasn't wandering around the house
with a Keely-vague look or crying in the bathroom.

I went into the kitchen to get Nancy a piece of the cherry
pie someone had left us in a labeled Tupperware container. The
cherry pie was red and hopeful, but somehow it tasted not so
hopeful and somewhat slimy. I figured I'd give it to Nancy, since
she was probably used to hospital food and might not notice.

I was in the kitchen, thinking about pie, but then the next
minute I was thinking about rabbits.

There used to be rabbits all over Birge Hill. They ate people's
gardens. They got hunted for dinner.

Then the coyotes came back from almost extinction. You
could hear them yip-howling in the woods.

When the coyotes came back, the rabbits disappeared.

In all my life, I only ever saw one rabbit, and Grandpa said it was a hare. It was as big as a raccoon and fat. It ran across the yard and jumped under the fence.

"A bunny!" I had said.

"It's a hare," said Grandpa.

I didn't know there was a difference.

"The coydogs didn't get him," he said, almost sounding amused. "Tough bugger."

That might have been the only time I ever heard Grandpa say something nice about anybody.

I never saw that hare again.

Like I said, the brain was weird. It made me mad.

They had asked me if I wanted to cremate or bury Keely's body. I knew Keely didn't want to be stuck here forever. She had wanted to float down the river to move on, away from me, but she didn't make it the first time. She crashed the pickup to try again. Only as ashes would she be able to move on far enough to get away from Grandpa and me.

"Cremate," I had said. One-word sentences were still all I could handle at that point.

Duck-Duck was going to be in the famous people cemetery, where the lady poet was, but in the new part. I was glad the lady poet would look after her when we weren't there. I tried to see them having juice and Yodels together instead of seeing Duck-Duck as cold, bloody ash all alone under the ground.

Molly still hadn't stopped crying. It was like the Cherry Road sound track.

25

Duck-Duck's funeral proceeded at the far end of a long paper-towel tube. Far away at the other end of the tube, people wailed and cried. At my end, miles away, I could hear only faint murmuring. Molly, Patricia, and I sat up front, Patricia between us holding both of our hands.

People kept standing up and talking about Duck-Duck and crying, one after another. They called her Chrissy, of course. It seemed all wrong, like they were talking about some other girl who had died.

Ellen talked about going to baseball games with Duck-Duck when she was little and betting on the teams. Duck-Duck won. Ellen lost.

Some lady with dyed-red hair and feathers in her belt talked about how we would all meet one another again in the end and how Duck-Duck was in a better place. Molly looked like she was going to puke. I felt like that too. Where would be a better place than with Molly and me?

The school principal got up and said nice things. He didn't really know Duck-Duck, so it didn't mean anything. You could tell he meant to be nice, though.

Molly had forgotten how to talk, like someone had pressed her mute button. In Molly's place, Patricia stood up and talked about Duck-Duck being born on the hottest day of the year.

"She was like a comet," she said, and a couple of tears ran down her cheek. "She was only here for a short time, but when she was here . . ." Patricia couldn't say anything else. She had on red high-heeled shoes, and when she came back to her seat, I could see that her black stockings had red threads running up and down the back. She sat down and wiped her eyes. She wiped carefully so her makeup wouldn't smear.

No one asked me to say anything, but I couldn't have talked even if I'd wanted to. Everything was glued shut. My stomach felt like a black stone.

Then they played music, and everyone got up and hugged and kissed. I hid behind Patricia, out of sight, as much as I could. I tried counting the times people said, "If you need anything, just call," and then ran away as fast as they could.

We hadn't had a service for Keely, but there at Duck-Duck's funeral, I could tell everyone knew about her. We all filed into another room with food, and I knew they were all looking at me because I was the daughter of the woman who killed Duck-Duck; my mother was the reason we were all there, crying and eating yellow cake.

I didn't eat any yellow cake. Eating cake without Duck-Duck seemed wrong. Molly didn't eat any cake either.

Molly and Patricia were huddled at the window side of the room. People kept coming up to them, to talk, to hug, to cry.

For a while, I hid in the bathroom, and then I sat down on a chair in the far corner, like it was an island in a lake of mud. Stuck on the chair, I didn't have to figure out where to stand or who to look at.

But I couldn't prevent people from walking over to me.

"Hi."

I looked up.

It was Worm, in a suit with too-short sleeves. He had shiny black shoes on his huge feet.

"My father said we had to come." He shrugged toward the huge man who was walking up to Molly.

My stomach still felt like a stone. My throat was welded shut.

We stared at each other for a minute, and then he said, "I'm sorry I pushed her."

I'd never been to a funeral, but it was weird how death did this to people. Made them talk about things that had happened a long time ago. Making the long-ago story different from it was when it happened.

"Why'd you do it, then?" I asked. I remembered Duck-Duck's eyes full of tears and her dirty yellow dress. "Why?"

"I dunno," Worm said, kicking his big foot a little on the carpet. "She was real pretty."

He pushed her because she was pretty? That was bad logic.

Worm still didn't go away. "You want a soda?" he asked me.

The table was covered with slices of yellow cake on little plates. Patricia had also bought tea, coffee, and soda for the kids. If Molly had been right in the head, she would have nixed the soda.

I shook my head. If I tried to swallow anything right then, I might have started crying.

"You look really nice," he said. He kept talking, even though I hadn't said a word. "My pop knew your grandpa when he worked in the prison. He said your grandpa was a real piece of work."

It startled me that Worm had said something so real and mean when everyone was working so hard to say only nice things. I looked up. It was the first time I noticed his eyes were brown with a spot of yellow right in the middle, like an egg or a star.

"Sorry about your mom," he said. "Sorry about Chrissy."

"Duck-Duck," I said.

"What?"

"Her name was Duck-Duck," I said, and the stone in my stomach hit the top of my throat and tears squeezed out my eyes. "Duck-Duck," I said. I put my head down on my knees, down on the velvet pants Patricia had picked out, and pretended they couldn't see me, all those people eating cake, while I cried snot on my legs.

Worm just stood there, a big black rectangle between me and the cake people. Then he got a napkin and pushed it under my face, into my hands. When I sat up because I was going to choke, he handed me another napkin and waited for me to blow my nose.

"My mom died, too," he said.

I hadn't thought of him ever having a mother. I had just imagined him and his father living in a house with lots of big shoes and maybe a pit bull.

"Sorry," I said.

Worm poured Coke into a glass of ice and brought it back to me. "If you drink it really cold, it makes the tears go back in your head," he said.

It didn't really, but it was nice that he thought it did.

Then Worm's father came over. He said something I couldn't hear through the black stone and the snot tears, but he nodded and patted my shoulder, so I guess it didn't matter.

"See you at school," said Worm.

I nodded quick and wiped my nose with the back of my hand. "Yeah," I said.

I had forgotten it was still only May.

Even when I went back to school, days kept moving on ketchup time. Sometimes I would look up, sure it was the next day, and no, it was only ten minutes later than it had been. Then, *wham!* the time would jump, like I hadn't been paying attention to dinner and now it was done and all the dishes were washed. I wanted to skip this part, the part where every time my heart moved, it banged up against my ribs and my stomach and made me want to cry, or throw up, or bite someone hard.

At school, kids looked at me like I was broken, like we looked at Carlotta Bennigan when her little brother died of cancer, like she had an extra arm sticking out of her head or a sign posted across her chest that said, *You Don't Want to Be Me.*

The school counselor asked me how I was doing.

"I'm fine," I said.

Patricia took Molly to the doctor, who gave her pills to help her sleep.

"It's just temporary," Patricia said to me, "because if she doesn't sleep now, she's going to get worse, not better."

I thought about what worse would look like. Maybe Molly would start acting like Keely, forgetting to go shopping, forgetting to come home, forgetting she was a mother. Maybe she would become like Grandpa, cursing everyone and only buying tomato soup. She wasn't doing any of those things yet; she was just crying all the time and not going to work. When I woke up at night, she would be walking around, just mumbling to herself. She would answer me if I talked, but she never came out and asked me if I wanted to watch a movie or if I would make more cookies. Maybe she was starting to wish I didn't live there. Maybe she was okay about me being there while Duck-Duck was there too, but now that I was the only one left, she wished I would go somewhere else. I sort of understood because I wanted to be somewhere else too.

Patricia did her California work by computer. She could see the California people on the screen and they would talk about numbers and orders and patents. She dressed up for these computer calls, like she was really going into the office, but she only dressed up the part the computer people could see. She would have on a fancy jacket and earrings and makeup, but down below she would have on exercise tights and no shoes.

"They don't have to know everything," Patricia said. "They think they do, but they don't."

I thought it was kind of smart of her, but it made me look at people on TV differently. If you couldn't see the newspeople's feet, were they wearing shoes? Did they have underwear on? It was the kind of thing I wanted to tell Duck-Duck. It was the kind of thing I would have told Molly, but before, not now. Now she didn't think anything was funny. She definitely didn't think *I* was funny. She would kind of pat me and try to smile and go into another room. I wondered if she would ever think I was funny again.

Then I heard her say what she was really thinking.

The Social Service lady caught me outside the house. I had been just standing on the doorstep staring at the sky.

"Fishkill," she said, walking up to the door. "How are you feeling? How's school?"

"Fine," I said. "No problem."

Then I let her into the house and hid. I don't know why, really. Maybe if I hadn't hidden and made her talk to me instead of Molly, Molly wouldn't have gotten worse. This was a new Social Service lady, because the old lady had quit, and she was talking about *options* and *long-term placements* or maybe *just adopt-*

ing, and then she hauled out all this paper and started pointing to different pages and shuffling them and pointing to other pages.

Molly was very quiet and didn't answer many questions. Even from behind the couch, I could tell she didn't want to consider *adopting* or *long-term* anything, but she didn't say so, and then Patricia came back from the drugstore.

"Thanks so much for coming," said Patricia. "We're going to give it all serious consideration." And she actually pushed the papers back into the Social Service lady's bag and opened the front door. "See you next month," she said.

I was still hiding, but I heard every word. Patricia sat down on the couch next to Molly. Molly leaned her head into her and started crying again.

"I'm sick of this shit," said Molly.

Molly never cursed, so I knew it must be really bad. Molly could always fill out paperwork, so I realized she must really not want me to be *long-term.*

That was when I knew I would have to move on. I would have to take care of myself. Some kids were born to have real mothers, and others weren't. I wasn't.

I could kind of understand. Once you had a perfect daughter, why would you want to have a pretend daughter who was only so-so? Probably you could only have one special child, one comet, and everyone after that was useless.

It wouldn't be right for me to stay anyway. If I thought about it logically, it was really all my fault. If Molly hadn't let me move in, Keely wouldn't have known Molly existed, and she certainly wouldn't have been following us, or whatever she was doing. If Molly hadn't let me live with them, her car wouldn't have been hit by Keely's green truck. Keely wouldn't be dead, and Duck-Duck wouldn't be dead. It was my fault that Duck-Duck was dead. No wonder Molly didn't want to be my long-term anything.

If I stayed, I might even make Molly worse. I had killed her perfect daughter. Who knew what else I might do?

I could call the Social Service ladies and tell them it was time to move on.

"Are you sure?" they would ask.

"Yup," I would answer.

Or maybe I would take the chance Keely never took. I could go west, like the pioneers. Or I could go to New York City and start a new life.

I didn't tell Molly or the Social Service ladies when I started getting ready.

Now that I knew what I had to do, it made things a little easier. I made a list, but I wrote it in code so if anyone found it, they wouldn't understand anything. Instead of *food,* I wrote *Yodels.* Instead of *clothes,* I wrote *Aunt Patricia.* Instead of *money,* I wrote *socks.* Then I wrote *Finish unfinished business.* I couldn't think of a code for that.

I tried to decide what to take with me. The cops had brought me Keely's purse. I opened it, and all I felt was a big black hole inside me. If only I had tried harder, if only I had been nicer to her, maybe she would have tried too. I pulled out Keely's lipstick and drew a red line on the back of my hand. If I stared at it just right, it looked like a big red vein that now pumped outside my body for everyone to see.

It took me a while to decide if I could take some of Duck-Duck's things. Should I take what I needed, or was that stealing? I needed to talk to someone smart like Duck-Duck to figure out if stealing was okay in this situation or not, but Duck-Duck wasn't here anymore. I started having a conversation with her in my head:

"I know you wouldn't mind," I said, "but what about Molly? I would sort of be stealing from her."

"Is it for the greater good?" asked the Duck-Duck in my head. "If it is, you can take it by eminent domain."

"Isn't that just an excuse?"

"The law isn't just an excuse," she said. "It's the foundation on which our whole society rests. What do you need?"

"Rain boots?"

I didn't have any rain boots. The tan-and-black pair in the bedroom closet must have been big on Duck-Duck, because they fit me fine. They weren't shiny or striped, like some of her flashy shoes, but that was good, because I didn't want to stand out. I wanted to blend in with all the other people in the big city where I was going. I guessed I was going to New York City, but I wasn't sure yet.

I found Duck-Duck's change purse, but I decided taking money was too much like stealing and left it in her top drawer. I pulled my allowance sock out from the bed springs and counted fifty dollars and forty-five cents. I knew I wouldn't have a lot left after I bought a bus ticket, so I decided to take forty-five dollars from Duck-Duck as a loan. I would pay Molly back when I had a job and an apartment in the city.

I bought twenty Yodels to take with me, but I bought them slowly, from different stores, so no one would get suspicious. I packed them away in my backpack with my new clothes, which were all folded up small, and some of Duck-Duck's socks. In the front pocket, I put the Yodel-from-scratch recipe Duck-Duck had printed from the Internet. Maybe someday I would be able to make it. I put it with Keely's lipstick and the tiger card Molly gave me after I took those tests. Then I stuffed in Keely's redacted file with Mary Esther's name on it.

I decided I would wear the white sneakers with red Velcro. I kept ripping the Velcro on and off, back and forth. It sounded like I felt inside.

I didn't know what to do with Keely's ashes. It wasn't like I could bring them with me, even though Keely probably would have wanted to go to the city too. I pushed the box into the way-back of Duck-Duck's closet and put the red boots in front. I didn't want Keely with me in the city anyways. She would just have been a pain in the neck. I would have had to explain everything to her.

Finish unfinished business was still on the list.

I decided I would go to Birge Hill one more time before I left. That was definitely unfinished business. The house wasn't mine anymore. The town was going to sell it because Grandpa and

Keely hadn't paid taxes in so long. I didn't think I was sorry about this.

"I'm going for a walk," I said to Molly, even though I didn't know if she could hear people or not. "Don't worry about me."

She didn't answer.

"I'll be back for supper."

Molly finally made a noise. It was between a grunt and a mumble. It would have made me sad if I hadn't been focused on my plan.

At least she wasn't crying. The day before, Molly had wept all day, in little bursts, in loud rainstorms, like she would never be a dry, quiet person again. Molly was soft, I realized; she had no stone inside to put a lid on all that water.

The walk to Birge Hill seemed much longer than it had when I lived there. The hill was steeper too. When I got to the fence, I saw that sections had caved in under the wet January snow. The town used to plow big, dirty snow piles and push them up against the fence. Sometimes they would plow snow across the driveway on purpose, and Grandpa would call up the highway guy and tell him his pisser wasn't bigger than a Tootsie Roll. That would make the highway guy mad, and he would plow us in even worse the next time.

Now the town had towed away the dead trailer, and they'd gotten rid of the rusty refrigerator, but they hadn't touched the dead trucks in the back yet. I stood by the fence while I talked myself into walking up to the door and stepping inside. I didn't need to stay long, I told myself. I just had to see if there was anything I should take with me before the town sold it off. Something I had forgotten. Something I had overlooked.

The house seemed to have shrunk. From the outside you could see the walls were leaning in, like there was a giant pushing on them. The roof tiles had separated from the house, exposing hollow black spaces, and when I opened the door, it smelled of mice and mold and dead people. If someone died in a house, was it possible to ever get rid of the deadness?

I started digging around and found a box hidden under Keely's bed. It looked like Keely had made a hole in the floorboards and covered it over with dirty clothes. I wiped up the dust and mouse poop before I pulled off the top. It was just papers. I was disappointed. It would have been nice to find money or a magic map. Then I realized there were drawings on the papers. Keely's drawings. Drawings of us. Drawings of the river.

I spread the pictures out on the bed. There were only ten, but finally I had proof. Keely could draw. She was good.

The first picture I pulled from the pile was of Grandpa. It was black and white, like Keely only had a pencil and drew with the side, not with the point. She made Grandpa look like a real person, not just a monster. He looked like an old man with a lot on his mind. I wondered if Keely really thought he looked like that or if she was imagining what he would look like if he weren't a monster. I guessed I would never know.

Then I found a drawing of a baby. I knew it was me. I wondered how she could do that—make it look like me, even though I was only a baby, and how she made it look like the baby didn't want to be there.

There were drawings of the river in the spring and drawings of the river in the winter. The winter river looked comfortable and familiar, like she had been there often and knew she would go back. I wasn't sure how you drew that into a picture. In a story, you could say it out loud in words, but in a drawing?

Why had she stopped drawing? There weren't any pictures of me after I was a baby. Maybe Grandpa threw them out. All that time in the shack and I never once saw her even doodle. If I could draw, I wouldn't have stopped just because Grandpa didn't want me to. I would've drawn until I became an artist and someone put my art in a museum, and then I would've moved out and lived with famous people and let Grandpa die on the kitchen floor all alone. The black hole that was Keely burned wordlessly in my belly.

I stacked up Keely's drawings and put them back in the box. Then I didn't know what to do. Should I leave them under the bed? The house could be sold at any time, or they could condemn Birge Hill and everything would be torn down on top of the drawing box. Maybe the Fire Department would use it to practice on, like they did with the cape house another old man willed to the town. He must have been mean too, because the house made everyone mad at one another and they fought for years about what to do with it. Some people wanted to sell it, and some people wanted to keep it. After twenty years, the Fire Department said it was a fire hazard and they were going to use it to practice firefighting. People were so tired of fighting, they let them do it. The firemen made it burn red and blue and green and jumped around a lot with their hoses and water. Everyone who had fought about the old man's house came to see the firemen burn it down. It was like a party on the Fourth of July.

I decided to bring the box of drawings to Duck-Duck's house and put it in the back of the closet with Keely's ashes. Molly wasn't going to be in shape to clean closets anytime soon and I knew her house wouldn't be condemned by the town. I buried the thought that by not taking the box with me, I was leaving Keely all alone. Again.

Just before I left Birge Hill, I checked my rock box. It was empty except for a torn page from the back of my old social studies book. I slid the rock over the empty box and walked down the hill.

26

My escape had to begin on Duck-Duck's bike. Buying a bus ticket in Salt Run was too risky. Someone might know me, plus the Salt Run bus schedule was way too limited; buses stopped there only once a day, in the morning. It didn't really make sense. People in a place like Salt Run probably wanted to leave town more than people in nicer, bigger cities. There should have been more stops, not fewer. Especially now that it was June, almost summer.

I knew I had to leave in the evening, to give myself more of a head start. Molly wouldn't notice I was gone until morning, if she noticed at all. Carrieville was ten miles south, past Birge Hill, in the opposite direction from school, the opposite direction from town. I could bike there and get a bus at nine at night. I felt bad that I would have to ditch Duck-Duck's bike behind the station, but I couldn't think of another way.

After I biked to the station, I would have to scam a ticket. I looked online and all the bus companies were out to screw kids. You had to travel with an adult or else have a form signed by the adult, have them drop you off, and have someone else pick you up at the other end with an ID to prove they were who they said they were. They had dozens of rules about which buses you could take too. You couldn't switch buses. You had to sit up front. It even cost five dollars extra to travel alone, which totally didn't make any sense, since you were taking up one seat no matter if you were with a grown-up or not.

I made a plan, plus a second plan in case the first one didn't work out.

In the first plan, I figured I'd wait for a big family that seemed disorganized and tag along behind them so no one would check for a form or an ID. Sometimes in food stores, parents made their kids bring their own money and pay for their own gum, just to teach them responsibility. You had to wait for each person to individually buy a soda, buy a Hershey's bar, buy a box of hair ties, when they all could have been rung up at the same time. Maybe there'd be a family like that at the bus station. I read an article on the computer about a boy who traveled all the way to Italy that way. If he managed to fly on an airplane with no ticket and no passport, surely I could get to New York City on a bus. I'd just get in line behind a "responsibility" family and buy my ticket to New York.

Before I left, I made a ham-and-cheese sandwich and put it in the backpack with my Yodels. Then I thought about it and made a peanut-butter-and-jelly sandwich too. There was only one juice box left, but I took it and put it in an outside pocket so if it leaked, it wouldn't get red juice all over my clothes.

The first night I tried to leave, I waited too long for a disorganized family. It was very late before I realized I should have gone to plan number two. I'd have to try again the next night. Biking to the bus station had been easy; it was almost all downhill. Biking back wasn't so easy. I was exhausted when I finally climbed in the window and into bed.

The next night, I went straight to plan number two. I'd printed out the form and signed it, faking Molly's signature, all loops and no closed letters. I brought it with me to the bus station. There wasn't anyone else in line when I went up to the one ticket window.

"A ticket to New York City," I said, and slid the form under the glass.

The man glanced up and started to open his mouth.

"My mom is over there." I motioned outside the door, where, indeed, there was a woman. She was smoking a cigarette, facing the other direction, and talking on the phone. She looked impatient.

"She's always like that," I said, and sniffed. It was an I'm-all-alone-but-I'm-not-going-to-cry sniff. "It's her boyfriend. He doesn't like me. They want me to go be with my dad." Then I bit my lip, like I was going to cry unless someone distracted me.

"Here you go," said the guy. He was young. Maybe younger than Keely. Younger than Keely had been. He was playing a game on his phone, and I could tell he didn't want to deal with a crying kid. He definitely didn't care about my fake mom and her fake boyfriend. "Bus leaves at nine o'clock," he said.

One of the other rules was that kids weren't supposed to travel at night without a grown-up, but the ticket guy seemed to have forgotten that.

"Th-thanks," I stuttered. "Do you have a tissue?"

"In the bathroom," he said, and went back to his video game. I was halfway there.

I waited for 9:00 in the bathroom so no one would see me and remember the kids-can't-travel-at-night rule. The bus arrived late, and I held tight to my backpack so they wouldn't put it under the bus, and when I got up to the driver, I turned and waved at the parking lot, as if there were someone there watching. The driver didn't say a word. I was starting to understand how that boy had gotten all the way to Italy without a passport.

I sat toward the front, but each time the bus stopped, I moved a couple rows back, finally getting to the back near the bathroom. It smelled a little, but I figured if the driver didn't see me, he would forget I was there. Then he wouldn't remember that someone had to pick me up at the other end. After a little while, I ate the ham sandwich and a Yodel.

I must have slept, because I woke up when the bus driver started talking to us.

"Excuse me, ladies and gentlemen," he called out. "We have a malfunction, and I need everyone to exit the bus at this station. Another bus will come to take you to your final destination."

"My God," said the man sitting in front of me. "Why do they have to stop every time a check-engine light goes on? It could be a stupid oxygen sensor, and still they're going to drop us off at a station in the boonies in the middle of the night and make us wait all night. JEE-sus." He stood up and grabbed his bag from the rack above us.

I clutched my backpack and tried to hear what the driver told the other passengers and what they said to him. *Wait. Don't wait. Another bus coming later. Quicker to rent a car. Why doesn't the bus company service these vehicles? Just my luck.*

Everyone got off the bus. They grumbled about being dropped at such a small station, and they called motels and rental cars, and one by one they all left. No one asked me what I was going to do. I hid in the station bathroom for a long time so no one would remember me and ask what I was doing in the boonies all by myself. When I came out, even the ticket man had left. I was alone in the one-room station. There were vending machines with potato chips and gum, and a video game that played a buzzy video song every five minutes. I timed it. The seats were hard orange plastic, bolted to the floor.

In the corner, there was a pay phone. No one used pay phones anymore, so the change slot was full of gum and cigarette butts. I checked for a dial tone, even though I knew it wouldn't work. I wanted to dial Duck-Duck's number, which now was only Molly's number, just to hear her voice. But it was two o'clock in the morning, and I was running away. If I dialed, I would listen to Molly say *"Hello? Hello?"* and then hang up.

My chest hurt like there was gravel moving along with my blood, but I decided I would be brave like the pioneers, or like Anne Frank hiding from the Nazis.

I tried to sleep on the bus station seats. If those orange chairs were movable, I could have put two together, like a couch or a bed. I would fall asleep, and then a truck would honk when it rumbled by or the video-game machine would suddenly play its whirly music, and I would wake up again. Finally, I pulled the machine's plug out of the wall. I fell asleep and dreamed of school lunches. I was walking the long cafeteria line, gazing at the soggy bagel pizzas and stringy gray meat in brown sauce. *What is that?* I kept asking. *What is that?* At the end of the line, the cash register rang me up, all by itself, and I gave it all my money. Suddenly, I was out in the cold winter air with nothing to eat.

When I woke up, the station door was open and swinging with each gust of wind.

There was no one there.

It was eight o'clock in the morning when the ticket man came back. He didn't say hello. He didn't even nod. You would think a kid all alone would make the guy say, *Hey, what're you doing here?* but no. I guess he wasn't really into his job.

There was still no bus labeled *New York City*. Finally, I went up to the window.

"They said there would be a replacement bus to New York," I said, and I held out my ticket.

"You missed it, kid. Came through at four a.m. Maybe you were asleep."

"When's the next one?" I could feel my armpits turning sticky and my hands starting to shake, which was stupid, since what was so hard about hanging out another few hours?

The ticket man tossed the schedule through the slot in the window. He turned around so I would know he wasn't going to read it to me, and then he started type-banging on the computer. I wondered if he would lose his job if his boss found out he ignored a minor stuck in the boonies all night.

Then I realized my backpack was gone. Did I really sleep through someone stealing my bag? Did I really sleep through the bus coming and going? All my Yodels, my clothes, the tiger card, and Keely's lipstick were gone. All my food and money too.

I don't know why I felt so bad just then. It wasn't like anyone had hit me. Suddenly, the walls turned grayer than they had been, and the stone in my stomach, which had never really gone away, squeezed up against my throat as hard as ever. I felt sick down in my belly and up in my throat. I had to go into the bathroom and press wet paper towels on my eyes really hard to keep from crying.

I didn't know what to do.

I stumbled outside, and it was then, in the morning sun, that I started to cry, even though Fishkill was never supposed to cry. My eyes and nose started hurting from the rising pressure of the stone in my throat, and I knew I could never win. I had lost my backpack. I had lost Duck-Duck. I had lost my mother. I was just like Grandpa, I was just like Keely. I would never get to New York City. I would end up on the street, eating food out of the garbage, never getting to go to the library. There was a sharp pain in my chest, like the rocks had broken up into pointy little shards and were pushing my heart right out of my chest.

It definitely wasn't my mother I wished for at that moment.

It wasn't even Duck-Duck. It was Molly who I wished would be in that blue SUV pulling up to the station. I ground my eyes into my hands and wished for a magic moment, like I was in a Harry Potter book, and then I cried even more because I knew Harry was just a story and magic rescues were just hog hokum, as Grandpa would say. I sank down on the bench and put my face against my knees.

"Fishkill?" said a voice. "What are you doing here?"

27

It was Worm. He was standing a few feet away from me. He wore a baseball cap and had three empty soda cups under his arm. His father was standing by the door of the blue SUV, unfolding a map.

I wasn't used to such big people. Worm's father was taller than the SUV.

Then I realized they had seen me crying, all by myself, with no backpack. I almost ran, but I didn't know exactly where I was or where I would run to.

"Yeah," I said. "It's me."

Worm's father folded the map and walked over, a mountain above me. "Is Molly here?" he asked.

"No." I didn't have the energy for lies. I didn't even have the energy to wipe the tears off my face.

"Are you all by yourself?" He looked worried, almost as bad as when Worm got beat on. "Where are you going?" I could have said I was going to my grandmother's and he might have bought it. But it was only a little voice that came out of my mouth. Nothing like my regular voice. Maybe a bit like my voice used to be, before I became Fishkill.

"I ran away," I said. I was almost afraid just those three words would bring the cops. Worm's father looked so sorry for me that I thought the big mountain was going to cry too.

"Come on," he said. "I bet you need breakfast."

Worm threw out their soda cups in the bus-station garbage can, and I got into the backseat of the SUV. I had to dig the seat belt out of the crack between the seats.

"It's brand-new," said Worm. "Top-of-the-line Ford Explorer. It's a V-six." He looked very pleased. "The old Jeep died. The clutch and the transmission and the exhaust system all went kaput at the same time. It was epic." He pushed a pile of Dunkin' Donuts napkins, two Coke cans, and a half-empty bag of Doritos off the backseat so we could both fit in.

Even though the car was big, Worm took up most of the backseat. I remembered how Duck-Duck and I would sit in the back of Molly's car, and there would still be lots of room — room enough for groceries or backpacks. The car was warm and the sweatshirt thrown across the back of the seat smelled of boy sweat. I would have thought it would stink, but it was actually kind of nice after sleeping in a bus station all night.

I tried to smile. "Where are you going?"

"We were going to a skeet convention, but my dad got lost.

We got up at four in the morning, and we're still going to be totally late."

His father gave a snort.

"The GPS died," said Worm, "and we drove the wrong way for forty-five whole minutes."

His dad apparently had figured out where we were, because he drove us straight through the little town and right up to a McDonald's.

"Let's have breakfast," Worm's father said, "and then we can decide what to do."

We went into the McDonald's and ordered. Both guys seemed to know exactly what they wanted without looking at the pictures and the descriptions even once. I knew I was taking a long time to choose.

"How about an Egg McMuffin?" asked Worm. He seemed fine about the fact that I had just crashed his weekend with his dad. He didn't even mention that I had been crying.

"Okay," I said.

Worm and his dad both ordered a Double Sausage & Egg McMuffin the size of my head, with hash browns on the side. Worm got a chocolate milk, and his father got a super-large coffee. I was going to get orange juice, but I changed my mind and got chocolate milk too. Breakfast was good. It was the kind of food you could eat without thinking about it.

"I ran away from home once," Worm's father said.

"Really?" I said politely. "How come, Mr.——"

"I'm Cork," he said. "You can call me Cork." He ate the last half of McMuffin in one bite.

"I wanted to go to Yankee Stadium," he said, "but I got on the wrong bus and ended up in Buffalo." He took a swig of his coffee. "What happened to you?"

I might actually have told him—he was so nice to buy me breakfast and everything—but Worm was sitting right there. There was no way I was going to say why I ran away in front of him—that Molly didn't want me, so I was on my own now.

"Let's check in with Molly," Cork said. "I'm sure she's worried sick."

I wasn't so sure about that. She might not be awake yet. She might not even have noticed I was gone.

Cork made me dial the number and then he took the phone.

"Hello?" he said. "It's Cork. Don't worry. I found her."

I went to the bathroom and stayed there for a while. I washed my hands and spent a long time washing bus-station tears off my face. When I thought the phone call was probably over, I went back out. What other choice did I have? I couldn't even run away right.

"Molly's sister is coming for you," said Cork. "We're going to meet her halfway."

Molly wasn't coming.

"What about your skeet convention?" I said.

"Hey," said Cork, "we were already late anyway, weren't we, Norm?"

He punched Worm in the arm, but not hard like Grandpa would have. He punched him in a playful way, like he knew there was plenty of Worm and he could just mush a little piece.

Worm punched him back. I figured it was a guy version of the hug-kiss thing Molly and Duck-Duck did. Used to do.

I couldn't finish my McMuffin, so Cork ate what was left. I watched as he tossed back the rest of my chocolate milk too.

"You pulled us out of the car," I said to him suddenly.

He looked at me, surprised. "You remember that?"

"Kind of," I said. "Not really." I picked up a McMuffin crumb with my finger, mashing it until it stuck, and put it in my mouth. "What did she look like?"

He didn't answer me right away, but he didn't say, *Who? Chrissy?* He knew.

"She was always beautiful, that girl," he said. "She was beautiful that day too." He didn't say anything else. I could tell he was trying to be nice to me. Then he just stood up and went and bought three cookies for later.

Back in the Ford Explorer, Worm asked his father to turn the radio on, and then there was music and a guy singing about losing his girl and his cows.

"Is it true you're going to skip a grade next year?" Worm asked.

I looked at him. "Who told you that?"

"Kids. You know," he said, not looking at me exactly.

"I'm not skipping a grade," I said. "I'm just going to the hard classes."

"Huh," he said. "Not me. I'm too dumb. You know that." He shrugged like he didn't care.

"I could teach you," I said. "It's like law. All it takes is a little logic and concentration."

"Huh," he said again, but it sounded like he might be saying, *Yes, I'd like that.*

We stayed on the highway for a while. Then Worm's father got off the highway and drove on smaller town roads. I had no idea where we were. I didn't know where he had agreed to meet Patricia. I felt like a lost package.

Finally we pulled up to a small store with a gas pump in front. We were on the top of a hill. The wind was blowing, and it was drizzling. It almost felt like we were near the ocean, even though I knew that was impossible. There was only one little red car at the store. It was Patricia's rental car. She was leaning against it, waiting for us.

"Oh, my God," she said. "Where on earth did you go? We were so worried." I'd never seen Patricia look so disorganized.

Patricia put out her arms and hugged me so hard we both almost fell over. It was funny, or it would have been funny if I weren't so screwed up.

Then she gave Cork a hug too, which surprised me a lot. It seemed to surprise him too, because he turned a little pink. They started talking about bus stations and police reports and Amber Alerts. I leaned against the front of Patricia's rental car. It was warm.

"Norm and I should get going," said Cork finally. "Are you ladies going to be okay?"

"We are," said Patricia. "Thanks again."

"Don't mention it," he said.

"See you later," said Worm.

"Bye," I replied, thinking of the yellow egg-star in his eyes, but I didn't look up. Then I was alone with Patricia.

"Where were you going?" she asked. "We were worried sick."

"Molly would have gotten worse if I stayed," I said. "It was better to leave. She doesn't want me."

"That's not true," said Patricia.

"She didn't even come to get me. She sent you."

Patricia folded her arms like she was suddenly mad. At first she was just upset. Now she looked like she wanted to smack me.

"My sister was up in the wee hours of the morning and found you were gone — nowhere in the house. She checked Chrissy's computer and found all your searches for bus schedules and left immediately, driving all the way to the Port Authority Bus Terminal in New York City. Does that sound like someone who doesn't want you?" Patty didn't have blue eyes. She had brown eyes, but they had the same squinty, mean power that Molly's did.

The stones rose up in my throat again.

"But it's all my fault," I said. It came out in a whisper. "Duck-Duck wouldn't be dead if it weren't for me."

And then we both cried, up there on top of the windy hill.

"It feels like that," said Patricia, "but it really isn't true. None of this was your fault. Don't you disappear on Molly too," she said. "You're the only one who really understands."

I thought about that while we were driving home. Patricia might have known Duck-Duck longer than I had, but she hadn't ever lived at Cherry Road with her. She hadn't eaten lunch with her every day. Maybe Patricia was right. Maybe Molly needed me around because there wasn't anyone else who knew

Duck-Duck the way she did. I had a headache from crying so much.

I thought about Molly finding my computer searches for New York bus schedules. Duck-Duck had been right. You had to be really careful about leaving electronic fingerprints. They were like muffin crumbs that someone else could follow. In a way, though, that was good.

"We're almost home," said Patricia.

But before we got home, we stopped at the mall and went shopping. Patricia bought me a new backpack, a swimsuit, and a funny hat for the summer.

"You're going to have fun again," she said, "even though it might be hard to believe, and even though it doesn't feel like it right now." She stopped and bought a pair of sandals to go with the hat. "I want you to be ready for good things."

Then we went to the uptown diner for lunch and had sliced turkey with gravy and mashed potatoes. For dessert, we split a piece of chocolate-coconut-cream pie. It made me cry again, but Patricia said good food sometimes does that. We packed a piece to bring home to Molly.

When we drove up to Cherry Road, it looked different, even though I'd only been gone a day. Everything was brighter and clearer. The grass was green with teeny pink flowers scattered through the lawn. The sky was warm blue. I realized I had stopped looking at stuff like that since the accident.

"Are you okay?" said Patricia.

"I am now," I said.

◆ ◆ ◆

It was dark when Molly finally got home. I was asleep on the couch. I woke up when she leaned over me, and then she hugged me and kissed me.

"I'm sorry," she said. "I'm so sorry." Her breath was warm on my ear.

"Yeah," I mumbled, because I hadn't quite woken up. "Me too."

28

When I woke in the morning, the house was still. I listened for Duck-Duck's sleep breathing. Then I remembered, and I got a sudden pang in my chest where I'd been holding my breath. I wondered if that was what a heart attack felt like, and if I was going to keep having heart attacks like this every morning for forever.

Then I remembered Molly coming to me late the night before. I remembered her saying *I'm sorry*. But now that I was awake, I wasn't totally sure what Molly was sorry for. Not stopping me? Not noticing I had a plan? Maybe that was it, because she had always noticed everything, and then she lost her voice and her mind and started crying all day. I wished I had said I understood. Instead I decided to make her French toast for breakfast.

There was me, Molly, and Patricia. I figured I'd make everyone three slices, since once you ate one, you wanted another, and what if Molly was really hungry after the long drive she had to take because of me?

I sliced nine pieces of bread, and broke egg after egg into a big blue bowl. I couldn't find the whisk, so I used a fork, sticky yellow clinging to the ends as I lifted and spun.

I poured milk into the eggs and whisked it again and again. It made me a little dizzy, watching it swirl around and around, like the river as it took Keely the first time.

I put in sugar and real nutmeg, and then melted butter in a hot pan. Was that what it was like to become ashes — liquid gold disappearing in a pan? I burned my finger a little because I forgot to use the pot holder. Could Keely feel heat anymore? What about cold?

I laid the bread in the egg, and it became an edible sponge. Piece after piece sucked up egg and milk. Piece after piece hit the pan and sizzled.

I watched and I flipped. I flipped and I watched. I'd made a stack the size of my head by the time Molly came downstairs.

She turned the fire off under my pan, and then she sat down and pulled me onto her lap. I was thirteen, but it was like I was six right then. She hugged me against her chest. "Promise you won't do that again?" she said. "I'm sorry I left you for a little while."

Like Keely, I thought, and my throat closed up.

"I'm still here," she said, as if she could hear me thinking.

It made me feel warm inside, having a mother cuddle me almost like I was little, or pretty like Duck-Duck, even though I knew I wasn't.

"The French toast is getting cold," I told her.

"Wouldn't want that," said Molly. "Should I wake up Patty? Where's the maple syrup?" And with a little squeeze, she let me slide off her lap. She was acting bouncy, but her face was a bit gray and her lips had lost color. Like pink with a bit of dust.

"I'm still not great," she said. "You know that, right? I haven't been able to go to work yet." She rubbed her head. "I haven't even been able to make a single phone call. Patty did all that."

I wondered which was harder, waking up to no daughter or waking up to no mother.

"I think if you eat the French toast, your face might at least stop being gray," I said, even though it was a little rude.

"It's good you didn't move to New York City," she said. She had big dark circles under her eyes.

"What do you mean?" I started divvying up toasts onto three plates.

"I would have starved to death," she said, and she made me come back over to her by tugging my hair just a little and then a little more. "My green-eyed girl." She gave me a squinty look, like she used to give Duck-Duck. Then she almost smiled, and she stood up to go wake Aunt Patty.

I put the butter and the maple syrup on the table and thought about how the heart-attack spot in my chest now felt achy but also gushy from Molly's hugs. I tried not to cry into the orange juice as I poured three glasses.

Aunt Patty went home to California at the beginning of July. She still called every evening and asked what we were having for dinner. Sometimes I heard Molly call her in the middle of the night. We sent her boxes of cookies wrapped in tinfoil and ribbon. She said she would visit us again at the end of the summer to take me shopping for school clothes.

Sometimes I'd be thinking about silly things, like what kind of shoes Aunt Patty would buy me. Then I'd remember that I had no mother and that I had no Duck-Duck, that I was alive, and that I had Molly. Why were *they* gone and not me? If Duck-Duck hadn't gotten in on the right side of the car, hadn't pushed me over to the left so she wouldn't get her shoes dirty, I would have been the right passenger. It made my brain feel like scrambled eggs, going back and forth between what happened and what should have happened.

Where was the logic in any of this? Why her, not me? Why Keely, not Molly? Why us and not some totally different family in a different city? One morning when Molly was in the shower, I opened up her purse and looked at all her belongings. I wasn't sure what I'd find there. I didn't take anything, like I might have before. I just looked. All her change was loose at the bottom of the bag. No wonder she was always complaining she couldn't find her pennies. She had a few of Duck-Duck's hair ties at the bottom too, a red one, a blue one, and a yellow one. I took out the yellow one and snapped it a few times. It hurt just a little when it cracked back on my finger. *Why? Why?* it snapped.

Molly also had a packet of gum and a really good Swiss Army knife with two blades, a pair of scissors, and a screwdriver. She had a little box of tissues, a bottle of aspirin, and her hospital ID.

And then, inside her wallet, hidden in a pocket, I found a picture of Duck-Duck. It was from long ago, when she was a little girl. Her blond hair hung in curls, and she had on a fairy-princess tiara. Maybe she was five. The picture was creased, as if Molly had been trying to hide it and not look at it, but kept taking it out and looking at it anyway. I put it back in Molly's wallet and closed her purse.

When I couldn't find a reason why, I got angry.

First I was angry at Keely. I didn't want to tell Molly, but she caught me hacking up the marigolds behind the house, and instead of getting mad that her yellow flowers were now confetti, she raised her eyebrows.

"So?" she said. Just like that. I knew if I lied and said something stupid like I hated yellow flowers, she would know right away that I was lying.

"If Keely weren't dead already," I said, "I would divorce her. Maybe she wasn't really my mother anyway. She was so screwed up, maybe she went to the store one day and brought home the wrong baby. Anyone who doesn't like mango couldn't be related to me." That's how it came out, but really I was thinking, *My life is just starting, and Keely's is already over.* Every time I felt good or lucky for just a second, I felt an instant pang of guilt for even thinking it.

But Keely had left me, and she had done it on purpose. I would be an orphan, a real orphan, for the rest of my life. It seemed like an incredibly long time to be motherless. But if Grandpa and Mary Esther had never had Keely, Duck-Duck would still be alive. I ground my teeth and pulled out another marigold.

"Yeah," said Molly. "I'm pissed too."

Pissed meant something light: some little annoyance. Someone killing your daughter? That was way beyond pissed. It made me mad at Molly for not saying the right words, the bad words, even when it was totally necessary.

"'Pissed'?" I said. "Keely's a fucking murderer, and you say you're *pissed*?"

Molly didn't yell at me for saying *fucking.* Her face crunched in a little. I could see shiny tears at the back of her eyes.

"Shit," I said. "I didn't mean to make you cry."

She hiccupped. "Like hell you didn't," she said, and we both laughed.

"I'll practice," she said. "Maybe I need a cursing teacher."

"No problem," I said. "At your service."

It was funny and all, but then later that afternoon, I was angry again. This time I was angry at Duck-Duck.

"She was like a comet," Patricia had said at the funeral.

Yes, I thought now. Fast and fabulous, so life down here on earth would make more sense. But then it just made me mad. She wasn't a comet. She was like one of those stupid butterflies teachers always talked about: pretty, with wings, got hit by a truck. Gone.

Why couldn't she have been just a little more boring or a little less pretty? Maybe she would still be with me and Molly, telling us how to be logical. Why did she leave us here all by ourselves?

I ran back outside and cried into the torn-up marigolds. Then I crawled under the picnic table. I don't know why. It felt like a safe fort. It felt safe until I looked at the bottom side of the table. There was gang graffiti written in the hand of a very young Duck-Duck. *GRRS,* it said on the underside of one board. *The Great Duk-Duk Farina conquers the world,* it said under another board. It was really dumb, but I cried again.

I never used to cry. Now it seemed like I cried all the time.

Molly found me under the picnic table. She sat down on the grass and looked in, as if I were a monkey in a zoo.

"We should decide what we want to do," said Molly. "What should we tell the Department?"

I knew she meant the long-term thing. *Long-term* sounded like a prison word, which sounded too much like Grandpa.

"Can I adopt you?" I said. "I think I'd rather do that than just be long-term."

"Adopt me? I would like that," she said.

Molly's hair had grown out a little. The blond spikes lay flat on her head now, and her face was thinner. I could see new wrinkles at the corners of her eyes and on her forehead. I reached over the picnic-table seat, through the monkey cage, and touched her ear. I thought of the first time I saw Duck-Duck, with her little pink ears and her bubble earrings of blue water.

"At Duck-Duck's funeral people kept saying I'll feel better eventually, like I'd forget her or something," I said. I thought of all the murmuring people. Had *they* forgotten Duck-Duck already?

"You never forget that kind of love," said Molly. She put her hand out, to draw me out from under the picnic table.

I took her hand, but I stayed in my spot underneath the table. What kind of love was it? I didn't know if Molly knew about the kisses or not. Maybe Duck-Duck told her, but I didn't think so.

I thought of Duck-Duck sitting up on the cemetery stone wall with the sun in her hair. Even if I got as old as Molly, how could I ever forget that?

"Who did you love like that?" I asked. I finally climbed out from under the table, and we sat on the bench. The wood was warm under my legs.

Molly laughed. It was almost the way she used to laugh. "Clarissa, in eighth grade. She was a terrific softball player." She smiled the best she could.

I wondered if Molly had wanted to kiss Clarissa.

"Where is she now?" I asked.

"I think she joined the air force and then got married to some pilot and had twenty children," said Molly.

"Twenty? Really?"

"No, not really. Probably just two."

When Molly laughed, she looked like Duck-Duck.

"Two's a lot," I said.

"At the time, that's what I thought," said Molly. "Now I think it sounds like a perfect number."

I didn't say anything else, because now she only had one.

We didn't talk for a little while. It was kind of nice that we could sit together and not need to keep talking to know we were still having a conversation.

"Do you forgive me?" I said.

"Forgive you for what?"

"For Duck-Duck."

Molly twisted around to face me. Her eyes were blue, but the parts that were supposed to be white were red from crying.

"You didn't kill her," she said. "A car accident killed her. It wasn't anything you did."

"But," I whispered, "my mother was driving that car. And my mother wouldn't have been there if it weren't for me. If I'd been nicer to her in the store, none of this would have happened."

Molly put her fingers in my hair. She scratched my head and then gave a huge sigh that made us both shake.

"Sometimes," said Molly, "I think, if only I hadn't stopped for milk before we picked Chrissy up, everything would be different. I could have changed everything by not getting milk but I did."

"That's not logical," I said. "What does stopping for milk have to do with it?"

"See?" said Molly.

I did but I didn't.

"I won't blame myself if you won't blame yourself," she said. She slid her hand down to my neck and looked like she was going to cry again.

So then, because I knew she was used to all those hugs and kisses, I hugged her.

"Okay," I said. "I'll try."

"I'll tell you a secret," said Molly. She kept playing with my hair but she didn't tug. "I was jealous of your mother."

I was stunned. "Jealous? Of Keely? But she was such a screwup." My insides clenched when I said that, but it was true.

"Yeah," said Molly, "but she was your mother, and she had a real claim on you. I was just a stranger. They could have taken you away from me in an instant if Keely had cleaned up her act. You could have moved to California, and I would never have seen you again." She buried her nose in my hair. "I wanted her to fail, and I felt guilty for wanting that."

I felt like my world was turning flip-flops. "Jealous?" I said again. "You? But you were always so normal and nice. Waving and telling me to say hi to my mother."

"I know," said Molly. "But inside I was totally scared that this would be it, and she would have fulfilled all her conditions, and she would take you away from me."

I started crying. I didn't even try to cover it up. I just held Molly's hand and let salt water run down all over my face. I never knew crying could happen because of a good thing.

After I had almost stopped crying, I whispered in her ear, "I'm sorry I ran away."

"I know," said Molly. "I wanted to run away too. Sometimes I still do. But I promise I won't."

And then we didn't talk anymore, because it felt like Duck-Duck might walk into the backyard at any moment, and because we both knew she wouldn't.

◆ ◆ ◆

When Molly went inside to make dinner, I fell asleep outside on the hard, warm wood of the picnic bench. The sun shone down on me, and inside those tall hedges, I felt kind of safe. Like I didn't have to go out if I didn't want to, and no one would come in.

I dreamed I was walking in the famous people cemetery. Duck-Duck was sitting under the quince tree, eating a Yodel. I knew she was dead, but I wasn't sure if *she* knew. It seemed rude to bring it up. She might be embarrassed that she didn't know. Could a person be embarrassed when she was dead?

She didn't look dead. She looked alive and ordinary with her golden hair and blue eyes. She had on her red boots, although I knew they were still in the bottom of the closet, and they were even a little dirty from the cemetery grass and moss.

"If you think about it logically," she said, "elevators should go sideways as well as up and down." She unrolled her Yodel and ate the white cream first.

"Why?" I asked. I kept looking at how blue her eyes were and at the unraveled Yodel in her pink fingers.

"So you could get where you were really going. You're going to do that, right?" she said.

In my dream, I didn't want to answer too quickly, because I knew if I answered she would go away too soon. So I leaned over to catch a piece of Yodel that had fallen into her lap.

"I love you," I said, but she was already gone.

29

It took us almost the whole summer to feel ready to do it. Finally, on August twenty-fifth—on Duck-Duck's birthday—we took a ride. I brought the cardboard box of Keely's ashes. Molly brought flowers. The bouquet had little pink and yellow flowers and white plumes that looked like sea spray. It was the hottest day of the year so far.

First we drove to the Birge Hill river. It was low now, since the summer had been hot and dry, but it still ran white and mad across the rocks.

I climbed up on a big rock and opened the cardboard box. It felt heavier than you would think a body burned to nothing would feel. *The Cremated Remains of Keely Jamison* and the name of the funeral home were printed on top. Inside the box was a plastic bag with the ashes. They weren't light and gray like fireplace ashes. They were darker and lumpy. I didn't look too closely.

"Do you want to say something?" Molly asked. "Or just say good-bye?"

I thought of Keely's first attempt to pass on. I thought of her drawings of me and Grandpa and of the Birge Hill river. I thought of her red lipstick. The black hole inside me squeezed and twisted. I tried to remember her face. If I forgot her, who was left to remember her? There was no one.

I opened the plastic bag and poured a few ashes into the fast white water. I watched as pieces of Keely raced away. The black hole squeezed again. I opened my backpack and took out another bag. It was the last bit of vanilla-shake powder.

"Cleaner, Concentrated, Secure, and Free," I said, and I emptied both bags into the river. "An answer will come to you."

We watched the dark ash and vanilla shake swirl downstream. In less than a minute, they had vanished completely. I tried to tell myself Keely had gotten her wish. When she got out to sea, maybe Keely would find Mary Esther, her mother. Maybe when I went to sea, I would find both of them waiting for me and it wouldn't be like it was but like it should have been.

As we walked back to the car, I found myself automatically looking for the green pickup. Any minute now, Keely would drive up, the truck coughing smoke. It was all a mistake, she would say, she had just been visiting Reno, and she would hand me a vanilla shake.

We got in the car, and Molly started the engine.

"She's not completely gone," said Molly. "People are still with us if we think about them and remember them." She didn't look like she completely believed that herself. If she wanted Keely completely gone, I wouldn't have blamed her.

"No," I said, "I know she's not completely gone, but she was never completely here either. She was like that."

Then we went to the cemetery. It was cooler on that side of town because of the big old trees. We walked up and down the rows, looking at old stones and the graves of famous people. I showed Molly where the lady poet lived, and the stone wall where Duck-Duck had appeared when I met her here that first time. The grass around the quince tree was shimmering green, and the trees hung over us like a summer canopy.

Then we made our way to Duck-Duck's stone. In my head it always appeared rough and worn like the lady poet's. In the real world, it was new and shiny, like a marble statue or a kitchen counter.

The writing on the stone said:

CHRISTINE FARINA

A COMET THROUGH OUR LIVES

WE ARE FOREVER CHANGED

"Patty told them to write that," said Molly. "I don't think I had a word left in me." Her face was wet.

The words were fine. It was the name, Christine, that I wished were different. But I didn't say anything; Molly was her mother and she had named her that.

Molly laid the pink and yellow flowers in front of the stone.

In silence she traced Duck-Duck's name with her finger.

"What do you want to do now?" she finally said.

I reached into my backpack and pulled out a Yodel. I split it into three parts: one for Duck-Duck, one for Molly, and one for me. I laid Duck-Duck's piece in front of her stone, next to the flowers. I handed another piece to Molly. Her hand was warm.

"Duck-Duck gave the lady poet a juice box too. I should have brought one," I said. "Next time."

Molly and I ate our Yodel. I thought of the lady poet and Duck-Duck, sitting on the big rock, swinging their legs, talking about poems and logic, eating their Yodels. The sunlight filtered through the leaves.

After a little while, Molly and I walked back down the path, past the stone wall, past the old trees. The sun watched us from behind. When we got back to the road, the day was still hot, and up in the sky a *V* of wild ducks was flying home.

Molly watched the ducks fly past the trees, over the dead people's graves, and then she looked at me with those blue blue sky eyes.

"I never called her Duck-Duck," said Molly. "Maybe I should have."

"Yeah," I said, watching the wild *V* soar. "You still could."